THE PILLBOX MYSTERY

BY

ANN DUPREY

Cover design by Kara Kniffen

ISBN#978-0-9973195-1-4

ACKNOWLEDGEMENTS

I want to thank Dr. Arthur P. Palombo, Jr. and his wife Lisa for their help and guidance regarding the drugs that were used in this tale and the overall flow of the story. Their help is greatly appreciated! I also want to thank my friends Michelle, Marietta and Amy for their input into making the story believable. Without your input, the story would not pass muster. Thank you to Missy, Kevin, Betty, Maria and your team for providing inspiration as I wrote this story. Thanks to Joseph W. Bebo for help building this book and finding a place to publish it. I want to thank my family for their support, encouragement and inspiration. And last but not least I want to give thanks to God for giving me the gift of storytelling.

Preface

A tall slender man jogged quickly with purpose and tilted his cap to shade his eyes from any unwanted stares of curious onlookers. He leaned against the brick face siding behind Jack's Diner, resting for a moment after jogging the four blocks from his vehicle. Pulling his burner phone out of his coat pocket with a gloved hand, he dialed a number and listened while the call connected.

"Hello... Yes, it's me. They crashed about five minutes ago. I was following them from the station where they picked up his car. I set the radio on a heavy metal station and turned the volume on maximum so he'd get a headache right away, just as you instructed me to do. I saw them go down the embankment. You should have seen them crash! It looks like you got lucky & your plan was executed much quicker than you expected. I think they're both out of the way permanently. When do I get my money?" The man listened a little longer, nodded his head in an automatic response to what was said on the other end of the call, then snapped the track phone shut and threw it in the garbage bin next to the wall he was leaning on. He straightened up, brushed off his coat and walked the four blocks back to the car he had hidden at a much calmer pace. He started the engine and began to drive away, checking his mirrors frequently to make sure he had not been followed. In an empty office a soft chuckle could be heard as the short, bearded man listened on the other end of the call. "I'm home free" the man said to himself ending the call. He slipped on his windbreaker, he left his office, humming to himself as he exited his building and walked down the sidewalk to his car. He slowed by the corner to throw his burner phone into a trash bin located there, then got into his Z-28 Camaro and sped off, leaving a trail of dust and dirt behind him.

Part One: Anderson Falls

Chapter 1

Jeff Weston slowly opened his eyes as he became aware of the sound of rhythmic beeping of the machines near him. As he wondered where he was and why his abdomen hurt so badly, he heard the strange sound of a piston and felt the sensation of a machine aiding his breathing. He took in his surroundings as he became more alert. The privacy curtain that hung from a track on the ceiling was pulled back and neatly folded against the wall. Looking at the ceiling tiles, he realized this was not his bedroom. He saw beams of light filtering through a window near his bed and noticed the plastic safety rail of his bed where the IV line was draped from its' pole to his arm. His head ached and his mind felt foggy. Gradually the IV pole and heart monitor came into focus. The blurry image of a woman started to take shape. He wiggled his toes and watched the blankets shift a little. Grateful that he was not paralyzed, Jeff tried to rub his eyes but felt the restraint of IV lines in his arm. With his other arm he touched his mid-section, feeling the bandages that were wrapped around his ribs. He groaned in pain.

"Jeff, you're awake!", his sister Monica exclaimed with joy, as she jumped from the padded chair next to his bed where she had been keeping watch over her brother.

"I was so worried about you! Thank God you are alive!"

Jeff tried to answer his sister, but the pain in his ribs was too much so all he could do was groan again. Another blurry figure came into sight. The figure of a woman in a neatly pressed white uniform came into focus.

"Don't try to talk, Mr. Weston, it will just wear you out. You have a few broken ribs on your left side and you have had a head injury. You have been in a coma for three days," the kindly nurse said as she strode up to his bed. Jeff looked up at her unable to speak. She handed his sister a pad and a pen. Turning to Jeff, she said, "I gave your sister a pad and pen. Do you think you can write on it okay? If you do, just nod your head and your sister can hold the pad while you write."

Jeff nodded weakly.

"Okay. Would you please tell me how you're

feeling? We've been watching you closely. The heart monitors alerted me at the nurse's station that you had wakened."

Jeff scribbled on the pad. Monica and the nurse read it together.

"Hmm, pain in the side, headache and hungry. Well, let's see what we can do to help you feel more comfortable, and what the doctor will allow you to eat." As she arranged pillows around Jeff to get him in a comfortable position she said, "Once I get you positioned, I'll check the chart to see when you can eat and what pain medications you can have." With that, she plumped the last few pillows around him and left the room.

An aide returned shortly afterwards with two bowls, one filled with Jell-O, and one with broth.

"Nurse Santor asked me to bring these in to you so you can get some nourishment. If you can handle this, you can try tea with toast later on and hopefully a full diet tomorrow. Then we'll be able to remove the IV lines."

Monica moved over to Jeff's side, looking down at her brother's bruised face. She thought of the brother who, just a week ago, could have passed for a GQ model. Inwardly she cringed, saddened that her handsome brother had suffered several injuries, worried they could mar his handsome features permanently. She stood at his bedside and laid one of her hands over his. With the other hand she smoothed his short blonde hair over the bandage wrapped around his head. As she helped him eat the food that had been delivered, she said,

"When I got the call from the hospital, I rushed right over. I was so worried that you wouldn't come out of it! All my friends at Church have been praying that you would wake up. Thank God you're back! Now that you're awake, I'll call Mom and Dad to let them know you're going to be okay."

Jeff smiled and thought of his mother and father living in a retirement community in Florida. They had moved there after his father had suffered a debilitating stroke. There, his mother had the necessary assistance in their new home to care for her husband properly. Jeff motioned for the pad and pen, then wrote a short note asking Monica not to worry their parents over him. She nodded and assured Jeff they would want to know his condition and how he was progressing. Jeff nodded in submission.

Monica looked at her brother and asked, "Do you remember anything from the day of the crash? Phil told me you had a bad headache and asked him for some aspirin. He said a little while later as you neared the diner, it seemed that you blacked out and just slumped over the steering wheel, causing your crash."

"No, I don't remember taking the aspirin, just asking Phil to hand me one from the pillbox I keep in the glove box." Jeff wrote on the pad.

Monica wiped Jeff's mouth and face when he finished the Jell-O and broth.

"Jeff, you look absolutely exhausted. I think all this excitement has taken its toll on you. Try to get some rest while I go talk to your doctor and then get some work done at home. I'll be back later on."

"Thanks, see you later", he wrote on the pad.

As Jeff lay there he tried to remember the events that brought him to this point in time and why it would have happened at all. He could not concentrate on anything at the moment. He was so groggy it hurt to think, so he decided to try and sleep. The nurse returned and put some medicine in his IV line that helped the process.

****

Phil Glass approached the Nurse's Station situated near his friend and patrol partner's room.

"Excuse me, please", he said to the blonde haired nurse sitting at the desk, as she wrote on a chart.

"My name is Phil Glass. I called earlier today to check in on my friend Jeff Weston. Now I'm here to see him."

Looking up from her work the nurse smiled at the lean, muscular man addressing her. For a moment she was dazzled by his cobalt blue eyes and rugged features along with the curly dark hair that framed his face. The deep tan he had from working in his garden every day made his features even more handsome and breath-taking. Regaining her composure, she smoothed the paper she had been writing on and replied, "Oh yes, Mr. Glass, I remember speaking to you this afternoon. Mr. Weston is in Room 207. He just got back from his Physical Therapy session."

"I bet he is giving you folks here a hard time, bugging you to let him go!" Phil joked.

The nurse chuckled and nodded. "He is anxious to go home."

"Well, I'm going to go make sure he stays in line until he gets the okay to leave. Thank you for the information." With that, Phil headed to Jeff's private room.

"Hi Jeff!" Phil said as he entered Jeff's room and pulled up a chair next to his friend, "How are you feeling today, buddy? The nurse told me you just got back from PT. Did they wear you out? If you need to rest, I'll leave and stop by later."

Jeff turned to his friend and partner from the Anderson Falls Police Department. They had been friends for the past nine years, ever since they entered the Police Academy as cadets.

"It still hurts a bit to talk, but really I am doing much better. They said I can probably go home at the end of this week. My ribs will just take time to heal, and I have to call Dr. Gromer for an over the phone evaluation in two weeks. To tell you the truth, I think I'll actually be able to sleep all night once I get home. I wake up every time the nurses come in the room to check on me. I mean, they use a flashlight to see if I am sleeping! Hah! - Plus, I need to get home to Shadow. Do you know who is taking care of my buddy?"

"The day we had the crash, Monica went to your house and fed your dog, let her out and crated her for the night. Once I was treated and released, I took Shadow over to my place to ease the burden on Monica. She was so upset and worried about you, I was afraid she'd have a nervous breakdown; she's such a sweetheart. Anyway, Shadow is fine. She is just as antsy for you to come home as you are to go home. She keeps walking to the door and whining – I think she's looking for you."

"Thanks for taking care of her. I know sometimes Monica can be intimidated by Shadow's size and strength. Shadow's sweet demeanor can fool a person into thinking she won't chase a squirrel or a cat!"

At that moment, Monica entered the room with a shopping bag that held several containers of food.

"Hey, boys! I knew you would be so busy

making plans for Jeff to break out, you'd forget to eat hospital food; I figured you should have a good home cooked meal before you escape from here!"

Monica pulled over a rolling table that held a plastic pitcher of water and a few packets of Graham crackers. As she put them on the bedside stand next to Jeff's bed and started to dish out some food, Jeff exclaimed, "Boy that smells like you've been working on it all day! Is this your newest creation?"

"Yes and no; it's Mom's beef stew and of course, I gave it my own twist."

The trio ate in a companionable silence. The only sounds were the comments about the tasty dish, along with the smacking of lips and the clatter of utensils. They finished off all the stew Monica had prepared.

After cleaning up the containers and the men complimenting Monica on her culinary accomplishment, they became serious, with Jeff asking Phil how the crash had happened.

"Well", Phil began, "after our last call of the day, we drove back to the station, dropped off the patrol car and decided to go get a bite to eat at Jack's Diner. You were complaining of a headache, so I got your pillbox out of the glove compartment and gave you a couple aspirin. You took them and we headed out to Jack's on the other side of town. We must have been less than a quarter mile from the place, you know, just before the exit for the highway, when you suddenly just slumped over the steering wheel and the car careened down the embankment, crashing into a boulder. I haven't a clue on what caused you to black out like that."

Monica's hands were trembling in horror. "Oh my God," she cried aloud, "you could have really been hurt- the both of you! What could have caused this accident? What were those pills?"

"I don't know," Phil said thoughtfully, "But you may have something there - I wonder if we can get the pillbox out of the car."

"Do you think there is any chance of that?" Jeff asked. "To tell you the truth, I don't clearly remember driving back to the station, much less getting into an accident. I remember having headaches that day, but, again, it's fuzzy."

"You cracked your head pretty hard when the car hit the boulder at the bottom of the embankment. I broke my arm protecting my head as the car broke through the guard rail. Thank God for airbags! Without them, I think you and I would both be dead!"

Jeff shook his head slowly, trying to take it all in.

"I just don't remember any of that. For the past week I've been wracking my brain, trying to remember anything of that day. The last thing I remember before waking up here last week is asking Phil for the aspirin. I must've had a whopper of a headache that day! Even that memory is fuzzy now."

Monica interrupted him, "Jeff, you were unconscious for three days. I'm sure you had a concussion, or worse. It only makes sense that you wouldn't remember the events just before your head injury. Don't worry about remembering right now. Just concentrate on getting better."

"She's got a point, Jeff," Phil said, "You'll be going home by the end of the week; let's just keep focused on that for now."

"It just seems like there's got to be a clue in all the hours I can't remember", Jeff sighed," Phil, can you think of anything we did or responded to that was unusual?"

Phil stroked his chin as he thought about that day and if there was anything odd that had happened on their shift.

"I can't think of anything out of the ordinary. The last call we had was at the Sunoco station where a guy drove off without paying. I'll have to go over the call log we had for that day and the days before it. Maybe I can see if there was something different that stands out."

"Thanks Phil, I'm curious what will turn up."

"I'll keep you posted. Maybe something will spark a memory for you, who knows?"

Changing the subject, Monica asked, "Who's ready for some dessert? I made cinnamon buns. I promised some to the girls at the nurse's station, so I'll drop theirs off and we can enjoy ours."

"Yum, that sounds great!" Jeff exclaimed. "Phil, you have to have one of Monica's famous cinnamon buns- They're fantastic!"

"I can't wait to try them!"

Monica took a box of the delicious pastries out to the nurses who began oohing and ahhing over the buns. She came back a short time later and opened the container that held the pastries she made for their little trio.

"Now this is awesome! Not like the food that's served here!" Jeff said as he wiped his mouth, "I am really lucky I have a sister who brings me something this tasty! "

"You are!" Monica teased, "Don't forget you have your partner who has been looking out for you too!"

"He is a great friend", Jeff agreed.

Looking at his watch, Phil said, "I better get going. I want to stop at the store and get some treats for Shadow; she's been so good; she deserves something special. I think I'll get her a nice marrow bone."

"Phil, I really appreciate how much you have done. Once I'm out of here I am going to treat you to a Texas-sized T-bone steak at the new steakhouse on Route 22." Jeff said appreciatively.

"It's a deal!"

An announcement was broadcast over the PA stating that visiting hours were over. Phil stood and bid Jeff good night. Jeff gave him a tired smile and lay back on his pillows, exhausted. Monica excused herself and ran to catch up with Phil at the elevator to the parking garage.

"Phil, wait for me", she said in a serious voice, stopping him at the elevator, "What do you think really happened? Do you think Jeff put the wrong pills in the pillbox by accident? Jeff is a smart guy; it isn''t like him to take the wrong pills! I mean, he is very vigilant about what he uses for headaches. He has always insisted on one brand of aspirin! He says the others won't touch his headaches! This really has me worried. Dad has the beginning signs of Alzheimer's. I hope Jeff's not getting it too!"

Phil looked at Monica with compassion. Her small frame was trembling with fear. He brushed back the long tendrils of hair that framed her face and said, in a reassuring voice, "If something fishy is going on with Jeff, believe me, I will make it my mission to get to the bottom of this. I've known Jeff since the Academy and he's like a brother to me. Right now, he's in a safe environment, so try to get some rest. Here's my card. On the back is my personal cell number.

Call me if you're uneasy about anything. We will get to the bottom of this." They stepped into the elevator and pressed the button for the garage level.

"Thanks, Phil. I feel better knowing you're looking out for us. Jeff isn't as rough and tough as you. He's more of a bookish fellow. He beats his foes with his brains. If he is beginning to lose that function, I don't know what I'll do." Stepping out of the elevator, Phil looked at Monica with genuine care.

"Don't worry about anything, Monica. I'll be watching out for him." With that, he lifted his key fob, pressed a button and unlocked the doors to his Camaro, as he waved goodnight.

Monica returned to Jeff's room, apologizing for being away so long. Jeff's nurse nodded to Monica, as she left Jeff's room, scribbling notes in his chart.

Monica felt real concern for Jeff, and asked if he really felt strong enough to be going home by the end of the week. Jeff countered that he felt great and was strong enough to go home right then if he could.

Chapter 2

Monica pulled the keys to Jeff's house from her purse and unlocked the front door of his brick ranch as Jeff walked slowly up the cobblestone path, bordered by the lush green lawn with his dog by his side.

As they entered the house, Jeff looked around, drew a deep breath and said, "Boy, does it feel good to be home!" Still looking around, he commented further, "Hey, did you clean up in here? Thank you!!"

"I didn't know if you would be angry at me for doing it, but I thought I'd clean up and arrange a few things so it is easier for you to get around. I'm glad you aren't upset."

"No I'm not mad, but if I can't find things, you're getting a call so you can tell me where you hid them!" Jeff laughed.

"No problem, big brother- I'll be there!"

Monica showed Jeff the various changes she had

made to ease his way around the house.

"I got you a decent answering machine. The one you had was so outdated; they don't even sell that type anymore!" See, this digital one time stamps the calls, so if the caller forgets to say when they called, you'll hear the machine's record of it."

"Thanks Monica, you really didn't have to do that, you know."

"After all you have done for me over the years, it's the least I could do", was her response. "When do they say you can go back to work?"

"I can go back tomorrow but I will have to be on light duty until Dr. Gromer talks to me this week. After that, I don't think I'll have any restrictions."

"I know you're chomping at the bit to get back in the swing of things but I hope you're not rushing it. Make sure you're strong enough before you go back to work. I don't want another call from the ER!"

"Not to worry, Monica. The doctor gave me instructions before I was discharged and I'm following them."

"Okay, but I worry about you sometimes."

"You really shouldn't worry," Jeff replied as he put the last of his groceries away.

Monica helped her brother stow the paper bags in the pantry and asked, "Would you like me to pick something up at the deli or the supermarket? If you like, I can warm up a meal for you. I stocked your freezer with care packages."

"You really are the best sister a guy could have! I think one of your home cooked meals would be great!"

The siblings sat on Jeff's comfortable living room couch watching TV as they ate. After cleaning the dishes together, Monica gave Jeff a tight hug and said goodnight.

****

That evening Jeff slept so soundly, he didn't hear his alarm ringing at 6 AM the next morning. It was the banging on his door that roused him from his slumber.

"All right, all right, I'm coming!" Jeff yelled, clearly annoyed both at the banging and at himself, for oversleeping. He quickly pulled on his sweat pants and made for the door.

Rubbing the sleep out of his eyes, Jeff opened the door to his home and was greeted by Phil Glass.

"Jeff, are you okay? I tried calling but there was no answer, just your machine. You're going to go to work today, right? You have 20 minutes to shower, shave, dress and eat! I'll fix breakfast for you."

Phil whipped up a quick breakfast while Jeff took a hurried shower and dressed.

"You can eat what I threw together on your way in. I'll brief you on what I discovered while I was checking the logs we talked about."

As they walked to the squad car, Phil said to Jeff, "Let's see if you come to the same conclusions that I did." Phil opened the trunk of the car where he had a box of papers. He reached in and removed a Manila folder marked Daily Logs. He handed it to Jeff once they were in the vehicle and had secured their seat belts. Jeff slid the file onto his lap, swallowed his last bite of breakfast, wiped his hands on a napkin and observed, "This looks pretty thick for just a few days. I didn't realize we had gone on so many calls."

"That's just it! We hadn't done that many calls - fifteen or twenty, at the most. The night dispatcher, Gary Phenton logged those in as completed calls by you and me. Notice in the log where the calls are reported to have been."

Jeff scanned the pages that were in the time frame for the day of the crash and the week after. "Boy, I'm amazed! The log shows me on a call the day after the crash. I was in the hospital and unconscious that day."

"That's right- now look where you supposedly went." Phil continued, "A drug bust on the outskirts of town, and the next day you caught a jewel thief at Kay Jewelers. Here's the kicker - none of the drugs or jewels that were supposedly recovered are in the Evidence locker! And it gets even better. I went to collar this guy, Gary Phenton, only to find he died three weeks ago! That's before we even had the accident. I never really knew Gary, so when the notice came out, I probably didn't pay attention, but I checked all the dispatchers that have worked here for the past few years just to be sure they are all legit. I think our computer system was infiltrated and used to cover up these crimes!"

"How do you suppose someone could do that? I thought IT Security deletes a person's profile right away upon their termination, whether voluntary or if they're fired. Do you think the perp got the log-on and password from somebody on the inside? This could be bigger than we think. If someone tried to kill us, it must be pretty high stakes."

"I don't know. We'll have to do some digging around to find out."

They pulled into the station, parked the squad car and walked into the building. Jeff was greeted by his coworkers with claps on the back and several choruses of "Welcome back!" as he made his way to the coffee bar for his morning brew.

Later that morning, as Jeff was writing out a report, a tall, beefy redheaded investigator approached his desk.

"Detective Weston?" he inquired.

"Yes, that's me", Jeff said cautiously, worried he'd already done something wrong, "How can I help you?"

"Phew, I wasn't sure which desk was yours! My name is Paul Z. Meyers. I'm from the crime lab downtown. My unit was dispatched to the scene immediately since the accident involved a pair of detectives. The unit is processing your car for fingerprints and DNA along with any trace elements that will help us find out if and how anyone could enter your car and tamper with your pillbox. When I found the pillbox I dusted for fingerprints. I found yours, Phil Glass', and another unidentified set. We brought the pillbox to the lab for analysis. The lab has already discovered a trace of Rohypnol in the pillbox that held your aspirin. It's quite possible the perpetrator fashioned a pill to look like your aspirin and took his chances on when you would ingest it. We are working to find out who the other prints belong to. We'll narrow the pool of suspects and figure out how someone could enter your car and put an illegal substance in your pillbox."

Feeling relief that he was not going to be disciplined for something he wasn't aware of, Jeff replied,

"Thanks for coming over to see me and give me this information. Is there anything I can do to help your investigation?"

"Yes. I would like to get a set of your fingerprints and your Patrol Partner's prints so we can eliminate them from the massive amount of prints we found all over your vehicle."

"No problem. I think Captain Egan has them on file from when Phil and I started here."

"Good, I'll get them from him." With that, Paul ambled off in search of the Captain.

Phil noticed the Investigator with Jeff, so he walked over to Jeff's desk and asked, "What was that all about? Did they find something worthwhile?"

"No, he just wanted a set of our prints so he can start sorting out whose prints should be there and who they should investigate." Jeff purposely withheld the information about the Rohypnol because he knew Phil would feel responsible for Jeff's blackout, or go on a rampage quizzing everyone in the station regarding their whereabouts on that day.

"Well, I was talking to Hal Edwards from the Cyber Crime unit and we had a good conversation about the logbook issue," Phil informed him.

"Really?" Jeff said sounding interested, "What did he have to say?"

"Well, he said whoever it is that used Gary Pentons' identity had to have known Gary pretty well so he didn't raise any suspicions when he logged into the daily logbook program."

"That should narrow the pool of suspects. We can check with his family, see who his friends were, and with the Captain to determine who he was close to here." Jeff said.

Phil agreed with Jeff then went back to his desk to pick up his assignments for the day. Jeff began printing the documents that he was to collate and file as part of his modified duty tasks.

Jeff took his armful of reports to the file room and began filing the completed reports. Captain Egan joined him.

"Jeff, how are you feeling? Are you pacing yourself so you don't have a relapse? The work you're doing here is very important; it helps to reduce our backlog. I need you well and here to keep things going smoothly."

"I'm hanging in there, just a bit tired. I haven't been here for a week or two and just need to get back into the groove."

"Yes", Captain Egan replied, "Once you do, things will come easier for you."

"Say, can I ask you some questions about Gary Phenton? He was one of our night dispatchers that died last month. It would really help me sort things out in my mind."

"I'm not sure how much help I'll be, but go

ahead", Captain Egan said, shrugging.

"Well, for starters, who were his friends here? And what was his security clearance? What was the cause of his death? Had he been acting strangely? Phil and I have discovered some disturbing things about him."

"Those are some tough questions; let me think about it." Captain Egan said stroking his chin, and then, turning to the detective he said, "Let's go and discuss this in my office where there's more privacy."

As captain Egan was reaching to shut the light off and open the door to the file room, he saw an odd shadow. "Something's not right," he thought. He shrugged it off and opened the door to exit the file room. There was the sound of scuffling in the back and a crash of boxes sounded behind them. Captain Egan instinctively pulled Jeff to the floor just as two deafening gunshots rang out. The wood above their heads splintered as the bullets intended for them were embedded into the wall.

"What in the hell is going on? Jeff, are you okay? Are you injured?" Captain Egan shouted.

Too stunned to even speak, Jeff laid still for a minute then looked up at the Captain and said in a voice laced with fear, "What was that!? Why are we under attack?"

Everyone in the station had come running at the sound of the shots fired, creating quite a commotion.

Phil appeared in the File room doorway first, showing concern for his best friend.

"Are you guys okay? I heard the shots and then someone hitting the floor." Phil huffed, out of breath from running across the office.

"We're not hurt. Find the bastard that did this", Captain Egan yelled the order over the chaos that had erupted.

"Did you see anyone come out of the File room?" Jeff called to his partner.

"No. I am checking the back offices and the parking lot to see if I can see anyone who can be that shooter." Phil called back. Troopers and detectives locked down the station and were frantically searching the surrounding offices, but coming up empty. Jeff and Captain Egan ran into the Captain's private office where the two men collapsed into the wing-back chairs by the captain's desk, still in shock from getting shot at.

"That was close!" Jeff breathed out, "If we lingered any longer, we'd be on our way to the morgue right now."

"You're right." Captain Egan reached for his radio. "Did anyone locate the shooter?" Captain Egan barked into the microphone on his walkie-talkie." "No sir, not yet." was the response that came from several troopers.

"Find him" Captain Egan ordered. "I want him in the Interrogation Room now!"

He sat back in his chair, running his hand through his hair in frustration and said to Jeff, "You are dismissed for now. You and Glass can meet with me in an hour to discuss this whole mess."

"I'll let him know." Jeff said over his shoulder, leaving the captain to his thoughts.

He went to the coffee bar to refill his cup. Phil was there doing the same thing.

"Captain Egan wants to meet with us in an hour. He'd like to discuss the crash and the shooting this morning. I think we should tell him what you found out in your research."

Phil agreed.

An hour later the three men sat in the Captain's office.

"Okay. Weston, Glass, what have you come up with?"

"Phil told me Phenton died a week ago. There are some things about the crash Phil and I were in that just don't add up."

Jeff then filled the Captain in on what he and Phil had gone over on their way in to work that day.

"Those are some interesting facts. So what's your plan of action? There were only a few people Gary was close with here. I mean, Melissa Sanchez was his girlfriend. He was obviously close to her. They were supposed to get married in the fall. He got along well with everyone but as far as people who were his confidants besides Melissa, there were not many. In fact, I think they broke up about a week before he died. "Let's see.... there was Dominick Mario, they were very close. I remember how we called them the Mario Brothers.""

Jeff scribbled these names down on his pad he kept in his uniform pocket.

"Thanks. Did either one of them have access to Gary's Duty Log or his PC, where they would be able to view and possibly steal his sign on and password? The logs have been altered for several days surrounding the crash Phil and I were in. In fact, it shows me going on a burglary call to a jewelry store on a day that I was unconscious."

"Well, let's go see Hal over at the Cyber Crime Unit. He's a wizard with computers and should be able to track down what was used to access the Duty Log on those days."

Phil excused himself to return to his desk and finish a report.

"I'll catch you both later, for lunch, Okay?"

Jeff and the captain nodded and stood. The two

men were about to walk over to the computer center when they heard someone approaching the office loudly saying "I said I don't care if we are on lockdown, I am going in there!" Jeff and the captain looked surprised when they saw a burly figure appear in the captain's doorway that stopped them before they could exit the office. The officer's bulky 6'4" frame blocked the doorway. His face had a permanent scowl etched on it and it only grew worse as he spoke.

"I'm Lieutenant Lester Gibson from Internal Affairs. We just received word that you both were involved in a 'shots fired' incident. I am here to find out more about it."

As the men started to settle around the Captain's desk Lt. Gibson squeezed behind the desk and assumed the chair the Captain usually sat in, then he snarled at them, "What did you do to provoke someone to shoot at you?"

Captain Egan, already put out by the Lieutenant's arrogance shown by taking his seat, spoke angrily.

"What do you think this is? Why do you assume we provoked someone!? Today is Detective Weston's first day back after being in a suspicious crash that could have killed him!"

Lt. Gibson appeared unruffled and said, "Easy does it, Captain Egan. There is no need to be angry, after all, I'm just doing my job." With this, he rocked back in the Captain's chair and stretched his legs out under the desk.

"Okay," he yawned "Now let's try this again. Do you know of anyone that wants to shoot or kill you? Have either of you had altercations with anyone recently that would have given them reason to harm you?"

The Captain replied with great restraint, "At present, the only person who would want to hurt me is my wife, and that will be if I forget to pick up bread, eggs and milk on my way home."

"That is very funny, Captain. "The Lieutenant drawled, "Seriously, have you any ideas on who would want to do this?"

This time, Jeff said sarcastically "Since you hopefully have done your homework on us before you showed up here, you would know that we just heard from the hospital that I had been drugged without my knowledge. How it got in my system is unknown right now, as is the drug. Their lab has to do some more tests to identify what it is, but it resulted in a car crash. I was on my way to Jack's Diner to get some chow with Phil Glass, traveling on Route Nine when it happened. I don't think anyone would get so upset over a traffic ticket I gave them recently to drug me and then try to shoot at both the Captain and myself."

Captain Egan added, "Obviously, we do not have the brass balls you do because we have not had any trouble until now. We don't accuse people before our investigations have begun, as you have. We have the brains to conduct interrogations that will produce answers, not anger. I suggest you rethink your strategy before someone pops you in the chops!"

"You two are regular comedians. This will go in my report." The lieutenant's scowl grew even fiercer.

"We are just telling it like it is!" the two men said at once.

"That does it!" Lieutenant Gibson growled, "Major Hoblock will be handling this case from now on. I suggest you treat him with a little more respect than you have shown me!"

"Hold it right there Lieutenant", Captain Egan said, "first, you barge into my office, show disrespect by sitting in MY chair and blurt out some inappropriate statements, and then you accuse us of provoking a shooting! Major Hoblock will get an earful regarding your behavior, you lowlife. Now, if there is nothing else, I suggest you leave", Captain Egan seethed through clenched teeth.

Lieutenant Gibson stalked out of the office, disappointed that he could not intimidate either man.

"That was interesting," Captain Egan said, "I think I'll call Major Hoblock and have a conversation with him, detailing our visit and hope he teaches this misfit to actually use some manners on his next interview."

"Good idea. Now, getting back to what we were discussing before he barged in, I'm thinking of talking to Melissa and Dominick. Phil is going to pay Gary's family a visit, that is, with your blessing."

"Jeff, why don't you talk to Dominick? You've known him for a few years. I'll talk to Melissa and see what she has to say. Tell Phil to go ahead and get in touch with the family. But let's all use some tact; don't approach it like Gibson did."

"I agree. Like the old saying goes about catching more bees with honey than with vinegar", Jeff chuckled.

As Jeff left the Captain's office and headed for his desk, Phil caught up with him and asked what had happened with Lieutenant Gibson.

"It sounded like he was getting kind of loud in there. After all the excitement this morning, I would think they'd give you both the rest of the day off. I saw Gibson stalk past me in the hallway. What was it all about?"

"He was supposed to question us about the shots fired in the file room. Instead, he accused us of provoking someone into shooting. I think the Captain's on the phone now, talking to Major Hoblock about Lt. Gibson's condescending attitude and his arrogance during the interview. As you probably heard, Captain Egan didn't take too kindly to it."

"I guess not; the way Gibson stormed out of here you'd think he was fired!"

"He might be, after Major Hoblock gets the earful Captain Egan is giving him!" Jeff responded. "Captain Egan wasn't going to let him accuse us of something that took us both by surprise. On another note, I think Paul Meyers will be stopping by the impound lot to see what's left of my car and to dust for prints later on."

Jeff and Phil continued discussing the events that had happened and the instructions Captain Egan gave regarding visiting the Phentons, Dominick Mario and Melissa Sanchez. As they stopped to get some coffee before tackling the tasks ahead of them, their attention was drawn to the front of the station where they could see the WANN TV cameras red lights flashing and the feisty reporter Lori Langorski saying in her squeaky voice, "Live from the scene of this morning's shooting, this is Lori Langorski, WANN Eyewitness news bringing you the latest developments in this case. Captain Egan", she said as she turned to him and he barred her way into the station, "Is it true that you and another officer were shot at, right here in the station?"

Captain Egan remained unruffled and said politely, "I'm sorry, but this is an ongoing investigation and I can't comment on any of the details pertaining to it."

"Really now, Captain," she insisted, "Can you tell

us how it felt to be shot at and have your life in jeopardy?"

"Lady, I was in the Vietnam War; this is nothing compared to that," he snapped.

Disappointed, Lori signaled to her cameraman to film the closing snippet and they left, dejected.

"Okay, everyone back to work, the show is over." Captain Egan said sternly, walking back to his desk. "Glass, Weston, I want you in my office. Now!"

"Yes Sir!" they answered as they came running towards the captain's voice.

The captain recapped what he and Jeff had discussed. Turning to Phil, he asked for his ideas on approaching the investigation.

"Like Jeff said, I want to go check out Gary Phenton's family and see what was going on with him away from work. Did he give any indication he was in trouble, or had enemies? What exactly was his home life like?"

"That will be our plan of attack. Let's get going." He dismissed the two detectives.

Chapter 3

Phil and Jeff walked slowly down the wheelchair ramp away from the Police station.

"Is your leg still bothering you, Jeff? You look like you have a slight limp."

"I was doing fine until I was pulled to the floor this morning, but to tell you the truth, I'd rather a sore leg than a bullet to the brain! I'm glad Captain Egan has quick reflexes; the man saved my life!"

They reached the bottom of the ramp and headed towards Phil's Camaro. There was a homeless man with a sign pleading for a few dollars. Jeff looked at the man, shrugged his shoulders and reached into his pocket withdrawing some crumpled bills. He peeled off a few and dropped them into the grimy coffee can sitting next to the unwashed homeless man.

"Get yourself a coffee or a burger and find a new spot to beg, buddy or we'll have to lock you up."

The scruffy faced man glanced up at Jeff and murmured thanks as he took his can and shuffled away. Something about the man seemed vaguely familiar. Jeff brushed it off as an errant thought. He said as much to Phil.

"You know, something about that guy does seem kind of familiar. I don't know, we may just be imagining things. Do you think we should bring him in for panhandling?"

"Nah, he's just a homeless guy. We've probably passed him loads of times and that's why he looks familiar."

"Yeah, you're right. Okay, let's get going. Monica made beef curry for dinner for all of us tonight. You'll love it!"

"Great! Let's go!"

Over another culinary masterpiece and a special dessert by Jeff's sister, the men told Monica of their excitement on Jeff's first day back. "...so, the captain told Lori Langorski he couldn't talk about an open investigation," Jeff concluded. "To tell you the truth, that reporter's intriguing and cute to boot!"

"That she is," Phil agreed, "But can she cook like your sister?"

"Nobody cooks like Monica, Phil!"

"You said it, partner", Phil laughed wiping his mouth, "That was the best chocolate mousse I have ever had!"

"Thank you, boys", Monica said blushing, "I just threw this together. It's nothing."

"It was awesome!" Phil laughed.

Monica laughed shyly and grinned at Phil.

"You are so sweet," She leaned over and gave him a peck on the cheek. "Thanks Phil!"

Now it was Phil's turn to blush, "Th-thanks Monica, you are too!" He squeezed her hand playfully.

"Okay you two, it's time to get serious," Jeff said, "We have to make a plan of how we are going to interview Gary Phenton's family and Dominick Mario. Captain Egan is going to talk to Melissa Sanchez."

"I'd still like to talk to the Phentons if you don't mind. I agree with the Captain that you should talk to Dominick Mario. I'll see if something was going on behind the scenes at home. We aren't sure what really caused his heart attack, are we?"

"No," Jeff said thoughtfully, "After I talk with Dominick, I am going to stop over to see Agnes Fisher, the ME that did Gary's autopsy. I want to find out if she found any anomalies in his cause of death."

"Good idea. I'll get started on the interview with the Phenton family tomorrow," Phil commented.

"Okay, I'm going to review my notes and jot down some questions I have for Dominick and the ME."

"Thank you for another great meal, Monica, I am going to have to go on a diet now, since you have been feeding me so well!"

"You work hard; you deserve good meals."

"Thank you again. I really do have to go home now," Phil stretched, "Today was a busy day with all the excitement that happened with Jeff and Captain Egan. The phones were ringing off the hook. We ended up helping Samantha Duprell, our receptionist, with the phones. Every news agency within 100 miles was calling!"

"Wow! That must have been awful."

"Between the reporters calling and the TV people showing up, we were swamped."

"Poor guy! Why don't you plan on having dinner here tomorrow? I have a special recipe I am going to make for you."

"I don't want to impose. At least let me bring the dessert."

"It's a date!"

Monica walked Phil to his car. As he turned to open the car door, Monica leaned over and gave him a quick kiss in the cheek, "Good night Phil, I look forward to seeing you tomorrow!"

Phil turned back to her, took her hands in his and said, "And I really look forward to seeing you tomorrow too." He kissed her lightly on the forehead, got in his car and backed slowly out of the driveway. Monica stood lost in thought about Phil, watching his car drive out of sight.

"You know, you two make a nice couple."

Startled, Monica jumped.

"Don't sneak up on me like that!" she reprimanded Jeff.

"Sneak up on you? Ha-ha, I was standing here for a full minute while you were staring dreamily at his car going down the street."

"I was just thinking of what I'll cook up for tomorrow."

"I have a feeling you and Phil are cooking something up!" Jeff said playfully.

"I have to admit, he's a nice guy. He was so helpful when you were in the hospital and his driving you to the station each day until you get your car replaced says a lot about him."

"He's a good friend and has been since we met at the Academy. We should get back inside so I can start working on what I want to ask Dominick Mario and the M.E. who did Gary's autopsy."

Together, Jeff and Monica went back into Jeff's house and were greeted by Shadow as the

Rottweiler trotted up to her master and covered his hand with kisses.

"Okay, Shadow, I'll feed you now. Go get your bowl!"

Shadow trotted happily over to her bowl, picked it up by the rim and dragged it toward Jeff. Monica laughed at the sight of the dog doing this trick.

"Hee-hee, that is funny! When did you teach her to do that?"

As Jeff put the dogs' food in her bowl he said, "She started doing that when she was a puppy. Now whenever I feed her, she drags her bowl over to me!"

"That is so cute! She is such a smart dog!" Monica exclaimed.

"That she is."

Jeff's tone grew more serious as he spoke to his sister.

"Do you mind if I bounce some questions I want to ask in my interviews off you?"

"Not at all, go right ahead."

"Captain Egan told me that Dominick and Gary were very close friends. In fact, the guys around the station called them the Mario Brothers. I'm pretty sure Dominick would know if Gary was in trouble."

"You mean, money trouble, or trouble with the law?"

"Probably money trouble. Maybe one of his family members was in debt to the wrong kind of person, or something like that. I'm sure he and Dominick would have talked about it, if they were truly as close as everyone says. Phil is going to talk to Gary's family, so he'll be able to ferret out what was happening in that area of Gary's life. I'm going to see what I can find out about his friends and what actually killed him."

Monica rubbed her hands together slowly and observed, "I get the feeling you don't believe he died of natural causes. I think you have another take on what caused his death."

"I do. I can't say I knew Gary as well as Dominick Mario, but from what I did know about him, he was a health nut. He was a runner; had a runner's lean body, and he was conscious about what he ate. He wasn't a junk food type of guy. I plan on asking Dominick if he knew anyone that would have had a grudge against Gary. I have to phrase it so it doesn't offend Dominick or make him uncomfortable about talking to me."

"Well, I would start by commenting on how close they were and how they were inseparable outside of work. I think I remember you saying they were both on your station's baseball team with you."

"That's actually what started the Mario Brothers nickname. They'd go over to Jack's Diner after the game to get a burger or some ribs. They both went to the same church too. They really were like brothers."

"It sounds that way. I think he'd probably be more responsive if you use the approach about what good friends they were and how he'll be missed at work, on the ball field and at church."

"I agree. I think that's the best approach. I'm a little less knowledgeable about the ME; I haven't met her yet."

"Her? How do you know the ME is a 'she'?"

"I spoke to her on the phone after all the excitement today. I set up an appointment to see her on Monday."

"What are you planning to ask her?"

"I'm going to ask if she found anything odd during the autopsy, or if things just weren't the way they should be for a guy that died from a heart attack, especially the way Gary was such a health nut. I just hope she's willing to share the information with me."

"Don't worry, big brother, she'll give in to your natural charm", Monica laughed.

"I'll have to turn it up a notch for her!" Jeff laughed back. "Hopefully she'll be swayed by it!"

"Oh, she will."

"I am going to say goodnight," Monica said as she yawned, "I have to think of something special to make for you and Phil for tomorrow's dinner."

"Do you want to go to Griffin's Steakhouse for dinner tomorrow night? Saturday is their Delmonico steak special. I hear it is supposed to be awesome."

"Let's see what Phil wants to do. After all, he'll be bringing dessert."

"Let's give him a call right now."

Dialing Phil's number, Jeff asked Monica what time he should make the reservations for dinner. They agreed on six in the evening. He nodded and then spoke to Phil, confirming six in the evening was good for him also.

The friends said good night. Monica kissed Jeff on the top of his head and left for her own apartment, still thinking of Phil.

Chapter 4

Saturday morning, Jeff was awakened by Shadow's licks on his face and her nudging his arm.

"Okay, okay, I'm getting up! Do you have to go out or do you want to eat?"

Shadow ran to her bowl and started dragging it toward Jeff as he headed for her feed bag. He had just finished portioning out her food when his phone rang. After three rings the machine picked up. Jeff grabbed the receiver just as his greeting was finishing on the machine. Shadow whined to go out at that moment.

"Hello, who's calling", Jeff said.

"This is Lori Langorski of WANN Eyewitness news. Is this Jeff Weston?"

"Yea, I can't talk right now, my dog has to go out."

"Jeff, just one quick question. I was wondering if we could meet and talk over lunch so I could do a short interview with you."

"I'm really sorry Miss Langorski, but I can't talk about an open investigation."

Not giving up, Lori Langorski tried another tactic.

"Okay, let's just have lunch."

"Lori, hang on a second, the dog is scratching to go out." He set the phone down and Lori could hear him opening the door, and then shutting it.

He picked the receiver up again.

"Sorry, but when she has to go, she really has to go. Okay, where were we?"

Lori laughed. "My dog is the same way. I taught her to ring a bell I have hanging from the door handle. If I don't let her out right away, she'll ring that bell like there is no tomorrow. Anyway, I was calling to see if you want to just have lunch. Just as two people. No interview. I really would like to get to know you and maybe I can help you by using my expertise in investigative reporting. You seem like a good guy and you certainly don't deserve getting used for target practice on your first day back at work."

"I don't like being a target either, especially on my first day back. It isn't a good way to impress my boss. It turned out to be quite a day." Jeff agreed.

"When I saw you the other day at the station, I knew I wanted to get to know you as a person, rather than a cop."

"I am flattered."

"I'll do anything to get you to go to lunch with me today", Lori said, chuckling.

Something in her tone appealed to Jeff and he wondered what harm could come of having lunch with her.

"Okay, but this is strictly lunch. I know you see a news story in here somewhere. I'll go to lunch with you with the conditions of no interview, no discussing the shooting."

"Okay!" she said cheerily, "Meet me at Jack's Diner at 12:30."

"See you there."

Jeff thought the perky reporter might try to wrestle information out of him and resolved to keep things strictly away from his work or the events of the past few weeks.

Jeff showered and shaved, put on a comfortable Polo shirt and headed for Jack's Diner. He arrived there about five minutes early and saw Lori sitting at a table in the corner that offered some privacy from the rest of the diner. He made his way over to the table.

"Mr. Weston!"

"Call me Jeff, please."

"And call me Lori."

"Okay, Lori, may I have a seat?"

"Please. I am glad you agreed to have lunch with me," she smiled sincerely.

Jeff sat down and the two ordered a light lunch. They exchanged pleasantries and got to know one another a little better. Finally, over coffee Lori asked Jeff if there was any way she could help him find the man who shot at him.

"Hold it right there, we agreed that we aren't going to talk about that, Lori. I like you, but I am not going to discuss an open case."

"I'm sorry Jeff. I guess I can't tame the reporter in me. I promise I won't mention it again, it's just that I can't fathom the idea of someone wanting to hurt you."

"Thanks Lori, now let's get back to you. Where do you hail from, originally? How did you become an investigative reporter?"

"Oh my, now who's doing the interview?" Lori laughed, "Well, I'm originally from a small town in northern Vermont. When I was in elementary school, then later in High School, I did well in English and was on the school newspaper. Mr. Stewart, my teacher for English in my senior year told me he thought I had great potential to be a reporter. I went on to Trinity College and double majored in English and Media Communications. What made you want to become a cop? Understand me, this is me asking, not the reporter." Lori explained.

"Well, I wasn't ever as brawny as my Patrol Partner is. Honestly; I never tried to be a muscle man. Sure, I exercise and eat right, but my body isn't built like Phil's. I always liked figuring out the whodunit novels before the end of the book, and I'm smarter than the average bear, so catching crooks became my passion."

"So was Anderson Falls the place you grew up in or did you move here? How do you like the area you live in now?"

"I grew up here and went to the Academy here as well." Jeff set his coffee down and as he did, he noticed Lori reaching into her purse. Jeff put his hand on hers to prevent her from retrieving money to pay for lunch. He was surprised when he heard a mechanical click of a cassette tape stop.

"Miss Langorski, what is that? I distinctly heard a cassette recorder stop." He reached into her bag and pulled out her hand which was gripping a mini cassette recorder.

"I thought I told you I would not be giving an interview!" he said sternly with fury in his eyes.

"J-Jeff, you have to believe me, I didn't want to do this! But that man, he threatened to hurt my Mom. After Dad died last year, she's all the family I have left!"

"Who is this guy that threatened you? Where are you supposed to meet him to hand over the recording?"

"He approached me when I was coming out of the grocery store. At first, I thought it was someone who recognized me from the 5 o'clock news. When he got next to me he hissed that if I wanted to see Mom reach her next birthday, I'd better do this."

Lori dropped her head into her hands and let out a sob.

"What have I done? Without the tape, he's sure to kill Mom!"

Jeff stroked her arm and soothed Lori.

"Just do as I say and both you & your mom will be okay. We'll re-record the interview and set this guy up to be taken down."

Jeff and Lori recreated the interview. Jeff gave all the information that Lori needed, but with a twist. The area he described as his was actually the address of the back entrance to the police station that was located on a residential street.

"Jeff, isn't that entrance marked as the Anderson Falls PD? Won't the man I am giving this to see a sign saying it is a police station?"

"It isn't marked as such. It has a house number

just like the rest of the houses on the street. It has a long winding entrance. The first time I went in that entrance, I thought I was at the wrong place. I thought I was at somebody's home."

"Well, if you think the station really looks like a house on the outside, I guess maybe it will work."

Jeff contacted the officer on duty to be on the lookout for this character and take him into custody should he show up at that location.

They paid the bill and walked out to the parking lot. Jeff walked Lori to her car, watching as she took a left out to the street. Just as she turned on to the street leaving Jack's, Jeff noticed the homeless man he had seen at the Police station dart behind several parked cars. Quickly he pulled his smartphone out and snapped a photo of the man.

"There's something odd about this guy. I'd like to bring him in for questioning. It's just hard to catch him." Jeff thought. "We're nowhere near the station where I saw him before. I can't bring him in by myself, even if I was on duty, I don't have my cuffs. Oh well, maybe he's just a panhandler who relocated." Jeff shrugged the uneasy feeling off and headed home.

That night at dinner, Jeff mentioned the strange appearance of the man to Phil.

"Phil, do you remember that guy at the station the other day? The one I thought was homeless and gave a few dollars to? Call me paranoid, but I saw him prowling around outside of Jack's Diner when I was there today. I'm not so sure he's some innocent homeless guy. I was able to get a picture of him on my cell phone. I think I'm going to run it for facial recognition and see what turns up. If there's a hit, I want to bring the guy in."

"Get in touch with Erma Honigbaum from the ID unit. She's Paul Z. Meyer's boss and the head of that unit. She's a very smart woman and very helpful." Phil suggested.

"I'll talk to her after I see Dominick Mario. The new ME, Agnes Fisher, gave me an appointment to meet with her Monday afternoon at one."

Monica interrupted their conversation as the waiter placed their bread and salads on the table.

"Okay guys, enough of the 'shop talk' for now. Let's enjoy our meal!" she reprimanded.

"Okay," they laughed and dug in. Soon, their entrees arrived and they were happily chatting about how the steak they ordered was tender and delicious.

"Mmm," Phil said, wiping his mouth with the cloth napkin, "I'm glad you invited me. Everything has been fantastic."

Monica agreed, saying, "From the salad to the steak, it's been perfect - the company as well." She gazed steadily into Phil's eyes.

“Yes, the company is great”, Phil returned her gaze.

The waiters brought them the bill that Jeff paid. Monica put the leftovers in the doggy bag and the three friends headed to Jeff’s rental car for the drive home for dessert. After they passed a gas station, a dark car began following them. Jeff noticed the car as he slowed and made a sharp turn into a side street.

“Whoa! Jeff, what are you doing?” Phil scolded.

"Phil, do you see that car behind us? It’s been following us since we passed the Cumberland Farms on Pleasant Street.”

Jeff made another quick turn into a shopping center. He pulled to a stop at the end of the parking lot. The car that had been following them pulled into the shopping center as well. Phil hopped out of the car, flashing his badge at the driver. The man looked frightened and confused. Phil walked up to the car and leaned over the driver’s window, signaling for the man to lower it. He complied.

“All right, why were you following us?” he demanded.

“Uh, well, the guy at the gas station gave me fifty dollars to follow you and see where you live. I have to go back there and tell him so I can get my money.”

“Who is this guy? What’s his name?” Phil said in

a menacing tone.

"Geez, I don't know. I was at Cumberland Farms getting a coffee when a guy in a suit came up to me and offered me the job. His hat was pulled over his eyes and he sounded like he had a New York City accent. That's all I know." The man looked sheepishly at Phil, obviously intimidated by him.

"Go back to the guy and give him this address", Phil said, writing down the address to the back entrance of the police station, located on a quiet residential street. Phil handed the man the slip of paper then walked back to Jeff's car.

"Who was that? And what did he want from us?" Monica blurted out. "This is really starting to scare me!"

Phil put his arm around her protectively, assuring her everything was okay. The rest of their drive home was uneventful.

Monica served the gourmet coffee and Phil cut them each a piece of freshly baked coffee cake telling them that the person who tailed them would be feeding his source poor information.

"What a surprise he'll get when he shows up there! Since the back entrance of the police station isn't well known and looks more residential, he'll assume it's your home address!"

The two detectives agreed it would be an eye opener for the fellow that arrived at a police station believing it would be Jeff's home. Jeff then relayed the story about the fake interview he and Lori Langorski had cooked up, sending her source to the back entrance as well.

"You'd better rest up tomorrow Jeff, because we're going to be busy on Monday! Captain Egan gave me the thumbs up to visit Gary Phenton's family and learn what I can from them. I'll be stopping by their home at one o'clock on Monday." Phil sipped his coffee, "Do you have your interviews scheduled?"

Jeff finished his mouthful of cake and took a sip of his coffee, "As a matter of fact, I do. I have to confirm that I'll be going to the ID unit at the crime lab to talk with Erma Honigbaum about the picture of the homeless man on my phone, and before that, I am going to meet with Dominick Mario in the break room at 9:00. Afterwards, I have an appointment with Agnes Fisher at her office. Captain Egan is going to talk to Melissa Sanchez after lunch. Then we should all meet in his office to compare notes and see what turns up."

"I have to admit you are well organized!"

Jeff smiled and replied, "The week and a half I was in the hospital I started thinking. I'm still frustrated that I can't remember what happened that day, but I'm not going to be worrying about that issue until I get to the bottom of this."

"Well we have a solid plan for unraveling this

mystery."

Monica had been listening intently to their conversation and spoke up, offering her thoughts. "Jeff, you were telling us earlier about Lori Langorski wanting to help find the truth behind all of this. Why not let her use her skills as an investigative reporter? I heard that when she worked at KCBL in Vermont that she uncovered some corruption in the government that had been ignored for years."

"NO!!" Both Phil and Jeff said adamantly, almost yelling.

"She's a TV reporter. We can't discuss this case with her. It's an open investigation!"

"You can't talk to her, but I can! I can ask her about her expose` on the homeless people at her last job. That series showed the homeless man who was scamming people. I could prompt her to go after the guy in the picture on your phone."

"I don't know if that's a good idea."

"I suppose that's the best thing to do. I still think Lori Langorski could expose this supposedly homeless guy. She really can get to the truth!"

"No!" Phil said forcefully, "Captain Egan has a team working all the leads. If she starts nosing around it could tip off this guy and he might leave town or even be better prepared for another attack!"

"Okay, I see your point. I don't want the guy that could've hurt you to get the upper hand."

****

Friday Morning, Jeff drove to the hospital to talk with Dr. Gromer. She sat with him, checking his reflexes and making sure he had no lingering effects from the concussion he had suffered.

"Okay, Mr. Weston, I am going to clear you for return to full duty with no restrictions on Monday. If there are any changes that effect your vision or balance, let me know right way."

"Thanks Doc."

Driving home, Jeff felt elated that he had no restrictions and could resume the work he felt was important.

Chapter 5

On Sunday, Monica and Jeff were surprised to see Phil at Saint John's Church. St. John's was a stone structure built in the late 1800's with an altar hewn out of marble, just as the large statue of Saint John was. The wooden pews were cherry with elegant carvings on the ends. The kneelers were well padded and covered in a plush red velvet.

"I didn't know you attended services here, "Monica whispered as he slipped into the pew next to her.

"I go to Mass here every so often, but I go more often to Saint Xavier's Church, near my gym," Phil whispered in response, "sometimes I go over to the gym after Mass because it's fairly empty on Sundays."

"The Pastor here is Father Ronnils Belleretz. He is a great homilist. I love his sermons!"

At that point Father Belleretz passed their pew on

the way to the Altar. The three friends stood as the entrance hymn was sung by the choir. As promised, Father Belleretz gave a moving sermon. After the Mass was concluded, Jeff, Monica and Phil walked to the entrance of the Church, where Father Belleretz greeted them.

"It's good to see you all." he said. Then turning to Jeff, "how is your recuperation coming along? Is there anything the members of St. John's can do for you? The Ladies Auxiliary has some wonderful dinners that they deliver."

"Thank you for the offer, Father, but my sister has been spoiling me with some pretty great dinners. I must have gained five pounds just in the past week!"

Father Belleretz laughed.

"Yes, she is a good cook. The last time I was sick, she treated me to her special chicken soup. It was delicious!"

Monica blushed at the compliment.

"It was nothing, Father. I just whipped it up at home."

Phil nudged Jeff while Monica was talking with the priest.

"Hey, Jeff, look over there, by the cars at the edge of the parking lot. Do you see that guy? He looks like that thug that has been working for the drug dealers we have been monitoring."

Jeff squinted his eyes and looked closely at the area Phil had pointed out.

"Uh, wait, yes! I see him! That's the guy that was outside the station on my first day back and again at Jack's Diner yesterday after my lunch with Lori. It looks like he has a suit on. He doesn't look too homeless to me. Can you get a picture of him now with your phone?"

"I already have it. I took it when I first noticed him."

"Let's get in touch with Captain Egan. Something is fishy here."

Just then a gunshot rang out; Monica screamed, grabbing her shoulder as blood spurted from the wound. Phil took Monica in his arms and dove to the ground where he pulled out his handkerchief and applied pressure to her shoulder to keep the blood flowing out of her in control. Jeff squatted next to them, unaware of the shots' origin.

"Did you see where that shot came from? Monica, I'm here next to you." He put his hand over hers, shocked that she had been shot. A crowd quickly gathered around them and a voice could be heard shouting, "Quick! Call 911! Someone's been shot!"

"Let me through here, I'm a doctor. Please, I need to attend to the injured person," a young female said loudly, with authority.

Jeff stood up and coaxed the crowd back to allow the doctor the space she needed to evaluate Monica's wound.

"Thank you, sir. I'm Dr. Sue Hogan from Anderson Falls General Hospital. Tell me what happened please."

"We had just come out of Church and noticed a suspicious character at the edge of the parking lot. My patrol partner, Phil, was sending a text to our boss, Captain Egan, when my sister was shot." Jeff reported.

"It looks like the bullet is embedded in her upper shoulder and arm's muscle. I would like to get her to the hospital and into surgery so we can safely remove the bullet and minimize any chance of infection or damage to the arm or shoulder."

The wailing sirens announced the arrival of the ambulance, followed by Captain Egan's patrol car. As the ambulance attendants lifted Monica to a stretcher and wheeled her to the awaiting vehicle, Captain Egan joined the doctor, Jeff and Phil.

"Is she badly hurt? Where did the shots come from?"

Clearly shaken, Jeff's words came tumbling out of his mouth, "I don't know where the sonofabitch shot her from. She's bleeding, can't you hear her crying? She's in awful pain!"

"She's going to be fine once I patch her up", Dr. Hogan told the captain. "Right now, she's in shock too. Please excuse me; I need to ride with her in the ambulance."

"What, in the name of God, is going on?" Captain Egan said to Phil, "First, you and Jeff are in a wreck, then someone shoots at Jeff and me, and now Jeff's sister takes a bullet to the shoulder!? This is crazy!" Captain Egan panted.

"We were just sending you a text with a photo of a suspicious character when Monica was shot. Let's get to the hospital so I can be with my sister, then we can get Phil's smartphone over to Erma Honigbaum. We were just sending you those pictures of the character that we have encountered too many times for it to be coincidence."

"Well, let's go!" the Captain nearly shouted. "Glass, stay here and secure the scene until Forensics arrives. I've got Brown and Monroe putting crime tape up now, securing the perimeter."

"I'll be with you as soon as I finish up here" Phil said to Monica as she was put on the ambulance stretcher.

Jeff turned to Monica, and assured her he was right behind her, and then watched as the ambulance sped away. He hopped in the Captain's patrol car and they took off behind the ambulance.

At the hospital, Captain Egan introduced himself

to the receptionist at the main desk in the Emergency room.

"I'm Captain Scott Egan from the Anderson Falls Police Department. One of my officers' relatives was just brought in with a gunshot wound. We'd like to check on her."

The receptionist checked the credentials Captain Egan offered and smiled up at him.

"Yes, she just arrived with Dr. Hogan. She's scheduled for emergency surgery in a half hour. She needs to be prepped for it. Nurse Coochart and Doctor Hogan are taking care of her now. They're in room 12. It is the fourth room on your right."

"Thank you", the Captain said as he and Jeff walked toward the room Monica was assigned.

As they neared her room, they could hear the nurse assisting the doctor as they were giving Monica an injection to numb her arm.

"I've prepped the site for the injection."

"Thank you, Miss Coochart. Monica, you are going to feel a pinch and some pressure. Okay, here we go; you're doing just fine. We'll just wait five minutes and your arm should be numbed. The anesthesiologist that just left has already begun his treatment; you should be feeling the effects of that shortly."

Dr. Hogan stepped out of the room, followed by

Miss Coochart, who was assisting her with the procedure. They noticed the Captain and Jeff standing in the hallway.

Captain Egan spoke to the doctor.

"How's she doing?"

"We just gave her a numbing agent so I can surgically remove the bullet and stitch the wound without her getting an infection or poisoning from the lead in the bullet. Once I've removed it, I'll preserve it if I can, so your forensics team can examine it. She's been alert the entire time, which is a good sign. If you'd like to go in for a few minutes you may."

"Thank you, Dr. Hogan. We won't be long."

The doctor and nurse headed toward the nurses' station as Captain Egan followed Jeff in to see Monica.

"Oh, hey guys", she said weakly, "Thanks for stopping by. I just got the happy juice in the IV so I may get a little goofy."

"Phil got a picture with the camera on his phone of the guy we think shot you, so I will get those pictures of the mystery man to Erma Honigbaum. She's the expert on facial recognition and if this guy has a record the captain will want to get an APB out for him."

"Sure," Monica slurred, "I didn't expect that to happen on the way out of church."

"I don't know if you will remember any of what I am saying, but we will be having that photo examined by our best facial recognition people we have and we'll catch him!" Jeff exclaimed.

"Okay Daddy, I'm going to sleep now."

Jeff and Captain Egan stifled their laughter.

"We're leaving you with Dr. Hogan. She'll call us after your surgery."

The men exited Monica's room and signaled to the nurse.

"Whatever you put in that IV is working. She thinks we're her Daddy!"

The nurse thanked them for notifying her as she stepped back into Monica's room. The doctor, with a sterile kit, followed her into the room and the nurse began the preparation for her surgery. Walking out of the hospital, captain Egan remarked, "I wonder which one of us is Daddy?"

Jeff laughed at that comment, but became serious once they reached his patrol car.

"Jeff, you stay here with your sister. Let us know how she is after her surgery is done. I'm going to reach out to Phil and enter his phone into evidence. Then I'll get the photo to Honigbaum. I hear she has the latest in facial recognition software. I''s 3D facial recognition and it's supposed to be excellent."

"Thanks, Captain. When you talk to Phil, please ask him to come up here after work. I know he must be worried about Monica and she probably would like to see him when she wakes up."

"Sure Jeff. Keep me posted on her condition, okay?"

"I will. If they decide to keep her here a few days, I'll report to work tomorrow and check on her during my breaks. After I talked to my doctor she cleared me to resume my full duties Monday, it will be no problem to take care of any business at work and be here for my sister. I know how overwhelmed I felt when I first woke up after the accident, so I'll spend my free time with her. I also remember how it seemed like the nurses were always hovering, waiting to draw blood or give medication. She'll be busy with them during the day."

"Jeff, you take whatever time you need. As I have always said, family comes first."

"Thanks, I appreciate it."

Jeff went back into the hospital's main lobby and took a seat. A volunteer from the hospital's auxiliary approached him, offering some coffee and magazines to read as he waited for his sister's surgery to finish.

"....and if you would like another cup of coffee, we have a carafe on the table in the corner that we keep full all night. Dr. Hogan will be out to speak to you when your sister goes to the recovery room."

"Thank you", Jeff said, His anxiety evident in his voice.

The woman set his coffee and magazines on a small stand near his perch on the couch, then scurried away to attend to other anxious family members awaiting news of their loved ones.

About an hour later, Phil arrived at the hospital, and spying Jeff, hurried over to him.

"Is she okay? Has the doctor talked to you yet? Is she in a room?" the words were rushing out of Phil.

"Monica went into surgery about an hour and a half ago. The doctor hasn't come out yet, but the volunteer said she'll come out when Monica goes to Recovery. There's coffee over there", Jeff pointed to the table on the opposite end of the room. Why don't you grab some and we can wait here together?"

"Good idea. Sorry I blurted everything I have been thinking all at once. I'm just so worried about her. I think you know she is very special to me."

Jeff looked up at his partner and smiled.

"You and Monica can't hide how you feel about each other. I can tell by the way she looks at you that you are very special to her too. Just don't get all mushy about each other when she wakes up."

An hour later, Dr. Hogan appeared in the doorway to the lobby, her eyes scanning the crowd. With a curt nod of her head she walked toward Jeff and Phil.

"Mr. Weston?"

"Yes," Jeff said as he stood.

"This is Monica's boyfriend, Phil Glass," he said, introducing Phil.

"Surgery went pretty smoothly, although there's some damage to the muscle from where the bullet was embedded. Physical Therapy will help regain her strength. We're going to keep her for observation overnight and probably release her tomorrow afternoon. Will one of you be able to stay with her for a couple of days?"

"Yes!" Phil said emphatically. "I, er, we will take care of her."

"Good. I'll talk to you tomorrow and give you the prescriptions that will need to be filled for her pain as well as an antibiotic for her to take.

Dr. Hogan left them, returning the way she came in. Jeff and Phil gave each other a man-hug, glad that their loved one would recover from the gunshot wound.

The next day, Phil drove to the hospital, received instructions about Monica's care from Dr. Hogan, and then drove Monica to her spacious two-bedroom apartment.

"I hope you'll be comfortable here. I put your things in the dresser in your room. I hope you don't mind me staying in your extra room until you are fully recuperated. I am going to put a tray with your food near your easy chair and put the TV remote and telephone there too. If you need anything, call and I'll come home right away. I'll pick up dinner on my way home from work." Phil leaned over to give Monica a kiss before he left.

"I cannot thank you enough for taking me home and caring for me here.   Jeff feels awful that he can't do it just yet."

"Don't worry about any of that. I love you and want you to feel as comfortable as possible." Phil kissed her softly on the lips, and left for work.

Monica leaned back in her chair, thanking God for Phil.

Chapter 6

Jeff sat across the table in the break room from Dominick Mario.

"Thank you for agreeing to see me, Nick.   I understand you and Gary Phenton were the best of friends.   I have few questions regarding him."

Nick looked at Jeff bleakly.

"Gary was like a brother to me. Really, like the brother I never had. I'll tell you something, but you'll think I'm nuts. I swear he did not die of natural causes - they all say it was a heart attack but that doesn't make any sense. He was a health nut, just like his whole family. He had just been to the doctor and only had a cold and I don't see how that could kill him!"

"I don't think you are nuts, and I don't buy him dying of natural causes. That's why I am going to see Agnes Fisher, the Medical Examiner that did his autopsy."

"Look, if there is anything I can do to help, please

tell me. Gary was my best friend. When I first moved to Anderson Falls, he befriended me and showed me the ropes at the station. He introduced me to everyone and got me involved in the baseball and bowling leagues. I wouldn't have known anyone if it wasn't for him."

"I appreciate your offer to help," Jeff said. "Can you remember if he was acting strangely in the weeks before he died? Was he troubled by anything or anyone?"

"I think something was bothering him, but I can't put my finger on it. At first, I thought it was his girlfriend, but he and Melissa were at the bowling alley a few weeks before he died and they looked totally in love. I know it wasn't a money issue because he was putting money away and the investments he made were giving nice returns. I don't know what it was. He just didn't seem like himself."

"I don't want to pressure you, but can you think of some examples of Gary not acting like himself, Nick?"

Nick sat silent for a moment then let out a long sigh.

"As I said, Gary was a health nut and loved biking, running and playing in our softball league. That last two weeks of his life, he was more interested in probing me about the evidence lockers and the computer logs. He didn't want to go running and seemed out of breath when we'd go biking in the trails at the park. This was unusual for Gary. He usually left me in his dust, then he'd rib me about how slow I was. The last two weeks, he was the one that was slow. I thought he was just being nice and easing up on me a bit. Oh, and one other thing: for a guy who was so health conscious, his clothes smelled like cigarettes. I mean when he walked by me, I could detect the cigarette odor. The Gary I knew detested cigarettes and their smell. I wish I had more information for you but I can't think of anything else." Nick slumped dejectedly in his chair.

"Well, thanks for talking with me. I appreciate your help with this case. If you think of anything else, please call me."

Jeff wrote in his notepad as he headed back to his desk, jotting down his thoughts and impressions from his short interview with Nick. He also jotted some questions he would give to Phil for his scheduled interview with the Phenton family at their home.

As he approached his desk, he noticed Captain Egan, Lieutenant Gibson and Paul Z. Meyers standing there engaged in an animated discussion.

"So what were they doing at the church?"

Jeff interrupted them with "It was Sunday, Lieutenant Gibson, and that is usually the day my sister and I attend Mass. Coincidentally, the church is where Mass is celebrated."

Jeff's lingering irritation with the lieutenant was evident.

"How dare-," Lieutenant Gibson started.

"No! How dare you question the actions of my detective and his family during his off duty hours?" Captain Egan cut him off.

"Obviously, he did something to make someone want to shoot at his sister and then at him...twice! Both times he was spared." the lieutenant said loudly.

Stepping between the captain and the lieutenant, Paul Meyers straightened up to his full height of six feet seven inches. He was not much taller than the lieutenant, but much more muscular.

"Lieutenant Gibson, I assure you, we are working fervently to catch this criminal. We have been taking prints from the car and from the pillbox. We sent the pillbox to the trace evidence section for examination - there may have been some tampering with it. You don't need to pressure us to check every angle, because we are making sure no stone is left unturned." Paul said with authority.

Deflated, Lieutenant Gibson excused himself.

"How are the Latent Examinations going Paul?" questioned Captain Egan.

"Well, we've collected hundreds of prints and through the process of elimination, whittled it down to about 20 unknowns. Those could be from the service station Jeff uses or the perpetrator. We'll be running them through the Automated Fingerprint Identification System, or AFIS, as it is commonly called. I'll get the results to you as soon as I have them."

"Thanks, Paul. Do you need any other fingerprint cards of our employees?"

"No, those that I need are all stored electronically. That's how we got the number of unknown prints narrowed down so quickly." Paul explained.

"Please keep me posted on the results you get from AFIS."

Chapter 7

As Dr. Agnes Fisher finished typing her report on her computer, she stretched and reached for her now cold coffee. She stood, carrying the coffee to a nearby microwave to reheat it. Just as the microwave beeped signaling completion, Jeff Weston knocked on the door to her office.

"I'll be right there," Agnes called as she took a quick sip of her warmed coffee and put it on her desk.

"Is that you, Detective Weston?"

"Yes, Jeff replied, "We set up a meeting for 1:00 today."

"Oh, that's right. I was so wrapped up in my report that I lost track of time! Please, have a seat. How may I help you?"

"You performed the autopsy on Gary Phenton, right?" Jeff began, "Did you find anything out of the ordinary?"

Agnes withdrew a folder from a stack of reports in her desk. Thumbing to the report she wanted, she said, "I did find a peculiarity regarding Mr. Phenton. His medical records indicated that he was in good health. No heart or cholesterol issues. Since the medical report I had on file for him is over two years old, I spoke to Dr. Sobol, our station's physician, about Gary's health. He told me that Gary was in top form. He had been in to get a physical the week before he died. The toxicology report came back showing acotine in his blood. That would have made people wrongly suspect a heart attack right away."

"Could someone have given it to him without his knowledge?"

"Sure. It dissolves quickly in a drink and if the drink has a strong flavor, the victim won't suspect anything is awry with it. Also, if it's an alcoholic beverage it speeds up the effect of the poison."

"Well, this has certainly been enlightening. I really appreciate your help."

"Detective, I have a question for you. Did Dr. Sobol talk to you when you came back to work?"

"No. Why?"

"Well, I may be talking out of school here, but they found traces of "roofies" in your blood when you were admitted to the hospital after your accident."

"What!? How the hell could that be?? Paul Z.

Meyers said they saw traces of rohypnol and the hospital had contacted me and said they found an unknown substance. It was roofies?? I don't do drugs!" Jeff exclaimed.

"Don't shoot the messenger", Agnes laughed. "I believe you. It's a mystery as to how it was administered to you."

Jeff sat forward abruptly, taking in this information. He was visibly shaken, realizing that someone, someone he probably knew and trusted, was really trying to kill him. He silently vowed to find out who it was.

****

Jeff's cell phone jingled as he was returning to the police station. He answered the phone and was greeted with a cheery hello from his sister, Monica. She informed him that Phil had picked her up and brought her to her two-bedroom apartment and would stay for a few days during her recuperation.

"Jeff, Phil is so sweet! He is going to stay with me; in the extra bedroom until I'm ready to be on my own. He makes sure I have everything I need before he leaves in the morning. I feel so pampered by him."

"If there is anything you need at all during the day, just call me. After all you've done for me while I was in the hospital; it is the least I can do for you."

"Thanks Jeff. Just between you and me, I think Phil likes doing this for me."

"You are very special to him, you know."

"I'm crazy about him."

Chapter 8

Phil Glass parked his car on road near the edge of the grass in front of the Phenton's modest Pine Street home. The lawn was well cared for. A rose bed abounding with fragrant American Beauty roses graced the walkway leading to the front door. Phil pressed the doorbell and heard the chimes resound inside the house.

"I'm coming!" a woman's tired voice called out and Phil was greeted by a motherly looking woman in an old flannel shirt and jeans. Pushing back a stray lock of hair, she opened the door. "If you're selling something, we don't want any."

"I'm not selling anything. I'm here on official business", Phil replied as he produced his badge and credentials.

"Oh, my!" the woman gasped as her hands flew up covering her face. "I can't take any other bad news! Is it Bill? Is he hurt?"

"Mrs. Phenton? I'm just here to ask you a few

questions. I didn't mean to upset you. May I come in?" Phil said in a reassuring voice.

"Oh, yes, please come in. I'm Madge Flanders. Phenton is my maiden name. Right this way, please. We can have coffee while we talk, if you'd like", Madge said as she led the way from the foyer to a large, comfortably furnished living room to the left of a spiral staircase.

"Yes, coffee would be nice", Phil answered as he sat in an overstuffed chair near a cherry coffee table.

A few minutes later, Madge returned with a tray holding two cups of steaming coffee. As she placed the tray on the coffee table and handed Phil his cup, she asked, "Cream and sugar?"

"Cream only, please."

Madge passed Phil the small pitcher with the cream. He poured a teaspoon of cream into the brew. Phil stirred his coffee and began with, "Mrs. Flanders, as I understand it, you are Gary Phenton's only living relative."

"Call me Madge. Gary was my brother; he was adopted when I was about two years old. He has a twin brother, but we have not heard from him in ten years. Our parents died last year; Mom first, from pneumonia. She was 85. Dad died just two months later. I am sure it was from a broken heart. He and Mom were like newlyweds right to the end."

Sipping his coffee Phil said, "I'm so sorry for your loss. I realize it must be especially hard now that Gary is gone too."

"Gary was a good brother. He was the kind of guy that would give you the shirt off his back. It's hard to believe he died of a heart attack; he was in such good health" Madge dabbed her eyes with her cloth napkin.

"We are actually looking at his death a little closer now," Phil explained, "something just wasn't right." Phil then gave her a synopsis of the events since Gary's death, leaving out his suspicions about the homeless man he believed to have shot at Jeff and himself.

"Now that you are aware of these things that have happened and what we discovered in the call log, did Gary give any indication that he was being coerced or that he was stealing from the evidence locker?"

Madge was quiet for a moment, taking in all the news Phil had given her. She finally gazed up Phil, her face set in determination.

"I will not speak ill of the dead, especially my own brother, but it seemed like he was withdrawn and not himself during the last few months of his life. He didn't come over for Sunday dinner anymore. Bill and I knew he had a girlfriend and thought perhaps they had some sort of disagreement that would have affected Gary. That is, until one Sunday when we decided to have a picnic lunch in the park. We saw Gary on the far side of the park talking with some shady looking characters. When we confronted him about it, he told us it was none of our business." Madge dabbed her eyes again.

"I truly did not mean to upset you. I'll be on my way now. Thank you", Phil said as he stood to leave, "You have been an enormous help."

Madge walked him to the door.

"I'm going to tell my husband about our conversation and if he thinks of anything else I will have him contact you."

"Please do." Phil reached into his wallet and retrieved one of his business cards.

Here's my card. He can call my desk phone or he can reach me on my cell."

****

Captain Egan offered Melissa Sanchez the wing back chair across from his as he closed the door to his office.

"Thank you for stopping by to see me. I'll try not to keep you too long. I just have a few questions about Gary Phenton that I'd like to ask you."

Melissa settled her slender frame into the

comfortable chair and said, "What questions about Gary? I didn't think there was anything wrong with him, but then in the last weeks before he died..." Melissa's dark eyes welled up with tears as she tried to stave back sobs. "He – he was not the man I fell in love with" she sniffed.

Captain Egan knelt beside her, offering her a Kleenex from the box on his desk.

"I am so sorry for your loss. I can see how upsetting this is. I have some suspicions about his death though and since you were the closest person to him, I think you would be able to help me the most."

Melissa blew her nose and dried her eyes. Then, sitting up straight, she said, "Really? Yes, I'll help in any way I can. I thought I was the only person suspicious of the circumstances surrounding his death - what would you like to know?" Melissa said eagerly.

Captain Egan opened his iPad, referring to it as he asked Melissa about Gary's demeanor in the last few weeks of his life.

"Well, as you know, we were planning on a June wedding this year, so we were excited about that. But there was something bothering him too, it seemed. I thought it was pre-wedding jitters. Now that I look back on it, there must have been something else going on, because he would plan a getaway weekend for us then at the last minute he'd get a call and cancel the whole thing. He kept blaming his job here, saying he got called in. I knew it wasn't true, but I never said anything." Melissa dabbed her eyes again and smoothed her slacks nervously.

"How did you know the calls weren't from here? And did Gary get these calls at home or on his cell phone?" Captain Egan asked.

Melissa sniffed then cleared her throat.

"Well, I know he got several of them on his cell phone and I don't know how many he got at home. He kept buying a new cell phone every few weeks. That's something else that I thought was odd."

"Hmm, throw away phones probably. Not easily traceable." he murmured to himself.

"What? I didn't hear that question."

"I was just talking to myself. Whoever was coercing Gary is very smart." the captain declared.

"Whatever I can do to help you catch this person, you can count on my help. I want to get justice for my Gary."

"Thank you. I really appreciate your help. You can go back to your section now. Please keep our conversation just between us. I'd prefer to only share it with the few who are investigating the matter."

Tuesday morning after the daily briefing for the Anderson Falls police station personnel, Captain Egan motioned for Jeff and Phil to follow him to his office. After the two detectives were seated, the captain closed the door and settled in.

"Gentlemen," he began, "I believe it's time for us to compare notes and see what we come up with."

"I'm still waiting to talk to Erma Honigbaum. She's been booked up all week with a homicide and the Latent Print Unit has been overwhelmed with work, so she's been busy. "

"Well, get together with her as soon as you can. Let's go over what we do have."

"I did talk to Agnes Fisher, the ME that did Gary's autopsy. She said the station's doctor said Gary was in top form. She did find acotine in his blood. It is a poison that works quickly when mixed with alcohol. People often mistake the cause of death as a heart attack, not poisoning." Jeff offered.

"I met with Madge Flanders, Gary's sister. Her story was that Gary was acting withdrawn the last few weeks before his death. He had become very withdrawn from the family, then the Flanders saw him meeting with a 'shady character' as they put it. Also - Did you know Gary had a twin brother?" Phil reported.

"No. Tell me more." The captain leaned forward, interested.

"Not much to tell. She just told me Gary and his brother Vito were adopted by the Phenton's when she was two and Vito dropped out of their lives about ten years ago. They have no idea where he is now."

Chapter 9

Jeff pulled out his cell phone and dialed Erma Honigbaum's number. Erma answered on the second ring, "FIU, Honigbaum here."

"Hello, Investigator Honigbaum. This is Detective Jeff Weston."

"Hello, Jeff! Sorry I haven't gotten back to you about the appointment you want to set up. I've been swamped with work on that homicide in Old West Tern this past week. What time tomorrow would be good for you to meet? I got the email with the picture of the unidentified person."

"Good. Is the quality of the picture good enough to use in your facial recognition software? I can come over anytime you say tomorrow."

"The picture is usable. I have to sharpen it up a bit because it came from a phone, but we can put it into the computer and see what we come up with. Let me glance at my calendar for tomorrow and see what time would be best. Hmm, how does ten o'clock sound? That way we can wait for any results and discuss them over lunch."

"I'll mark it on my calendar. Do you want me to pick up anything for lunch?"

"That's not necessary. We have Woody's Cafe next door to us. They have a nice variety there and it is fairly private, so we can speak freely about the results of the facial recognition testing."

"Good. I'll see you at ten o'clock tomorrow."

"See you then."

Jeff replaced the receiver on the phone and felt a sense of accomplishment. If he could get a match on the face of the homeless person, he would be able to unravel this case.

Jeff had barely replaced the receiver when his phone rang.

"Detective Weston."

"Hi, Jeff, Malcolm Bradley here.

"Malcolm! It's good to hear from you! It's been some time since we have seen each other. How are you?"

"I'm doing well. I was just promoted to supervisor. Actually, I'm calling in that capacity to speak with you," Malcolm said, his voice becoming more serious, "I just got a call from Dr. Fisher about the results from your blood work at the hospital. Got a minute?"

"Sure, what can I do for you? I did not know Dr. Fisher was going to discuss the results from my blood test with everyone. I wish she would have told me she was going public with the results."

"No worries about that issue with me. She said you were probably unaware you even took the drug. Did Captain Egan speak with you yet today? He asked my group to assist in your current investigation."

"No, he didn't mention anything about it when we met earlier today," Jeff said, somewhat surprised.

"You might want to talk with him before we discuss any details." Malcolm suggested.

"I agree. Let me look into it and I'll get back to you."

"Okay, talk to you later."

Jeff sat at his desk pondering the odd call from Malcolm. He knew Malcolm had a real talent for finding trace elements in tough cases, but why involve his group? The Captain had instructed Phil and Jeff to keep the investigation private. Jeff decided to ask the Captain about this sudden turn of events. Walking slowly to the Captain's office, Jeff thought about how he would confront his boss. Should he just ask him bluntly about the new involvement of Malcolm's group, or should he let the Captain introduce the subject? Jeff decided to use a combination of both.

Jeff knocked on the oak door to the captain's office.

"Yes, come in."

Opening the door, he said, "You'll never believe who I just heard from; my old pal Malcolm Bradley! He says we're going to be working together on this case. You know the one we're looking at regarding the homeless guy? It's funny, because I thought we were keeping this quiet, not knowing who we can trust. He says you gave him the go-ahead on this."

"Jeff, I'm doing my part of the investigation. We can all speak about this on Friday when we regroup."

"Maybe we can meet earlier," Jeff started, "because I found out some interesting stuff from Dr. Fisher. I guess the autopsy found acotine in Gary's bloodstream. They also found rohypnol in my bloodstream when they brought me in from the car accident."

"Well, this is news. Maybe we should get Phil in here now and see what we have." The Captain said, picking up the phone and dialing Detective Glass' number. He spoke briefly then hung up.

Phil joined them in a moment's time and the two detectives sat with the Captain to discuss their new findings.

"Looks like Jeff found some interesting things here", began the Captain, "eye opening information from Dr. Fisher, and I have brought Malcolm Bradley on board to help us with the investigation. Have you come up with anything new, Phil?"

"Well, yes. I spoke with Madge Flanders, Gary Phenton's sister. She enlightened me a little bit on his childhood and the changes in his life just before he died. Did he ever mention a twin brother to you?"

Captain Egan stood and walked to a file cabinet behind his desk. He opened it and retrieved a thick file.

"Gary was already a Dispatcher when I was promoted to Captain and came here. He had been here for five years already and was the first person to help anybody that was new to the station. This is his personnel file. It's filled with letters of appreciation and glowing reviews from his supervisors. He was going on 15 years here. Let's see if his application or the background check revealed anything about a brother."

He flipped the file open and thumbed to the section that contained Gary's original application and the subsequent background check.

"Let's see here," he said, "He lists his parents as the Phentons, but didn't Madge say he was adopted, Phil?"

"Yes, when she was about two years old is what she told me."

"How did she happen to mention his brother?"

"She told me about Gary's adoption and added that he has a twin that they haven't heard from in ten years. I just assumed they were both adopted at the same time and the brother just took off ten years ago. I haven't been in touch with my brother for a while. He moved across the country and we don't talk as much as we used to."

"But you still keep in touch enough to stay in each other's lives," Jeff interjected.

"You could say that. I send him birthday and Christmas cards."

"Madge said this twin just dropped out of their lives, right? Did she attempt to contact him when her parents died?" Captain Egan asked.

"I didn't ask her. She was pretty upset. Her parents were like newlyweds right up until their deaths. Gary has just died. Probing her about a missing brother just didn't seem right."

"We might have to pay her another visit. Don't worry; we'll be very tactful with her."

"I'll give her a call and set up another appointment for us to go see her," Phil said grimly.

"Good," Captain Egan said, "see if you can convince her to see us both, preferably on Wednesday while Jeff is with Erma Honigbaum checking out that picture of the homeless guy.

That way we can kill two birds with one stone."

"Her number is at my desk. I'll call her once I get back there."

"Just email me the appointment. I'll add it to my calendar. Is there anything else we need to discuss?"

"Yes," Jeff said. "What exactly will Malcolm Bradley and his group be doing in this investigation? He said you asked for his help. Did you fill him in on all aspects of the case?"

"I gave him a brief outline of what has happened so far. He is unaware that it could be someone within the department." the Captain explained. "His expertise is in Trace Evidence and electronics. He and his team have helped solve some very puzzling cases. I think he'll be able to take a look at the reports from the church shooting and give us an in-depth report on each item that was gathered as evidence."

"I wish you had just given us a head up on this," Jeff complained, "I treated him with such suspicion; he probably thinks I am a jerk."

"I think Malcolm will understand your suspicion once we're all working together. He'll be sweeping my office and your cars for anything unusual. If the person or persons that have made attempts on your lives is from within, we need to find out how they got the roofies in that pillbox.

We also need to find out if they're listening in on us."

"Good, I've always thought he's a good guy. I hope he and his team can shed some light on the case with what we already know."

"When are you going to meet with Honigbaum?" Phil and the Captain said in unison, then broke out laughing since they spoke their thoughts at the same time.

"To answer you both, I am meeting with her at 10:00 tomorrow morning and we'll discuss the results over lunch. She says we'll start the facial recognition of the cell phone picture right away and then once we get the results we can go over their probability of being a person we can lay our hands on."

"Good! Phil is going to set up another appointment with Madge Flanders – she's Gary Phenton's adoptive sister. Maybe he can schedule it for us to talk to her tomorrow because I have more questions for her to answer."

"I'll try and set it up for the time that Jeff will be with Erma." Phil replied.

The three men parted company and each headed back to their desks to prepare for the next day's activities.

While Jeff jotted down questions regarding the facial recognition process, Phil dialed Madge Flanders' home.

"Flanders residence, who's calling, please?" a man's voice greeted him.

"Good afternoon, this is Detective Phil Glass. Is Madge available?" Phil asked.

"Oh, Sorry, detective. Yes, I'll get her for you. Please pardon the brusqueness, we've been getting some prank calls lately and it's been upsetting her. As he cupped his hand over the receiver, Phil could hear him call to Madge. A moment later she was on the line.

"Hello?"

"Hello, Madge. This is Phil Glass. We spoke yesterday about Gary. I was wondering if I could stop by again tomorrow with my boss, Captain Egan, and go over a few more details with you."

"We aren't in trouble are we? I don't know what Gary was up to before his death." Madge said in a worried voice.

"Oh, no, you have nothing to worry about. We just want to clear up some minor details so we can figure out how and why Gary died. If it is not a good time we can schedule our visit for another day." Phil said in a reassuring voice.

"Do you mind if my husband Bill joins us? I'd feel more comfortable if he is with me."

"Madge, we want you to feel at ease when we talk. Bill might be able to add further details to what we already know. Is 10:00 in the morning a good time to stop by? Remember, we want don't want you feeling pressured or uncomfortable."

Phil overheard Madge consulting her husband about the appointment for the next day.

"Yes, 10:00 will be fine. Bill will be able to join us also."

"Good, then we'll see you tomorrow at 10:00."

After Phil hung up, he marked the appointment on his calendar and emailed the details to Captain Egan. As he stood to get a fresh cup of coffee, an idea struck him and he sat down abruptly, tapping out a private message on his cell phone to Hal Edwards in the Computer Security department. He read it over, making sure he was clear in his request.   Once he was satisfied, he stood, stretched, and grabbed his mug and headed for the coffee bar. As he passed Jeff's desk he saw him huddled with Malcolm Bradley, discussing reports that were spread across the desk. He stopped to see if there were new developments he should know about.

"Well, we swept the office and didn't find any bugs. We're working on the trace evidence from the pill box that we retrieved from your car. Erma and her team have been busy with the homicide at West Tern, but felt your case was a high priority so they sent Paul Z. Meyers out to gather evidence from your vehicle. That's about all for now." Malcolm gathered his reports and put them in a file folder, then stood to leave.

"Thanks for filling me in, Malcolm. Oh! This is my patrol partner, Phil Glass", Jeff said as he waved Phil over to his desk.

"It's good to meet you." Malcolm said and shook Phil's hand. "I need to run but Jeff can fill you in on our discussion." With that, Malcolm headed to his next appointment.

Jeff gave Phil a synopsis of their meeting as they walked to the coffee bar.

"Well, it sounds like he got right on the job and is good at it too." Phil commented.

"He's tops in his line of work." Jeff responded.

Chapter 10

Hal Edwards frowned as he read the message from Phil Glass. If what Phil suggested was true, then there had been a major security breach within the agency. He reread the message, ensuring he understood the seriousness of the allegations it contained. The message read:

"Hal, I am wondering if it's possible for someone to see my email correspondence without my knowledge. I have a suspicion one of our associates may have provided information to whomever it was that took a shot at the Captain and Detective Weston last week Also, I don't believe the person who shot at Monica Weston at the church entrance was just some random nutcase. Am I within reason to have these suspicions?"

"How do I explain this to him so he isn't confused by technical jargon?" Hal said to himself, and then with a confident nod, he hit reply:

"Phil,

Someone with advanced technical knowledge
in computer programming could install a key
logger program on one of your systems and get
the passwords for your computer and email
account. They could log on remotely, access your
emails & read them. A person without that level
of technical knowledge would be unaware the
email had been read. If you truly suspect this is
happening, please let me know so we can report it
to the proper personnel in my department and they
will rectify the issue."

Hal hit send on his phone, hoping Phil's
suspicions would go unfounded.

****

Jeff laid his briefcase on his desk, opened it up
and carefully laid Phil's cell phone in it, laying
out notes containing his questions for Erma next
to the phone. He snapped the briefcase shut and
looked up to see Phil waving him over to the
coffee bar.

"I'll be right there; I just want to make sure I have
everything ready for my meeting today."

Jeff took one last look at his desk and decided
everything was in order. He walked over to Phil
and in a puzzled tone asked, "What's up?"

Phil answered in a hushed voice, "Follow me."

"Okay, but I have a 10:00 meeting at FIU with Investigator Honigbaum."

Phil wordlessly took Jeff by the arm and led him to Captain Egan's office. Rapping quietly on the door, he eased it open. Captain Egan was at his desk reading some files. He looked up and quietly motioned them to the chairs opposite his own.

In a hushed voice Phil started the conversation.

"I'll make this quick; we all have appointments to keep. I've been thinking about all that has been happening lately. It seems someone that wants to harm us is always one step ahead of us and is able to see the emails we sent without have been seen by you, me or Jeff. I emailed Hal Edwards in Computer Security, asking if it is possible for a person to do this. His answer was yes, but the person would have to be a highly skilled computer programmer. This is why I am speaking in person to you both. I have a feeling that someone within our agency is supplying Intel to the person who has come after us three times now."

"I've been looking over the personnel files from the IT department, trying to determine if there is anyone that fits the profile Hal provided. I've found a few possibilities that we can take a closer look at. I've enlisted Hal's help."

"Good idea," Captain Egan said,

"He's great with all this stuff. I don't have any

expertise in programming."

"I can see he'll be a real asset to us, especially if the shooter is someone we know and trust." Jeff observed.

"I agree, Phil chimed in, "If this unknown person has been reading our correspondence, that would explain how he knew Jeff was in the file room the first day he was back here and how he knew Jeff and I were going to meet at church on Sunday. Here's what I did today, as a test. I wrote that we're meeting Madge Flanders today at Jack's Diner. In reality, we're going to her home; let's see if anything odd happens at Jack's."

"Good thinking, Phil. Okay boys, it's time to get going. What do you say we meet back here tomorrow and compare notes again?"

They agreed on their next meeting and then headed to their respective appointments.

Chapter 11

Jeff slowed his car to a stop at the guard booth in front of the laboratory where Erma Honigbaum worked. He showed the guard his ID and appointment information. The guard checked his clipboard, making a call to Erma announcing Jeff, confirming that he indeed had an appointment with her. Once he was satisfied, he waved Jeff into the parking lot and gave him directions to Erma's office. Erma, a tall slender woman with a runner's body met Jeff at her office door and showed him into the area where the facial recognition process was performed.

"It's nice to put a face to the name, Jeff. No pun intended!" Erma's wise face crinkled into a genuine smile. Her hazel eyes shone.

"It's a pleasure to meet you, too."

Becoming serious, she said, "Okay, let's get started. Let me take a look at the image on the phone. My printout was quite grainy. With this latest software, we can email the photo directly to the computer that does the facial recognition, rather than scanning the poor printout that I have."

"Sure. I have the phone right here in my briefcase."

Jeff opened the briefcase, turned on the phone and loaded the picture for Erma to view.

"Phil took this picture just before my sister was shot. This is the same fellow we saw once at Headquarters and then at Jack's Diner. We grew suspicious when we saw him lurking around the church parking lot. I'm curious to see if we can put a name to that face."

Taking the phone and studying the picture, Erma said, "Yes, this is much better quality than my printout. Do you mind if I access the email program so I can send it to the facial recognition system?"

"Not at all", was Jeff's reply.

Erma opened the email program and loaded the picture into the special facial recognition program. Satisfied, she said to Jeff, "Now we will wait for it to read the picture and compare it to the countrywide database." Erma explained, "Did you say you had other questions for me?"

"To be honest, I thought I would have lots of questions, but I think they should wait until we get results, if any."

"That's fine. If you think of anything, just ask.

We have to wait a while for the results to start coming in. Would you like coffee or some tea? I am going to pour myself a fresh cup of coffee. The office has a gourmet coffee maker that grinds the beans fresh for every cup. I highly recommend it."

"Sure, I'll try a cup." Jeff said.

The two headed off to a nearby break room where they sat at a small table drinking their coffee awaiting any results from the comparison software.

"This is good coffee, Erma. Thanks for insisting I try it!"

"No problem, Jeff. Relaxing and having a cup of coffee while things are processing helps make the wait a little easier. If all goes well, we will be able to review the reports over lunch."

****

Phil motioned to the house on the right.

"There," he said, "That's their house. We can park on the side of the road a few houses down and walk back to their place."

"What's wrong with parking in their driveway?" Captain Egan asked.

"I don't like being so obvious. It's a quiet neighborhood and I don't want the Flanders being questioned by nosy neighbors. They're a nice couple and have been through a lot with Gary's sudden death."

"So that's why we took the unmarked car! Okay, I suppose we can do as you say. After all, they've been very cooperative." With that, the Captain slowed to a stop on the side of the road, put the car in park, reached over the seat and grabbed his suit coat.

The two men approached the Flanders's house on foot. An old pickup truck and a Volkswagen Jetta were parked in the driveway.

"I hope they didn't forget our appointment and invite company over." Captain Egan said.

"No," Phil replied, "That's probably her husband's truck. When I was here before there weren't any cars in the driveway, but I noticed a Jetta through the garage window."

Phil reached the front door first and pressed the doorbell. The two men waited as they heard the sound of footsteps approaching the door.

As Madge Flanders opened the door, Phil couldn't help but notice she looked rested and much more composed than the last time he saw her.

"Hello, Detective Glass. Come in, come in!"

Extending her hand to the Captain, she said, "You

must be Captain Egan. It's a pleasure to meet you."

The Captain shook Madge's hand and the three went to the living room. This time, the tray with the coffee service was already in place, along with small sandwiches. Bill Flanders, a slender man with graying hair, was already seated on the couch, but stood to greet his guests.

"Good morning, Gentlemen. I'm Bill Flanders, Madge's husband. She filled me in on the visit she had with the detective last week and said it would be helpful if I was here today. Anything I can do to unravel this mystery about Gary, I'm willing to do. Gary was a devoted brother to Madge and treated me as if we were brothers. Please have a seat and get comfortable."

The group took their seats with Madge and Bill on the couch and Phil and the Captain on the armchairs across the coffee table, facing the Flanders.

"Thank you for meeting with us," said the Captain, "we just have a few more questions for you regarding Gary just before he died."

"Certainly, "Madge replied in a more relaxed tone," We'll do our best to help."

"That's right," Bill agreed.

Bill poured coffee for each of them, setting a small sandwich on each plate.

"Thank you. The coffee and sandwiches are very tasty," complimented Captain Egan.

"Mm, I can't agree more," the Phil said as he wiped his mouth.

"Mrs. Flanders, could you fill us in a little more on Gary's childhood and the twin brother he had?" Captain Egan asked.

"Sure. What would you like to know?" asked Madge.

"Do you have any pictures of the two of your brothers? I mean, before the twin left? Also, what is his name and did you contact him when your parents or Gary died?"

"His name is Vito. He was Gary's twin."

Then she turned to her husband, saying, "Bill, would you get that box of pictures marked Cape Cod from the closet for me, please? I think I have a few photos of Gary, Vito and myself."

Turning back to the Captain, Madge continued, "The photos are from when we were all in our mid to late teens, some from just before the boys went off to college; Gary to the Police Academy and Vito to the State College. It was after his second semester in college that Vito stopped communicating with us. When Mom and Dad would write to him, their letters were just returned with 'addressee unknown' written across it. That broke their hearts, really."

"So you weren't able to let him know his adoptive parents had died?"

"Gary tried tracking him down. Some of his friends at the Academy and the Post Office looked up the address and tried to find out if it was valid or not. It came back as a frat house and unfortunately nobody would admit to knowing Vito. We were at a loss, not knowing how to get word to him about our parents. What we ended up doing was putting an obituary in the paper where we thought he lived."

Bill returned with the box of photos, setting it on the couch between Madge and himself.

Opening the box, Madge thumbed through several pictures, reminiscing as she did. "Oh, those were some of the happiest days... Ah, here we go!"

Madge produced a photo of three teens at a clambake, looking very happy. Madge hadn't changed drastically. Her hair was gray now instead of the brunette color in the photo. Vito and Gary had matching T-shirts in the photo, their blonde hair ruffled by the wind. The three of them looked as though they hadn't a care in the world.

"That was our last year of high school and a bunch of us went to Cape Cod for a week in the sun. Vito's girlfriend took this picture."

"Do you keep in touch with her? Can she contact him?" Phil asked.

"I'm sad to say no to both of those questions.
She and Vito split up after they went to college.
They were both attending the state college when
Vito started partying a lot and began hanging
around a rough crowd. That group was more
interested in parties and sex than they were in
their studies. Isabella Coziole, Vito's girlfriend,
was studying pre-med and was an honor student.
Vito had started in pre-med also, did poorly, then
switched his major to communications and
wanted to work either in radio or television. His
grades took a big hit when he began partying all
the time. He asked Isabella to get him narcotics.
It was when she refused to do so that they broke
up. That was also about the same time he broke
off communicating with us." Madge's eyes welled
up with tears. She dabbed at her eyes and
continued, "Thank God Gary didn't follow that
path! Mom and Dad were crushed by Vito's
actions. If Gary had done the same, they would
have both died right then from a broken heart."

Phil pulled out his smartphone and asked Madge
if he could take a picture of the three of them at
the clambake.

"This will be used as a reference only", he
explained, "We have no intention of circulating it
without your permission."

"Well, I guess it's okay", she said, holding the
picture out for Phil.

Thank you very much. Please tell me: when did

Gary start to withdraw from you and behave differently?"

Bill Flanders answered this question, "Gary and I used to go to the gym on Saturday mornings then over to my Elks club in the afternoon to mingle with the other guys and watch sports on the big screen. About two months ago, he suddenly quit going to the gym, saying he had other things to do. You have to realize that before this, Gary was at the gym religiously every Saturday morning. Then he started blowing me off about going to the club! He said he had other things to do that were more important. Our friends at the club were startled by this."

"Did he ever mention the men you saw him meeting in the park? Were they his friends or anyone you recognized?" Phil inquired.

"No", Madge said, "I would have recognized his friends. We used to have Gary, his friend, Nick and a few of his other pals over for Sunday dinners. That's another thing! He just stopped showing up for our Sunday meals!"

Madge dabbed her eyes and bleated, "I miss my brother so! It seemed like he wasn't himself at all!"

Captain Egan stood. Phil followed his lead and rose from his seat.

"We should be heading back to the station now. Thank you for your cooperation."

Bill Flanders walked the men to the door. Just as they were about to leave, he motioned for them to wait. In a low voice he said, "I'd prefer that Madge doesn't hear this. Just between us, the characters Gary was meeting in the park were thugs. I've seen them at the last construction site I worked. They were hanging around the dilapidated building my crew was tearing down. I've heard it was a spot for the drug dealers to meet and was part of the reason we were demolishing it. I can't bring myself to tell Madge. It would destroy her image of Gary."

"Thank you for that, Mr. Flanders."

Captain Egan and Detective Glass turned to walk to their car.

"Thanks again to you and your wife for the coffee and sandwiches," Phil called over his shoulder.

Once the two men were in their vehicle, they compared notes.

"Let's send that photo off to Erma Honigbaum. Jeff is over there with her. Hopefully, she's willing to put this photo in the system and share the results with him."

Phil tapped out an email, attached the photo and hit send.

Pressing a few buttons on his phone Phil said, "There, it's sent. I asked her to reply whether she can do the recognition or not. Just as Phil finished speaking his email chirped, alerting him to an incoming message.

"Good news; she says she'll put it through the paces shortly," Phil reported.

"Good. Now, what is your gut feeling about Gary's twin brother?"

"Well, I'd have to say that I think he's bad news. He enters college studying pre-med and somehow winds up doing drugs. Where did he go wrong? What influenced him to make such bad choices?" Phil wondered aloud.

"What is it that makes any kid go bad? The Phenton's home was a loving one, according to Mrs. Flanders. I imagine he felt secure enough to be able to do well in school and be accepted at the state college. Maybe he was overconfident and figured nobody would catch on that he was dealing." Phil continued.

"I wonder if he fell prey to the lure of a quick high and started using them himself."

Captain Egan responded, "In my twenty years on the force, I've seen that happen all too often and the dealer has to either come up with outrageous amounts of money for the thugs they get their drugs from, or they need crazy amounts of drugs for the folks they are selling the drugs to. Either way it doesn't end well."

"I wonder if Vito was murdered and that's why they never heard from him," Phil mused.

"That's another lead we need to check on. Let's contact the state college and see if they have any record of him disappearing. If they have a set of fingerprints, we can run them against the John Does that have died."

"That sounds good. When we get back to the station I'll put a call in to the college."

Chapter 12

Erma Honigbaum's alarm on her phone chimed. She glanced quickly at the message, and said, "We have some results waiting for us. Shall we gather them and go over to Woody's to discuss?"

"Sure, sounds good." Jeff said eagerly.

Selecting a fairly private booth, they ordered as Erma withdrew the manila folder with the recognition results from her bag.

"Let me give you a little background on facial recognition. The computer software program compares facial features with a database; we can have it search in a certain area or have it connect with other databases nationwide, much like AFIS does with fingerprints. The program will collect the best matches, then our office ascertains if the matches correspond with living or deceased individuals. If the good match is living, then we can search for their current residence. If the person is deceased, we can find the locality where they died. So," Erma continued, "on to our John

Doe."

Erma spread a few sheets with printouts on them in front of her.

"Are those all possible matches?" Jeff queried.

"Some, yes. Other printouts show possible locations for these hits and other options available to us in order to find our John Doe."

Erma selected a few printouts and arranged them so Jeff could easily read along as she explained their contents.

"This one here," she said, pointing to the sheet in front of Jeff, "shows a likely match to a Vito Anstenini in Pleasantville. Although it's relatively far from here, we can check and see if it's actually a match. Now this one," she pointed at another sheet, "isn't so likely because it's a poorer match and the person is from New Mexico. See how the rating system gives it a much lower grade than the first one?"

"Yes, yes, I see," Jeff said, peering at the documents, "the one from down south has some of the same features but not enough to be considered a good match."

"You have the right idea. Good job!" Erma said in a praising tone, "Let's track down this possible match in Pleasantville."

****

Phil replaced the phone's receiver, then stood and walked to Captain Egan's office. He tapped lightly on the door, entering when the Captain replied.

"Find anything, Phil?" Captain Egan asked.

"Yes. Vito was on the Dean's List in his first year at college. In his second year, he started getting C's and D's. Apparently, he dropped out because there is no record of him after the second year. They had no forwarding address, so all correspondence went to his parents. It's like he vanished!"

The Captain stroked his chin thoughtfully, "What about that photo you emailed to Honigbaum? I wonder if they have someone on staff that can do age progression then use the facial recognition software to look for possible matches. Let's call Jeff and see if he can get her to accept our request."

"Good idea," Phil replied, pulling out his cell phone, "I have his cell on speed dial." Phil punched a few buttons then handed the phone to the Captain.

"Weston? Captain Egan here. Did you get the email with a picture attached?" He paused, listening, nodding his head to Phil that the email had been received successfully.

"Yes, hello Investigator Honigbaum. The boy on the right is the one I'd like you to work your magic on. See if you can do an age progression and a facial recognition as well."

The Captain sat in his chair, straightening some papers on his desk as he listened to Jeff relay the requests. He sat bolt upright with a beaming smile as Jeff gave him an unexpected surprise.

"You can and you will!?I owe you big time!"

Captain Egan hung up and gave the phone back to Phil, clapping him on the shoulder at the same time.

"Erma says she'll get her associate, Larkenvar O'Dea, to do the age progression."

"Great. Now we're getting someplace." Phil said.

"Let's just hope and pray she can get results. That photo is at least 30 years old. Realistically, if Vito wanted to really get lost, he could have altered his looks by now." Captain Egan reflected.

"I hadn't thought of that. Well, we can only hope for the best."

Chapter 13

Erma Honigbaum examined the new photo and considered the requests Captain Egan made over the phone.

"Hmm, let's see," Erma said more to herself than to Jeff, "I guess I could do something with this. Sharpen it up a bit and then I'll send it to my associate for age progression."

Turning to Jeff, she spoke in a clearer voice.

"Tell Captain Egan we'll do what we can."

"We appreciate your help." Jeff replied with enthusiasm, "The captain will be pleased." He turned to Erma, rubbing his hands, and asked, "Do you think that's usable? I mean do you think there's a chance you can do the age progression and facial recognition, too?"

"Well, I am going to see if my talented associate, Larkenvar, can do the age progression. If he's successful and the picture isn't too grainy, I'll put it into the facial recognition software."

Erma sent the picture off to Larkenvar, silently hoping he could do an age progression of Gary's twin, taking into account the possibility of the subject having smoked and used illegal drugs, since those activities age the skin also.

"Let's see what Larkenvar comes up with, if anything", she said, standing and stretching.

"I guess we can only hope for the best and expect the worst." Jeff replied.

"Thanks for your help. Please call me on my cell if you hear anything."

"Oh, it's no problem, Jeff. Thanks for the lunch. I'll call you as soon as I have anything."

Erma walked Jeff back to his car, waving goodbye as he pulled out of the lab.

"I hope we find something for Jeff", she thought to herself. "I wouldn't mind having lunch with him again. He seems nice."

Jeff was having similar thoughts as he drove back to the police station. He felt instantly at ease with Erma when they met. He was glad they had lunch together and had gotten to know each other a little. He couldn't help but feel she was a great asset to the investigation, but more than that, he wanted to strike up a friendship with her.

Pulling into his spot at the back of the police station, Jeff was still thinking of the conversation he and Erma had. He exited his car and considered seeing the Captain right away to update him on his progress. Jeff found himself so engrossed in his thoughts he didn't hear the sound of a car approaching the back entrance to the station. The loud sound of the gate broke into his reverie, just as he found himself inexplicably under attack. A man, clearly outweighing him by more than a few pounds, tackled him, knocking him to the ground. His attacker wrestled a chloroform-soaked cloth over Jeff's mouth and nose. Jeff tried to call out, struggling briefly before going limp. Maneuvering Jeff into the back seat of his nearby car, the man noticed a uniformed officer coming towards him.

Sprinting into the parking lot, the officer shouted, "Hey! You! Stop right there!" The fracas attracted the attention of the detectives in the bullpen area of the station as the hooded man jumped into his car, speeding off leaving a trail of dust in its wake.

"Did you get the plate number?" huffed Detective Glass, who was the first to reach the scene, realizing the uniformed officer was Captain Egan. Glass had his hand-held computer ready to enter the registration.

"No", coughed the Captain, "he kicked up so much dust and dirt I couldn't see anything."

"Did you get a look at the guy? No matter, we can look at the security camera's tapes." Phil sent one of the responding detectives to examine the

surveillance tapes for a clear view of the
license plate number.

"Put out a call to all units that Weston has been
kidnapped. Call the main communications for the
State Police and all law agencies with the same
message!" barked the captain.

Phil opened his hand-held computer and tapped
out a teletype to the main communications,
instructing them to broadcast the message to all
agencies throughout the state. Then he picked up
his cell phone and punched in a number, waited as
the call connected then gave some orders to the
person on the other end of the phone. He listened
a moment then hung up.

"The teletype will go out right away and the other
Departments in the area are on high alert. We'll
get him back, ASAP!" Phil declared.

****

Jeff blinked slowly and rubbed his eyes. "Not
again," he thought. His head hurt badly. The
barrel of a gun pushed into his ribs, "Get out of
the car. Now!" a harsh voice sounded, reminding
Jeff he was not in the safe environment of a
hospital but rather crammed in the back seat of a
dirty, foul smelling compact car. The gun barrel
prodded him into the present as Jeff felt for the
door handle. As Jeff started to move toward the

open door, he noticed his dog sitter, Alice, walking a large dog in the park across the street.

"I said GET OUT!" the voice said louder, this time, prodding him even harder. Jeff slowly got out of the car and let out a low whistle. The dog in the park jerked away from the woman walking it, leaving her watching in dismay as it galloped towards him. Within seconds, the large dog was at his side barking, startling Jeff's attacker, allowing Jeff to wheel around and snatch his attacker's gun.

"Good girl, Shadow! Keep this guy down." With that, the dog jumped on the now unarmed, trembling man and knocking him down. Shadow started growling, causing the man to shake uncontrollably. Seeing the scuffle, Alice came running to retrieve the dog, not knowing Jeff was there. She stopped about thirty feet away, realizing Jeff and his dog controlled the situation.

"D-don't let her hurt me!! Please," the man whimpered.

"Just stay put and you'll remain unharmed." Jeff commanded.

Shadow laid her 100-pound body on the man's legs and stomach, still growling. Jeff reached into his pocket and pulled out his phone, dialing the Anderson Falls PD.

"Captain Egan, please." Jeff looked at his captive and shook his head. Watching his captor-now-turned-captive closely, he said, "Mister, it's going to be a long night for you."

Chapter 14

The sirens died down as two police cruisers pulled alongside the stolen car that had been used to kidnap Jeff Weston. Their lights were still flashing as two patrolmen jumped out of one car, batons and handcuffs swinging from their utility belts as they sprinted to where Shadow held her victim at bay.

"You have the right to remain silent ...." started the young officer with a body-builder's frame who reached them first. As he read the Miranda to the man, he cuffed him, brought him to his feet and walked him back to the waiting patrol car. The Captain exited the second car and quickly strode over to Jeff.

"How did you pull that off without getting you or your dog shot!?"

"When Shadow was a puppy, I taught her a few tricks. One of them was to come to my side when I let out a low whistle. At first, I did it just to be able to recall her if she got loose in the park. It came in handy today, didn't it?"

"I guess so!" laughed the captain, "That guy looked scared to death."

Jeff rubbed Shadow's head, leaned over and gave her a kiss.

"You are one smart girl! I'm so proud of you!"

The dog looked lovingly at Jeff and gave him a big sloppy dog kiss.

****

Phil Glass met Captain Egan and Detective Weston at Anderson Falls PD Headquarters. When the Captain and the two Detectives entered the station they were surprised to see Paul Z. Meyers there, leading Lt. Gibson into the Booking Area in handcuffs.

"Paul! What's going on here?" Captain Egan questioned in an astonished voice.

"I'm sure you remember when I ran the prints from Jeff's car? I had dismissed anyone from the station because they had reason to be around the vehicles. Yet, something bothered me when I found this guy's prints in the car. When the APB went out about Jeff's kidnapping, Erma came to me and asked me to recheck Gibson's activity.

The fella that's in Interrogation right now threw Gibson under the bus right away - it seems that the Lieutenant here has a taste for dope. He hid it pretty well and the prisoner in custody supplied him with dope in exchange for information. You can get the details from him while I take this dirty cop to Booking."

Jeff, Phil and the Captain all went in to the Interrogation room together, a fair sized room with a cement floor, a long metal table with a few folding chairs. A Sergeant had just shackled the prisoner to a ring in the center of the table. He turned to the three men, before they went into the room and handed them a sheaf of papers and said, "This is everything we have on Vito Anstinelli, aka Omar Tullio, Fineas Underwood and Vito Phenton. Pick whatever name you want. I just got word from Honigbaum that the facial recognition results all led to those identities. He has a laundry list of former names as well as crimes, ranging from small scale drug pushing to money laundering and now murder of his twin brother along with impersonating him and stealing evidence from the evidence lockers. You should've heard him sing! He was so scared he started confessing to everything."

"He didn't ask for a lawyer?" Phil asked.

"Surprisingly, no. He signed a waiver saying no lawyer. All the information and his confession are in those pages I just gave you."

"I think we should still talk to him," Jeff insisted.

"I do too." Phil agreed.

"Let's do it," Captain Egan said, he's already waived his right to counsel and signed a confession. Maybe he'll tell us why he committed all those crimes."

The three of them went into the Interrogation room. They sat across from Vito.

"Okay Vito, how about telling us your true name, for starters?" Captain Egan waved the papers the Sergeant had given him.

"Then you can fill us in on why you committed all the crimes you've confessed to this evening."

Chapter 15

"First, my real name is Vito Phenton. Our birth mother, - Gary's and mine, got pregnant when she was just eighteen." Vito began, "She married our father because of the pregnancy, but we were never accepted because, really, we were unwanted. Then, when Gary and I were about a year old, our parents were in a terrible accident that killed them both. Their families did not want us because we were illegitimate. The Phentons took us in shortly after we were put up for adoption. I was glad that Gary and I were able to stay together. I never tried to find my birth parents, - the only parents I knew were the Phentons."

"Why not?" questioned the captain.

"Gary was the curious one, the smarter of the two of us, and looked up the information on our birth parents. I have to admit, Mom and Pop Phenton were good to us, and they gave us a good life."

"Go on."

"I was going to college with my high school sweetheart, Isabella. I was going to study pre-med with her. My second year there I fell in with a bad crowd. I had been getting okay marks, you know, B's mostly and some A's. That second semester I couldn't make the grade. I learned enough to make me dangerous. Then I started using drugs and selling them too. I transferred into drama/communications program in the beginning of my sophomore year and did well in that area, so when the drug dealers came after me I could create a disguise for myself. I left college and the city it was in."

"Your sister said you stopped communicating with your family about then. What happened?"

"First of all, I didn't want them as targets of the drug dealers. I know it sounds harsh. Anyway, I was able to slip into another identity easily at first. I was making plenty of money pushing drugs to the college students. The drug dealers kept coming after me. I assumed another identity and moved to another state, but somehow they found me every time. That's when I came back to Anderson Falls and reached out to my twin brother for the money to pay off the thugs that were after me."

"Why didn't you just turn yourself in?" Jeff asked.

"I couldn't. I am still an addict. In fact, I was so

scared I would get caught that I kept some acotine dissolvable powder in my knapsack in case I was cornered by the guys that were after me I could take it and end it all. But something kept me from doing myself in."

"When I arrived in Anderson Falls I decided to watch Gary and study his routine. Two months ago I broke into his place. He was surprised to see me in his apartment when he got back from running his ten miles that was part of his routine every day. I could see him breathing hard and offered him a cold beer. He knew I was still using drugs, but I think he hoped I wanted to turn a corner and reform, but you know I didn't. I asked him for some money to keep the dealers off my back and he flat out refused. Then the idea struck me that I could take on Gary's identity pretty easily. I just put the acotine powder in his Bud Light beer and slipped out of the room under the pretense of having to use the bathroom. It sounded like the acotine started working quickly because he started hallucinating and was pounding on the bathroom door asking what I slipped him. He said to come out so he could throw up in the toilet but I just locked the door. I heard him retching then he went into cardiac arrest. I stood behind the door and did nothing."

"Wait, you just stood behind a locked door and listened to you own flesh and blood in agony, dying?" Investigator Glass asked, stunned.

"Yea, at the time I needed the money more than

anything else. I drove him out of town and dumped his body in the woods. Then I stole some of his work clothes, did some quick makeup work and assumed Gary's identity. Of course, I made sure 'Gary' was back at work the next day. I had observed his routine and knew his every move. Gary was so predictable it was easy to copy his movements when I took on his identity. I was able to appease the drug lords for a few weeks, but they wanted more and more money. I started giving the drugs and jewels to the thug's right out of the evidence lockers. Then Gary was found in the woods by some hikers, and they assumed right away that he died of a heart attack. That's the beauty of acotine! I should have used that on you", he sneered at Jeff.

"Look pal, you'll be going away for a long time and prison life isn't pretty, so I won't be taking the bait on that one." Jeff leaned back in his chair and stretched, then stood up.

Captain Egan leaned forward and asked the next question. "So when did you involve Lieutenant Gibson? And why?"

"Gibson liked dope, so it was easy to manipulate him. Since he worked in Internal Affairs, he had the authority to command the IT department to put key loggers on the computers and taps on phones. He kept me informed of your every move and I gave him his dope fix. We knew we had to eliminate any threats to our operation, so when Gibson and I saw how quick Weston and Glass are to pick up on things we knew they would see the discrepancies in the dispatcher's log. We decided that Gibson's authority with Internal Affairs would be useful in planting the roofies. I had seen Weston go for his pill box after complaining of a headache. It was easy enough for Gibson to get Weston's car door open and plant them in his pill box. Then we just hoped he'd take an 'aspirin' soon."

Captain Egan shook his head in disgust.

"That'll be enough to lock Gibson away for attempted murder. That's good enough for me."

Jeff walked forward, leaning on the table, his face inches from Vito's. He was about to ask another question before he jumped back and exclaimed, "Wait! Phil - that clue I was trying to recall - it was the odor of cigarettes I smelled on Vito as he impersonated Gary! I smell it now!" Jeff smacked his head in amazement. Phil nodded emphatically as he realized the same thing. His partner addressed Vito again, "This bothers me about you. If you're so good with poisons, then why did you shoot Monica? Why didn't you just slip her something when we were at the restaurant you were lurking around? That charge can land you in prison for a very long time, just for attempting to take her life."

He stepped back, and waited for Vito's response.

"That was the one thing I did that really was spur of the moment. I've kept a gun on me ever since the last time the drug dealers found me. I wanted to scare you guys away from tracking me and discovering my identity. You never know who's in cahoots with the mafia or the drug dealers in the world. She was collateral damage."

"You never know. Maybe you will meet up with them in prison!" Phil scoffed.

Vito dropped his head in his shackled hands and moaned loudly.

"Then I'm be dead for sure."

At that moment, the Captain motioned to Jeff and Phil to exit the room with him for a moment.

"Sit tight, Vito. I want to talk to the detectives a minute."

In the hallway leading to the Interrogation Observation Room the Captain said, "He can stew in there for a little while. I have an idea."

Captain Egan picked up the phone in the Observation Room, dialed a number and spoke in a hushed voice to the person on the other end. He soon thanked the other party and hung up. Turning to Jeff and Phil he said,

"That was the Prosecutor I just spoke with. He's willing to protect Vito if the names of his suppliers are turned over to us."

"That sounds fair. Do you think he'll go for it?"

"We'll see", he said and led the two detectives

back to the Interrogation Room.

"Let me offer you a deal, Vito. There's a way we could keep you safe while you do your time," the Captain said in a stern voice. "Give us the names of your suppliers and any of their suppliers. We can haul them in and get ahead in our war on drugs."

"Okay," Vito said, "can I just tell you? Are you taping all this or should I write the names down?"

Sliding him a pad of paper and handing him a pen, Captain Egan asked Vito to write the names and ranks of his suppliers down. Vito scribbled fervently, sliding the papers back to the Captain.

The Captain scanned the pages, saying, "Very good. Yes, very good. We'll see to it that you're kept safe while you serve your time."

"Thanks; At least I'll be able to do my time and not worry about getting snuffed out by one of the drug gangs hired killers."

At the signal from the Captain, a Sergeant came in and took Vito to his cell to await arraignment by a judge. A much meeker Vito went with his guard.

"I guess he's ready to spend a lifetime behind bars", Phil remarked.

"It's sad to see a life wasted like that", agreed the Captain, "There was so much potential in that young man and it was ruined by drugs."

"At least we'll make a dent in the illegal drug trade around here with the information he gave us", added Jeff.

****

The next day Jeff called Erma Honigbaum to thank her for her invaluable help.

"We want to thank you for getting those results to us so quickly - how did you do it!?"

"When I heard the APB go out saying you were kidnapped; I couldn't sit still. I called Larkenvar O'Dea to see if he had the photo of the young man you gave me. He said he did, so I had him get to work right away on the age progression. He did an amazing job in a short amount of time. I took his results and ran the facial recognition program. It returned the results that I brought over to the station right away. You can't believe how happy I was to hear you're okay!" Erma paused to catch her breath, "This may sound mushy, but I've developed a bit of a soft spot for you."

"That doesn't sound foolish at all. I'll be honest with you - I feel the same way about you. Do you think we could discuss this over dinner sometime soon?"

"That sounds wonderful; I'd love to go to dinner with you."

"Well then, how about tonight? I know a good steak house on the other side of town. What time and where should I pick you up?"

Erma was so overcome with joy, it took her a moment to reply but when she did, Jeff could hear the happiness in the lilt of her voice.

"There's one more thing, Erma. Is it okay if we double date with my partner? He recently began dating my sister."

"That sounds like a wonderful way to end to our case."

(SIX MONTHS LATER)

Vito Phenton plead guilty to a host of crimes and was sentenced to fifty years to life in the state prison with the stipulation that he would not be in the same population as the thugs that had been trying to kill him.

"That's one more criminal off the streets!" Jeff Weston exclaimed to his partner as they high fived. "Good job!"

Phil smiled in agreement.

"Plus I got to know Monica better. I think the few days I spent at her place was the turning point for us. We got to know each other better. At first, we did not really know each other that well, but we had some intense conversations. It's hard to believe that was over six months ago. I just love being with her."

"You've been taking her out almost every night. Are you independently wealthy or something?" Jeff said jokingly, "I only take Erma out once a week, although we go running every day. She really is into that stuff."

"Well I don't go to Griffin's every night with Monica. Sometimes we stay home and make something there. She is a real chef. I've seen her make gourmet meals from the simplest ingredients. Other times we just go to the park and relax by the pond. Other nights, we just veg on the sofa and watch TV, or go to the park and lay on the grass watching the stars come out. I will point out some of the constellations I know."

"You two have really become a serious item!"

"So have you and Erma." He countered.

Phil kicked the toe of his shoe on the rug. Hesitating a little, Phil said, "I have to ask you something serious."

"Go ahead and ask away!"

"You know how special Monica is to me, right?"

"Yes, and she's head over heels for you, too. What are you driving at?"

"How would you like to be my brother-in-law?"

"Are you proposing?" Jeff laughed.

"I will be tonight, but not to you. I'll be proposing to Monica!" Phil practically shouted.

"Fantastic!" Jeff rejoiced, "That will be great! I'm sure she's going to say yes!"

That night Phil took Monica to their favorite spot in the Town Park. As he went down on one knee, he opened a jewel box holding an engagement ring and asked Monica to be his bride. She agreed through tears of joy.

Later that same evening, as Jeff was drying his hands after cleaning up his dinner dishes, his phone rang. Jeff picked up on the first ring, seeing it was his sister calling.

"Hello!" Jeff greeted his sister.

"Oh Jeff, Phil just proposed to me! I'm so happy; I wanted you to be the first to know!"

"Congratulations, Monica! You couldn't have landed a better man!" Jeff exclaimed.

"We're thinking of a spring wedding. When are you going to pop the question to Erma? I know how you feel about her and you've been seeing her so much, you might as well be married!" Monica burbled.

"You know," Jeff said playfully, "We could have a double wedding."

"That's a great idea!" Monica said gleefully. "Hurry up and propose to her so we can start planning the wedding." She clapped her hands. "This is so exciting!"

The next day, Jeff went to the Jewelers with Erma under the guise of seeing the ring Phil bought for Monica. Erma's eyes glowed when she saw the ring.   Jeff took the ring from the jeweler, knelt on one knee and said, "Will you spend the rest of your life with me? Erma Honigbaum, will you marry me?"

Erma's mouth formed a surprised "O".   She stepped back and leaned on the jewelry case.

"Jeff! Yes! A thousand times, yes!! I love you so much!!" she practically shouted. She wrapped her arms around Jeff and hugged him so hard he could barely breathe. He kissed her passionately, wrapping his arms around her, lifting her off the floor, spinning joyously. The staff at the jewelry stored gave a hearty congratulatory applause.

"You two young lovebirds make such a nice couple!" the jeweler exclaimed.

The happy couple drove back to Jeff's house, talking excitedly, planning their wedding. Erma was ecstatic at the idea of having a double wedding with Monica and Phil.   She pulled out her iPhone and called Monica.

"Monica!" she said excitedly, "Jeff proposed to me!" She listened to Monica's excited reply and responded, "Well of course I said yes!"   She listened again, nodding her head.   "...yes, mmhmm, we can do that! A double wedding sounds awesome. That's just five months away. We have a lot to do!"

The next five months flew by. The wedding was wonderful.   Erma and Jeff, Monica and Phil honeymooned in Hawaii. The two couples had a great time, learning how to surf and for added pleasure, windsurf. They were feeling like they had become accomplished at the two sports by the end of their three-week honeymoon. Upon their return home, Phil and Monica moved into their new house, just a few blocks from Jeff and Erma's home. Life was good.

****

Madge and Bill Flanders were having their morning coffee and reading the newspaper together. The headlines screamed the news of Vito Phenton killing his own brother for drug money. Madge read the article with horror and dismay.

"Bill, look at this! It is so hard to understand how both of my brothers could come to this end. Gary was so loving and good. We thought Vito had just turned his back on his family and left us. I don't know if I can ever forgive him for killing Gary."

"Madge, he is going to pay his debt to Society. He will be a very old man if and when he ever gets out of prison. Maybe by that time, you'll be able to forgive him. Father Belleretz has always preached forgiveness."

"I'm not so sure I will ever be able to do that Bill.

It is a pretty tall order."

Bill leaned over and kissed his wife gently on the forehead. "Honey, I will be here for you always, we'll get through this together."

Part Two: Cell Block A

Chapter 16

Missy Barone felt the vibration of her cell phone in her pocket. Completing one of the martial arts moves she was currently teaching her early morning class, she pulled her phone out, looking at the display. Recognizing it as an urgent text, she instructed her assistant to take over the class. She stepped into the locker room, dressing hurriedly. As she was driving to the FBI field office she began wondering what the reason is for this urgent text. At the same time, Kevin Leestaud O'Hara received a similar text as he was preparing to teach his Special Forces unit the latest techniques in a stealth attack. He quickly dressed and hopped into his car, also wondering about the urgent text. The two agents arrived within minutes of each other, entering the building and hurrying to the conference room.

Investigator Don Rennips finished reviewing his

notes as he approached the conference room. He began to address the detectives gathered for the impromptu meeting.

"Good Morning, Ladies and Gentlemen. I called this meeting today to give you an update on the criminal activity in Anderson Falls. Two years ago, Vito Phenton was sent to the State Prison for the murder of his brother, Gary. Many of you remember Gary as the Anderson Falls Police Department's night dispatcher. Vito was dealing drugs at that time and was convicted on those counts. He then became a Confidential Informant in exchange for protection from the members of the cartel he was working for. Those members are now serving time in the prison system. During these past couple of years, he has provided vital information to us that have greatly aided our war on drugs. He's proven to be a valuable asset."

The investigator turned on the laptop next to him and opened a PowerPoint presentation. An image appeared on the screen beside him. He shuffled through his papers, selected a few that were clipped together, then continued.

"This is Vito Phenton just before he entered prison," He went on to the next PowerPoint slide. It showed an old Italian with an angry look on his mustached face. "This is Mario Carmeletti, head of the biggest drug cartel we've brought down. He and several of his henchmen have been confined to the Golga Correctional Facility, thus protecting Vito. We've been keeping them under surveillance as well." He advanced to the next slide. "Yesterday, it was brought to my attention that Vito had fallen ill and was taken to Anderson Falls General Hospital. He was treated and released to the prison guards. He was supposed to return to his cell by 1600 hours yesterday. He did not. An APB was issued immediately. We received word at 1800 hours that the prisoner was taken to Golga instead of having been returned to the state prison. This slide shows a transfer order for Vito Phenton from the state prison to Golga Correctional Facility. Needless to say, it was either a grave clerical error or a forged document that will bring about the demise of one of our best informants. We need to come up with a plan to rectify this issue before Vito is seriously injured or killed. Let's develop a plan to get to the bottom of this and preserve Phenton's life."

The detectives huddled in groups and began discussing various options for returning Vito to the state prison safely and the risks involved. Some plans included breaking him out of Golga, but were rejected immediately. A couple groups discussions grew quite heated. Finally, a plan was devised that everyone agreed upon. Investigator Rennips thanked everyone for their help and dismissed the meeting.

"Lt. O'Hara and Detective Barone, could you stay for a moment?"

The pair walked over to the investigator.

"You wanted to speak with us, sir?" Lt. O'Hara asked.

"I'd like you two to head up this mission. Vito Phenton has proved to be an important source of information in Narcotics Enforcement. We need him alive and well. Use whatever resources you need, human or otherwise. Vito is an indispensable asset."

"Yes, Sir," Lt. O'Hara replied. Detective Barone shook her head in agreement and said," You can count on us to get the job done, Sir!"

Chapter 17

Monica Glass opened the back door of her new home, carefully balancing a plate of steaks and two bowls; one filled with her special German potato salad and the other with an ambrosia salad.

"Phil! She said, "Jeff and Erma just called. They should be here in a few minutes."

Phil walked over to her quickly, relieving her of the steaks. Monica put the bowls on the picnic table by the door, then turned to Phil, smiling and patting her growing stomach.

"Honey, do you want to tell them, or should I?"

Phil adjusted the flames on the grill and replied, "Let's both tell them! This news is too exciting to hold in!" He wrapped one arm around Monica's waist and nodded toward their soon to be bundle of joy.

"Here's to our own little miracle!"

Just then they heard the crunch of gravel as Jeff's

car came to a stop in their driveway.

"We're out back", Phil called. Soon, Jeff and Erma could be seen as they rounded the corner of the house.

"I have the grill fired up and the steaks are ready to go on. How does everyone want their steaks done?"

"Medium, for me", Jeff answered.

"Same for me too" chimed in Erma.

"Well, Phil, you might as well make that three" Monica giggled as she turned to Phil, "Let's tell them now!" she burbled.

"Tell us what!?" Erma and Jeff said in unison.

"We're having a baby!" both Phil and Monica practically shouted.

"We have the same news as you guys! Erma's nine weeks pregnant!" Jeff exclaimed.

"This is a great reason to celebrate!"

Hugs and handshakes were aplenty. The ladies compared notes on their progress and then everyone sat down to eat. Monica and Erma were still bubbling with excitement throughout the meal. Once all the dinner plates were washed and put away, the foursome relaxed in the comfortable lawn chairs set up in the shade of a towering elm tree.

"That was a delicious meal!" Jeff observed.

"You certainly know how to make a great German potato salad. My mom's version cannot compare with this!" Erma complimented.

"Thank you", Monica blushed.

Just then, both Phil and Jeff's cell phones started to ring.

"What the…." Jeff exclaimed as he looked at the caller ID.

"Captain Egan", Phil said as he glanced at his phone and answered it.

"Hello, Captain Egan", Jeff echoed as he joined the call on his phone too.

"I conferenced you both in to this phone call because Lt. O'Hara and Detective Barone have uncovered some important Intel that you should be aware of."

"It was important enough to call us both on a Saturday afternoon?" Jeff asked.

"Yes," Captain Egan responded in a grim voice, "This is serious enough to call you both in to my office on a beautiful day when I would rather be relaxing with my wife."

"We'll be at the station in 10 minutes, Captain", Phil said and disconnected his call. Jeff hung up, grabbed his windbreaker, kissed Erma on the head, and followed Phil to his car.

"We'll be back as soon as we can!" Phil called out.

Once the two men were on their way to the station, Jeff wondered aloud, "What could be so important that Captain Egan is calling us in on our day off?"

"I don't think he'd call unless it was really important. Maybe another sleeper cell plot was uncovered in a city near us. Other than that, I can't even hazard a guess."

Chapter 18

Captain Egan met the two detectives at the door to the station and ushered Phil and Jeff into the department's conference room.   "Let me introduce you to Lt. Kevin Leestaud O'Hara and his counterpart, Detective Sergeant Missy Barone." He motioned toward the table next to a pull down screen.

Lt. O'Hara was a tall, trim man with short brown hair. His boyish face did not reveal the Marine training he had received during his time in the military.   His uniform was smartly pressed; the short sleeves revealed well-muscled, tanned arms. He had a pleasant a southern drawl. He stood and addressed his audience.

"Good afternoon, Gentlemen. Please call me Kevin. I'll be handling the duties formerly carried out by Lt. Lester Gibson. Our office has received some unsettling news. Special Agent Rennips brought it to our attention just this morning. I'll let Detective Barone explain."

Detective Barone had her red hair pulled back in a

neat bun, with a few wisps of hair falling across her forehead. Her slender face was peppered with freckles. She was fair-skinned, with soft brown eyes. She also looked unassuming and with the name her parents gave her fooled people into thinking she was immature or a pushover. The majority of people that do not know her very well are surprised to find out under her petit frame is a martial arts instructor.

"Thank you, Kevin. As you all recall from personal experience with this case, two years ago Gary Phenton, our night dispatcher, was murdered and his twin brother, Vito. Convicted of the crime, he was sentenced to 50 years to life in the State Penitentiary, with the stipulation that he would not be in the same population as the guys he turned over. He's being treated as a confidential informant. That is, until last week, when the Golga Correctional Facility presented papers authorizing his transfer to them after he had been released from Anderson Falls General Hospital. Mr. Phenton is now in the same unit as the people he turned over to us two years ago. We have reason to believe his life is in jeopardy. Detective Barone will explain our plan further."

The detective booted up her laptop, hooked up to the video screen on the wall and started her PowerPoint Presentation. A photo appeared of Golga Prison, a drab looking three story building, appeared on the screen beside her. She pointed to one section of the prison and continued:

"This is where Vito and the convicted Carmeletti

drug leaders are housed – Cell Block A. A clerk for the Golga Superintendent apparently made a grave error by having Vito transferred there. We don't believe it was just a clerical error. If that was so, Vito would be back in the state prison. We believe this goes deeper. There has been an influx of illegal drug activity in the community near the prison an in the prison itself. We need to find the root of this. Is it just small time corruption or is it widespread? The plan that Lt. O'Hara and I are proposing is dangerous, but necessary. We need the two of you to go in there, undercover of course, one to see to Vito's safety, as his cellmate, while we correct this error. We need the other to pose as a new clerk in the Superintendent's office and observe the existing clerk, Tim Effabee. Tim may simply be incompetent, or he may have ulterior motives, such as money or notoriety. If he's doing something illegal, we will have to see how far the repercussions go. A Confidential Informant's life is at stake here. Are you two men willing to take this assignment on? We need you to be committed to the success of this mission, so please take a day and think about it. The two of you are the most qualified to do this since you dealt with Vito previously. If you refuse this assignment, we will have to find other qualified candidates to go in there. Remember, we've gotten valuable information from Vito and he's been a model prisoner. If he's killed now, we'll take a big hit in our operations to bring down top drug dealers.   Do you have any questions?"

Captain Egan spoke up.

"I have a few questions and concerns. First, how do we stay in contact with my men, if they agree to take on this mission? Is there an escape plan if they get into a critical situation? And how long do you think this mission will last?

Lt. O'Hara addressed these questions. "I'll be going to the facility on visitations, posing as the southern cousin that grew up with whoever is at the prison. The escape plan for that person will be a wireless transmitter that needs only the press of a button and we will extract your man immediately. As for the person posing as a clerk, Detective Barone will be also in close contact with him, posing as a friend who got him the position in the prison system. She will meet with him after hours at the motel where your man will stay. As for the escape plan, whoever poses as the clerk will be given a laptop and a secure email account that can be accessed by voice. If that person is in a situation where they're away from the laptop, they will have a keyword that activates the emergency email. The mike for the laptop will be disguised as a button. It is actually a Wi-Fi mike that works similar to Siri or Cortana on smartphones. The laptop has its own Wi-Fi hotspot installed. Finally, we estimate that the mission should last about a week."

"I have a question," Phil said, "Who will be posing as the clerk and who will be in the prison? And how are we going to explain why we are in those positions?

"Detective Barone, would you explain this part of the plan, please?"

"Assisted by what we have learned from your personnel files, we have set up profiles for the infiltration and determined the best fit would be Detective Weston to the Superintendent's Office at Golga. There, he will be working directly with Superintendent Bryce Wixmor and the clerk, Tim Effabee. Weston's role in this mission will be to find out if the transfer is a means of getting Vito into a life-threatening situation, how this got by the checks and balances and how far this type of corruption goes. You will be accessing highly sensitive documents at the prison. Hal Edwards in our IT department has created alternate backgrounds for both of you. You have them in the packets Lt. O'Hara gave you. Please familiarize yourself with them. If it was human error, we'll initiate the paperwork to transfer Vito back to a safer population. If you determine that it's a plan for his demise, find out who's behind it and let us know. We'll handle it from there. Remember your escape plan if things get out of hand and you find yourself in danger. We don't want anyone hurt, if we can help it."

Turning to Phil, Detective Barone said, "Glass, we're going to be placing you in Cell Block A as Vito's cellmate. As you will see in your packet, you are in prison for the assault and battery of a health club trainer. We'll be adorning your arms with tattoos." Seeing the look of apprehension on

Phil's face, she continued, "No worries; they're temporary. Your mission will be to keep a watchful eye out and protect Vito from being harmed. If you hear of or become aware of an attack plan, contact us right away. Use the escape plan."

"Thank you both for the briefing. Phil, Jeff, you two should go home and decide if you want to accept this assignment. Let me know what you decide by tomorrow. We will begin the mission on Monday. We need to get this under control as soon as possible." Captain Egan instructed the men.

"Yes Sir, we will" Jeff said as he and Phil departed.

The ride back to Phil's house was a quiet one, filled with uneasy tension. Worry emanated from both men. They entered the home to find their wives sitting on the couch flipping through baby magazines and giggling happily.

"….and I think this will look so cute in the baby's room, don't you?" Monica burbled.

"Oh yes, and the mobile that hangs over the crib will go perfectly!" Erma exclaimed.

"Uh, girls" Jeff interrupted, "Phil and I need to talk to you about something important."

"Oh, don't worry guys", Monica said, "We won't max out the credit cards!"

"No", Phil said slowly, "That's not it. We just got some disturbing news from Captain Egan."

Jeff slid his easy chair closer to the couch and took his wife's hand in his. "It seems that the case we worked on a couple of years ago has come back to haunt us." Phil explained, "Remember the one with Vito Phenton? Erma did the facial recognition on that case."

Erma looked at Jeff and said worriedly, "What do you mean? I thought that the guilty parties were sent to the State Penitentiary."

"They were. Vito had agreed to become a confidential informant in exchange for protection while he's in prison. He's been very valuable as an informant but now he is in trouble. Jeff and I are going in undercover, for about a week."

"The folks in the Electronic Equipment Section made an emergency device for us to wear so if we get into a dangerous situation, we just need to press the device and help will come immediately. Besides, they anticipate that this mission shouldn't last more than a week."

Erma gripped Jeff's hand, looked steadily into his eyes and asked him, "Do you really have to do this?"

Monica nodded in agreement. That's right. I am used to seeing you come home every night, Phil."

"It's supposed to be only for a week. We can't give you any other details except that it is our assignment." Jeff said.

Chapter 19

Sunday night, the couples went to dinner, then went to Jeff and Erma's for coffee and dessert. Erma made some strong coffee in her French press and served it with the carrot cake Monica brought over for everyone to enjoy. Sitting around the kitchen table, the conversation turned to the upcoming assignment.

"I wonder when you are going to get your tattoos Phil. And I wonder if I am going to have to wear some nerdy outfit to work in that office!" Jeff joked.

"You are getting tattoos?!" Monica exclaimed. "I hope you can cover them up! I don't like ink!"

"Don't worry, dear" Phil said calmly, "They'll be airbrush tattoos and will wash of in a couple weeks."

"Okay, they better!!" she laughed.

Phil leaned over and kissed his wife. "You're so cute. I'll miss you, even if it's only seven days away from you!"

Monica hugged Phil, saying, "I'll miss you too!"

Jeff patted Erma's hand. "You know I'll miss you and our little soon-to-be bundle of joy. I don't know if I'll be able to call you during the mission since I'll be staying out near the prison. I'll know more tomorrow." Jeff yawned and stretched. "I think we should call it a night. I want to be well rested and prepared for whatever Captain Egan has in store for us." He stood and carried their dishes to the sink. As he was rinsing them off and loading the dishwasher, Phil wondered aloud how Lt. O'Hara and Detective Barone would pull off their personas in order to remain in contact with them.

"Well, I don't think he'll have any problem playing your southern cousin. His natural southern drawl is perfect for the part. Detective Barone is very professional. As my friend who got me a job in the office, I think she'll do fine. I am eager to wrap this up quickly."

"I am too." Phil agreed.

Monica hugged her brother tight as they parted and she warned him to be very careful while on assignment. Jeff gave her his word that he would. The men agreed to meet in the morning.

****

Monday at nine a.m. Jeff and Phil went to Captain Egan's office after the morning briefing for the Headquarters staff.

"Ah, Gentlemen, come in and have a seat." Captain Egan said in greeting.

"Did you tell your wives you are going undercover?"

"No, we told them we are going on a week-long mission, no further details." Jeff said.

"Thank you. Golga is far enough away from Anderson Falls that the chances of you being recognized are slim. However, we're going to alter your looks temporarily, like we will with Phil. We'll give you contacts that will change the color of your eyes and perhaps give you a little facial hair to alter your looks. Since you're posing as an office worker moved who from England with his wife, it will be important that you go "home" each night. Here is the address of the motel you'll be staying at. You'll have a fully stocked refrigerator in the room with enough foodstuffs to last a week. Phil, we have a tattoo specialist that will ink your arms up with airbrush tattoos; they'll last a couple weeks. The tattoo artist will give you instructions on making the tattoos last the duration of your undercover assignment. Our makeup specialist will be applying a scar to your face that will stay on even in the shower. Have you both read and memorized your new profiles?"

"Yes, Sir. We have," both men responded.

"Okay, Tom. What is your last name and tell me about yourself"?

Jeff straightened his tie and responded, "I'm Tom Mickson. I'm a graduate of Her Majesty's College in London with a bachelor's degree in Business Administration. My past job at Fillson Brothers Department Store was as a Human Resource Manager. When Fillson Brothers downsized, I was let go. I recently became employed at Golga Correctional as Clerk to the Superintendent. Hopefully, I will be able to become a manager there, too."

The captain smiled broadly. "That's very good, Weston! You were convincing. Keep it up when you are at your "job" tomorrow!"

Captain Egan shuffled a few pages and said," Okay Donny, care to explain that rose between a skull and crossbones tattoo?"

"Donny Sarmanson, or Spike, to my friends. Got this here tattoo after my gang initiation. Had to find a broad named Rose and whack her. It was easy; I snuffed her like the wind blowing out a candle." Phil said in a gravelly voice with a leer at the Captain.

"Yes! If you can keep up that attitude and voice for the mission, I'm satisfied. Okay, what type of music do you boys listen to?"

Phil growled, "Spike don't listen to music, that's for sissies!"

"Pardon my uncouth accomplice please", Jeff said in a prim voice, "Music soothes the savage soul. Classical music suits my tastes, of course."

"You boys have got it down pat! Before we go to see Towanda, our makeup artist, let me tell you how you will be inserted into the Golga system. Jeff, Detective Barone will be a friend of the HR Liaison who will get you set up in the same office as Tim Effabee. You will contact her at the number on your profile sheet tomorrow at 9:00 A.M. Phil, Sgt. Stanton will pose as a Sheriff and take you through the intake process. Unfortunately, we need to stage an arrest first. Lt. O'Hara's contacts at Golga will make sure you're in the same cell as Vito. Both of you must remain vigilant in your posts. The sooner we get this wrapped up, the better."

"You can count on us, Captain!"

"Okay then, let's get the ball rolling! Phil, you know where to find Towanda, right? Head over there and get started on your transformation. I'll call Brad Geller and have him pick you up from there after she airbrushes some tattoos on your arms and back. When she's finished with you, come back here and we'll set up your arrest with Lt. O'Hara."

"Thank you, Sir. I'll see you both later" Phil said as he headed for his first stage of transformation.

"Jeff, let's go over to the station's vision center. Stella Rackman is the station's personal eye doctor. I've been in communication with her regarding the colored contacts. She has your records and has prepared a couple sets of contacts for you. You can head over there and get started. Once you're done there, call Mike, the head of our undercover wardrobe and disguises. He'll get you set up with the wardrobe you'll need as an office clerk. He's read your new identity's profile and is putting together some things that will reflect that persona. Report back to me when your transformation is done and we'll meet with Detective Barone."

"Thank you, Sir. See you later!" Jeff called as he left the office.

Captain Egan straightened some papers on his desk then sat down and let out a sigh. "I hope this mission is a success and goes quickly. I don't like putting my men in harm's way," he thought to himself.

Phil sat in a chair with his arms stretched out on a padded table as Towanda Wardarno created several tattoos on his arms. Patti Finnegan had just finished applying the "scar" to his right cheek. "Don't scrub this area when you shower. I've used a waterproof glue on it, but if it is rubbed too hard, it may come loose." She warned.

"Thanks," Phil said, "I'll remember to keep away from that area when I wash my face."

"I read over your profile and am creating some artwork that will help convince your cell mates that you have been hanging with a rough crowd. Where would you like the skull and crossbones with the rose?" Towanda asked Phil.

"How about on my shoulder or neck? And will it last long enough for this mission?"

"I think the shoulder would be a good choice. To preserve the tattoos, once you are out of the shower powder them completely. That will keep them from fading."

Once she finished her artwork on Phil, Towanda had him stand in front of a full length mirror and appraise the tattoos.

"If I saw these on someone I arrested, I'd believe that person was in a gang or seriously demented. You did a great job! Thank you."

"Oh, no problem, Detective Glass. I believe Brad Geller is here to take you to your next appointment. "

In Miss Wardamo's waiting room, Sgt. Geller sat on a couch, flipping through an old issue of Sports Illustrated. As Phil passed through the door to the waiting room, Sgt. Geller gave a whistle of admiration.

"Those are some impressive tattoos, Phil! Towanda, what a great job you did!"

She said her thanks to Brad and wished Phil good

luck. She exited the waiting room the way they came. Brad escorted Phil back to Captain Egan's office through back corridors so no one would recognize him after his staged arrest.

Stella Rackman and Jeff Weston sat in the dimly lit exam room. Jeff was given the standard eye exam and fitted for his new contacts.

"Will the colored contacts obscure my vision? I'm posing as a clerk and will be doing a lot of paperwork on the computer."

Stella laughed. "No, not at all! The coloring on the contacts will be covering where your irises are, not your pupils. In fact, since your vision changed slightly, the new prescription I wrote for the contacts you are getting, they will ease your eye strain. It looks like the team that set this up wants you to go from blue eyes to brown. I sent the prescription and the request over just after we finished the exam. I asked them to expedite the request, so we should be hearing back from the lenscrafter at any moment." A knock sounded at the door to the exam room. Dr. Rackman answered the door and a young man handed her a medium sized package. She thanked him, closed the door and turned to Jeff.

"Here they are! Let's put a pair in and see how you like them."

Jeff took the contact lens box from the doctor. "Is there a place I can wash my hands? I don't want to get any dirt on the contacts."

"Sure, right in the back of the room here I have a small sink."

Jeff washed and dried his hands then gingerly put the contacts on his eyes. He blinked a few times, adjusting to the feeling of wearing lenses.

"I haven't worn contacts in so long, it will take a little while to get used to them."

"Yes, it will", Dr. Rackman said. "Would you like to see how you look with brown eyes?"

She handed Jeff a mirror.

"I'm so used to my reflection having blue eyes. Hey, they go well with my blond hair!" He returned the mirror to Dr. Rackman.

"They do change your appearance. I've included a bottle of saline drops. If your eyes feel dry, or start to itch, just put a couple drops in each eye. By the way, once this assignment is over, please come back in to see me. I would like to do a follow up exam and make sure your eyes are healthy."

"Sure. I'll do that. Thanks again for getting me in on quick notice. I know Captain Egan will be pleased. Jeff waved goodbye as he left the vision center and headed back to meet with Captain Egan and Detective Barone. He stopped at the Undercover Wardrobe department, was given two suitcases containing his wardrobe for the mission.

Sergeant Geller wished Phil good luck on his

upcoming mission as he left him at the door of Captain Egan's office. Phil stepped inside and was greeted by Lt. O'Hara and the Captain.

"Phil! I like the new look! Are you ready for your arrest? IAB has your alter ego in the system with your prints. Nobody in Booking will recognize you!" Captain Egan explained.

"Good! I would really rather they don't think I went to the dark side."

"Lt. Rafferty will accompany you there momentarily. First, here's some equipment you'll need. Here is the button mic. Find someplace on your prison garb to place it that's inconspicuous. Remove it at night in case the clothes go out to the laundry. Once you're entered into the prison system Lt. O'Hara will come to visit. If you have any issues you can discuss them with him. If it is an emergency, use the button. We don't want to lose you. Or Vito."

Phil put the button in his pocket and was led away by Lt. Rafferty. They passed Jeff in the entryway to the Captain's office. Neither man recognized the other.

Chapter 20

The gate leading into Cell Block A clanged shut behind the prisoners as they shuffled into their new surroundings, carrying heavy woolen blankets and thin cotton sheets in their arms. Their dingy orange jumpsuits were so baggy it was hard for them to walk, thus the shuffle. Cat calls and shouts of "Fresh Meat" echoed through the corridors, taunting as each new prisoner as they passed the cells.

"Open 518", the guard commanded. The steel barred door slid open, revealing a rectangular sixteen by fourteen-foot cell. On the long side of the of the cell, metal framed bunk beds stood opposite one another. At the far end sat a rusted sink and a small toilet. Laying on the lower bunk of the set of beds, Phil saw Vito Phenton. His haggard appearance revealed the stress of fearing for his life in this prison. The upper bunk had a rolled up mattress that looked like it had seen better days.

"Sarmanson, you get that bunk", the guard said, "Get busy making it up!"

"Spike is my name, don't get it wrong again, Screw," Phil growled. At that, the guard pulled his baton from his belt, brandishing it towards him.

"Look, Spike," he said in a menacing tone, "You try talking like that to me again, I'll break so many bones in your body that you won't be able to move. Now get busy making your bunk!" For emphasis, he cracked Phil in the ribs with the baton.

"Oomph" was the only sound Phil made as he clutched his ribs. He unrolled the mattress, taking a slow breath to control his temper.

"Close 518", shouted the guard   The cell door slammed shut as the guard sauntered away.

Phil finished making his bunk up in silence. He walked to the old sink and splashed water on his face. As he turned to go back to his bunk, Vito said in a low voice that wasn't much more than a whisper, "Hey man, er Spike, don't mess with that guard. The fellow in the cell across from us warned me on my first night that Officer Thomas is brutal. He had that transgender surgery and is loaded with testosterone. He killed an inmate just for fun, and that was when he was a woman."

 "Thanks man," Phil replied, "now I know which Screw I'll have my gang brothers jump on his way home."

"What are you in for anyway, Spike?" was Vito's next question.

"Gang initiation killing", Phil said in his rough voice," I had to find and kill someone named Rose. He pulled his shirt off revealing the skull and crossbones with the rose on his shoulder.

"Once I did the deed, I got this. My lawyer was pretty slick and got me off. I'm only doing two years. Better than the electric chair."

Vito looked at him in awe. "You mean they knew you killed her and you only got two years!? Hell, I got put away for my brother's murder and am doing at least fifty! I wish I'd had your lawyer!"

****

Early the next morning, Jeff Weston, Captain Egan and Detective Barone met in the captain's office

Captain Egan welcomed Detective Barone into his office by pulling a chair out for her.

"Detective Barone, please have a seat. Weston, Detective Barone will be posing as your friend and former supervisor. She will accompany you to Golga's Admin offices and will meet with you frequently. She'll introduce you to your new coworkers."

"I've been in contact with the office manager, Ann Cody. She's expecting us at her office in an hour, so we better get moving. Your rental car will be parked in Lot R at the facility. I'll drive you over to Golga now", Detective Barone said.

Jeff stood and removed his suit coat from the back of his chair.

"Well, I guess we better get going. Wish me luck, Captain!"

"Jeff, here's the button mic. Just press it if you get into dire straits. If we get a distress call from you, we'll be at your side within minutes. Good luck in there. Ferret out the truth about the Phenton transfer."

Jeff affixed the button to his suit coat. "Thank you Captain, I'll do my best to find out what is really going on up there."

Detective Barone reached for her coat as well. "I'm parked right outside the front entrance. Let's go."

The thirty-minute drive to Golga Correctional Facility went by quickly.

Detective Barone and Detective Weston walked up the sidewalk to the front entrance of the prison.

"We'll stop in to the Personnel office and get your ID card made, and then we'll walk up to the administration office."

After passing through the metal detectors, the security guards directed them to Ann Cody's office.

"I'll summon the elevator for you. Take it to the fifth floor and turn right. The Personnel Office is the third door on your right. I'll call them and let them know you're on your way."

Jeff and Detective Barone stepped on to the elevator, pressing the button for the fifth floor. As the elevator ascended, Detective Barone said, "Jeff, please, call me Missy. Remember, I'm your former supervisor and also your friend. Outwardly, we have to pose as old friends."

"I think we can pull this off" Jeff said as the elevator doors slid open with a swish.

They stepped out of the elevator into a carpeted hallway and turned right, following the guard's directions to the Personnel Office. They walked in, admiring the potted plants on the floor. A receptionist greeted them.

"Good Morning, how may I help you?

"Would you let Ann Cody know Missy Barone and Tom Mickson are here to meet with her, please? We have an appointment for nine o'clock."

The receptionist looked at her computer screen, then smiled at the visitors. "Yes, I see it here.

Mr. Mickson, you'll be starting work today in the Administration Offices, right"

Jeff nodded and said, "That's right. I was told to report to Ann Cody before I go up."

"Sure. Have a seat and I'll go get Mrs. Cody now, then once you've met with her we'll get you an ID and an access card. Please have a seat while I fetch her."

Jeff and Missy sat down. The receptionist walked down an inner hall to the Personnel Manager's office. She returned a few moments later, accompanied by a medium built, athletic looking woman.

"Ann," Missy said, "This is my friend, Tom Mickson. He moved here recently from England. Today is his first day in the Administration Office. I didn't know you were the same Ann Cody I knew in college!? What a surprise!"

"I didn't recognize the name at first, Missy. So you married Tony, didn't you? We all thought you made the perfect couple!"

"Yes, I did. He's at home with Champ, our dog, today. We'll have to get together sometime. Right now, I'm bringing Tom over to his new office. I can give him more references if you need. I was his supervisor at the state offices."

"Nice to meet you, Tom", Ann said as she shook his hand. I can see that you will be a real asset here, especially with Missy's recommendation.

Let's get your ID and access card taken care of, then I'll escort you to your office."

"Good luck, Tom," Missy said and hugged him goodbye.

"Thanks, Missy. Tell Tony I said hello."

Missy left the office with a wave over her shoulder to Ann. "Take good care of my friend!"

Ann led her new employee into a back office, where he had his photo taken for his ID badge. A printer churned out his ID in a matter of seconds. Another printer produced his access card. Putting both cards in a plastic sleeve, then attaching a lanyard, Jeff was now official.

"Tom, make sure you have your ID on at all times. Some of our supervisors get cranky if they don't see it on you. Also, try to keep the access card away from your credit cards. The two don't play nicely. I had my access card erased by the chip in my credit card."

"Thanks, I'll remember that."

Ann led the way to the same bank of elevators he and Missy had used earlier. She pressed the Up button. The doors slid open and they stepped into the elevator.

"Your office is on the sixth floor, Room 614. Sometimes people get lost up here because the room numbers are a little squirrely. Here we are, sixth floor. Follow me."

Jeff followed Ann through a long hallway that opened to several rooms at funny angles to one another.

"Normally, the rooms in a circular area will ascend in number clockwise. Not here. I think the architect for this floor was cruel." She pointed to the first door on the right. The room number was 601.

"One would expect that the next door will be 602 and so on. Yet, look to your left. See how that is 602? The room numbers ascend in a zigzag fashion. One can get confused easily on their first few days here."

They walked further around the circular area.

"Here we are, room 614. Your new office. Let me introduce you to your coworkers."

Ann led Jeff to an inner office with the name Bryce Wixmor, Warden stenciled on the frosted glass. Ann knocked lightly on the door.

"EFFABEE!" a man's voice shouted, "Get in here!"

A pudgy man with a head that looked too large for his body jumped up from a desk behind them and came running. He pushed Jeff away from the door roughly.

"Out of my way, fella! The boss wants me!"

Taken aback, Jeff said, "Pardon me, Sir."

Ann, however, stepped directly in front of Tim Effabee, blocking his path.

"Mr. Effabee, that is not the way we act in this organization," she reprimanded him. Mr. Wixmor is expecting us." She apologized to Jeff for the rudeness of Tim Effabee.

"Miss Cody, when the boss calls to me, I have to go to him immediately. After all, I'm his right-hand man!" Tim said defensively.

"I'll discuss your rudeness with your Unit Supervisor, Sir." Ann retorted.

Tim Effabee seemed oblivious to her reprimand and plowed into Bryce Wixmor's office.

"Yes, Mr. Wixmor, you called?"

"I did. I am expecting Mrs. Cody and our new employee, Tom Mickson, to be here any second. Show them into my office as soon as they arrive. And show some manners when you greet them."

"Yes, Sir" he answered meekly, "As a matter of fact, they're right outside your office now."

"Well, show them in!"

Tim Effabee timidly opened the door to the warden's office where Ann and Jeff stood waiting patiently.

"Mr. Wixmor is waiting for you. You can go in to his office now."

Ann led the way in to the spacious office with a polished Mahogany desk and expensive leather chair for the on one side, a set of windows that overlooked the prison's exercise yard on the other. Next to the window was a bank of monitors, each with a different feed. One showed the intake area where prisoners were processed, another showed the main eating area for the prisoners, and another monitor displayed the main corridor of Cell Block A. Bryce Wixmor reclined in his chair. He stood as Ann and Jeff entered the room.

"Mrs. Cody, it's good to see you. And this must be Tom. Have a seat. I just want to talk to you before we get you set up at your desk."

Ann and Jeff sat in the two metal folding chairs intended for visitors.

Bryce Wixmor reminded Jeff of the old movie actor Basil Rathbone except for the way he carried himself. Bryce Wixmor did not exude the intelligence Basil Rathbone did as Sherlock Holmes. He limply shook Jeff's hand as if he had better things to do.

"Mickson, eh? You look strangely familiar. Have we met before?"

"No, Sir. I don't think we've met. I've read of your excellent facility and that prompted me to apply for a position here."

"Ah, well, you must have a twin out there" he

said, more to himself than to his two guests.

"I'd like to get to know you a bit before I put you to work. Have you ever worked in Corrections or a Police facility before? Are you married?"

"No, I worked only in some state offices in West London. When they downsized due to budget cuts, my position was eliminated. I'm married and fortunately my wife has a decent job with benefits because we're expecting our first child this year." Jeff said, thinking to himself how easily he was able to mix fiction and truth.

"Let me give you a brief history of Golga Correctional. We were established in 1966 and at first housed only the overflow from the other prisons in the state. We expanded in 1972 when we started taking in violent offenders. Cell blocks B, C and D are for the general population. That is where the majority of your work will come from, such as new visitation policies and forms for visitors to fill out, amongst other duties." He tapped one monitor. "This is Cell Block A. The most violent offenders are kept here. The guards in that section have to be disciplinarians, especially when the inmates get rowdy or show disrespect. Just a month ago, one of the guards had to use lethal force on an inmate. Our internal investigation revealed it was justified."

"I rather hope I do not have to visit that cell block," Jeff said, "By the way, has there ever been an escape attempt here?"

"Not on my watch" Wixmor said haughtily, "My guards keep the prisoners in line! I think the warden before me had one attempt, but it was unsuccessful. The inmate was shot down by the snipers in the tower above the exercise yard."

"It seems like you run a tight ship, Sir." Jeff said with false admiration.

"Let's get you set up at your desk and you can familiarize yourself with your new duties." He picked up the phone and punched a few numbers. "Kimble, please." Holding his hand over the mouthpiece he said to Jeff, "Tom, your unit supervisor is Mr. Kimble. He'll show you to your desk and give you a tour of the building." His attention was drawn back to the phone as Kimble answered his call. "Tom Mickson, yes, the new employee. Right, okay, yes. The desk next to Effabee? Okay he'll meet you there. Thanks." The Warden hung up his phone.

"I'll escort you to your desk. Are there any other questions you have?"

"Just one. Does Mr. Kimble work for Mr. Effabee? When we first encountered Mr. Effabee he told us he's your right hand man."

"Goodness, no!" Wixmor laughed, "He works for Kimble. Kimble is my right hand man. Effabee is lazy and full of himself."

"I suppose I should take what he says with a grain of salt?"

"It depends. If he is trying to be authoritative, then yes. He's pretty smart about how the prison is run."

"Thanks for the information. I better get to my desk now. Mr. Kimble will think I deserted him!"

Looking at his gold Rolex watch, Wixmor said, "I didn't realize I'd kept you so long. I'll escort you to your new work space and explain to Mr. Kimble that I was late letting you go."

"Thank you, Mr. Wixmor. I appreciate it."

Bryce Wixmor led Jeff to a fair sized metal desk at a corner cubicle. Waiting patiently was a man of medium build, with closely cropped dark hair and a handlebar mustache.

"Warden, thank you for escorting Tom to his desk. I assume you took a little longer than planned."

"My apologies, Mr. Kimble. Tom and I were engaged in an interesting conversation. It's a good thing he reminded me about getting settled, or I would still be talking!"

"That's fine" Mr. Kimble replied, "We're just going to get Tom settled in today and show him where everything is. We'll start him working on the routine tasks tomorrow."

"Very well then. Tom, I leave you in capable hands."

"Thank you, Mr. Wixmor" Jeff said politely.

"Dean Kimble." The man said to Jeff, introducing himself and extending his hand, "Nice to meet you."

"Tom Mickson", Jeff said falling into his new persona, gripping the man's hand and pumping it firmly, "The pleasure is mine."

"Please, call me Dean. This is your work space. We've tried to anticipate the supplies you'll need and have put them on your desk. If you need anything more, just Let Tim Effabee know. Have you met him yet?"

"Yes, briefly."

"Yes, well, Tim tries to attend to the Warden's every need. He overdoes it a bit, but you'll get used to him. Would you like to get a short but informative tour of your new workplace?" Dean Kimble offered.

"That'd be great. I do want to know where I'm going. Mrs. Cody said it can be daunting, finding one's way around."

Dean Kimble produced a map of their building and gave it to Jeff. He showed him around, pointing out the break room, the rest rooms, the conference rooms and finally a large bank of elevators.

"The elevators with the green numbers on them will bring you directly to the front doors. Those elevators are crowded at 5PM. The elevators with the yellow numbering bring you to the exercise rooms, if you'd like to work out before or after work. You can also take the stairs" he said, pointing to a door to the right of the elevators, marked Authorized Personnel Only. "I take the stairs frequently, since I don't work out that much. It lessens my guilt!" he laughed.

The two men made their way back to the desk Jeff was assigned. To his surprise, there was already a nameplate on his desk.

"This is impressive", Jeff admired, "My first day on the job and I have this fine piece of artwork bearing my name."

"You came with such impressive recommendations, we ordered this the day you accepted the position."

"My wife will be bowled over once she hears about my day."

Chapter 21

Missy Barone parked her Honda Accord in a lot adjacent to the Extended Stay Motel. She picked up her purse and sweater, got out of her car, pressing the lock button on the key fob. The roadrunner-like beep sounded, ensuring the car was secured. She walked into the motel and located Room 116. Jeff answered her knock with a cheerful, "It's open, come in!"

Missy opened the door to Jeff's room and surveyed the spacious area. On one side stood a small kitchenette where Jeff sat at a small, round table sipping coffee. On the other side of the room was a door leading to a full bathroom with a shower. Beyond that was a double bed facing the wall-mounted television. Jeff stood and pulled a chair out for Missy.

"Please, have a seat; I have a lot to tell you."

Missy laid her sweater and purse over the back of the chair and sat down.

"Before I start my story may I get you a coffee or a soda?" Jeff offered, playing the polite host.

"No thanks, Jeff. I'm fine. I'm anxious to hear about your first day. Did it go well?"

"Oh, it was a very interesting day. After you left us, Ann Cody brought me up to the office of the Superintendent. The Administration Offices are in the same area. We were to meet with Bryce Wixmor at 9:00 sharp, so we went up to his office a couple minutes early. Effabee literally ran into us! It was an odd way to meet the guy I am going to have under surveillance for sure."

Missy leaned forward, interested in Jeff's recounting of his day. "Why would he run into you? Did he not see you?" she asked.

"I'm pretty sure he saw us because he told us to get out of his way. He was in a hurry to get into the Warden's office for some reason. Ann Cody chewed him out for not even slowing down or apologizing. I guess he thought he could impress the warden by answering his call within nanoseconds."

"That would be impressive!" Missy joked.

"It would be more impressive if he was more careful. He almost knocked the both of us over. Anyway, my, or "Tom's", interview with the Warden went pretty well. I learned that the Warden doesn't hold Effabee in much esteem. He seems to think Effabee is lazy and full of himself and pretty much inept. I'll have to get to know Tim Effabee more, so I can see how much of this a show he's putting on."

Jeff took another drink of coffee and leaned back in his chair.

"I was busy after meeting with the Warden. I met so many people, I doubt I'll remember all their names! Then, I was led around the building and shown the break room, the exercise room and a plethora of elevators that take people to each of those locations as well to the front door. They're all color coded."

"Sounds like you can get lost easily there!" Missy observed.

"Well," Jeff said as he refilled his coffee cup, "Mr. Kimble, my supervisor, gave me a map of the place. It lists all the places I have access to and gives the layout of each floor. I made a copy of it for you."

"Good. If Lt. O'Hara and I need to infiltrate the building, this will come in handy. Have you had a chance to see where the private files are kept yet?"

"No. Kimble must've thought I'd get lost if he wasn't next to me the whole day. I hope that tomorrow I can break away so I can do some looking around. I have to find Vito's file and see if the transfer order was tampered with or if it was a simple mistake."

Missy felt a vibration from the phone in her purse. She removed it, glanced at its screen and put it back in her purse.

Missy's concerned look troubled Jeff.

"What is it? Did our mission fail already!?"

"No," she said slowly, "It's just that I received a message that Phil was assaulted by a guard just after he was left in his cell. Vito witnessed the entire event. In fact, he used his informant status to let Lt. O'Hara know what went on."

"Is Phil okay?"

"He has a few sore ribs and several bruises. Officer Thomas has a history of beating prisoners. This was one too many times. They will be conducting an investigation. In a way, this fits perfectly into our plan because you will be gathering information on the guards and the prisoners and the paperwork relating to them."

"My sister is his wife and is pregnant; she doesn't need to know about this."

"Don't worry. Kevin will make sure Phil is okay. If he is injured, Kevin will bring him to the hospital and we'll abort the mission."

"I better get into those files quickly and see if those transfer papers are legit."

"You're right; if you need authorization to get into those files, get in touch with Ann Cody. I'll make sure she gives you access to them."

"How are you going to do that? She thinks I'm Tom Mickson, Clerk. Why would she give me special consideration over anyone else?"

This time Missy doubled over, laughing. "Oh, Jeff, you were completely fooled! Ann is actually Madeline Gilmore, one of our top agents. She could be Ann Cody's double. Ann Cody is actually in Chicago doing specialized training in HR. We inserted Madeline into Ann's position when we developed this plan and she was so good that even her coworkers can't tell the difference. That's how we'll be able to get you access to the private files for Vito Phenton."

She won't be challenged by other supervisors?" Jeff queried.

"I don't believe they would question someone with her authority, especially since an internal investigation is being conducted to determine if his cell mate was disciplined without cause. Vito and the guard are the only ones who witnessed it."

"That would make sense if I am assigned the task of gathering vital information regarding everyone involved in the incident. I would have to have access to that guard's file as well if I am to be genuinely completing the task."

"I can arrange that with Madeline as well."

Jeff took the maps out of his suit jacket. He spread them out on the table between Missy and himself.

"Let's go over these and see which areas I'll need to access to get the documents that will show if Vito was transferred here inadvertently or if it was as a means to get him killed."

The two detectives bent over the maps of the Golga Correctional Facility office building.

Using the tip of his pen, Jeff tapped the map's layout of the sixth floor.

"This is where I'll be working. See how the office is built in a clock-like fashion? The office of Bryce Wixmor is at twelve o'clock. The Office Supervisor, Mr. Kimble, has his office at six o'clock. I'm at the nine o'clock position and Effabee is at eleven o'clock. I met the other twenty clerks in the office. I noticed a few locked cabinets in Wixmor's office. One cabinet was labeled Personnel Files, the other one was labeled Inmates. I think I am going to have to take a peek in that cabinet. I don't anticipate a problem, since I'm tasked with gathering information for the probe into Officer Thomas' behavior."

"I'll have Madeline call Mr. Kimble and alert him regarding tasks assigned to Tom Mickson."

"Good, then he won't be suspicious."

"Well, we both need to get some rest before tomorrow. I'll meet with you again tomorrow night. Sleep well," Missy said as she gathered her things.

Jeff stood and stretched. "Good night, Missy. It's going to be a long day again. My shift starts at seven."

Missy left Jeff's motel room and walked slowly back to her car, going over everything she and Jeff discussed. Just as she reached her hand out to unlock her car a gloved hand covered her mouth and a strong arm wrapped around her mid-section. Instinctively, she bent over rapidly, lifting her attacker off his feet. She twisted and used the momentum to disengage herself. The masked man looked up at her from the ground in confusion and anger, struggling to get up. Missy swung her heavy purse and struck her attacker in the jaw, knocking him out. He fell over, limp. Missy took her handcuffs from her purse, pulled the man's hands behind his back and cuffed him. Flipping him on his back, she pulled him up into a sitting position. Reaching into his pocket, she withdrew his wallet and checked his ID.

"Hey, you! Wake up!" Missy shouted.

The man's eyes fluttered and he quickly became aware of his predicament.

"What the hell! Who are you!?" the man sputtered.

"The question is – who are you and why did you attack me?" Missy barked at the man.

"Get me out these cuffs and I'll tell you anything you want to know," he pleaded.

Missy helped the man to his feet warning him that if he tried anything, she would have him held overnight in the local jail.

"Okay lady, just get me outta these things; they're hurting my wrists!"

Missy asked him again for his name and why he attacked her.

"I don't have to tell you anything!" he yelled. Missy yanked him to his feet and walked him to Jeff's motel room. She quickly recounted her encounter with her captive to Jeff. They started peppering him with questions. Jeff demanded the captive tell them his name and why he attacked his partner.

"I'm Royal Wixmor."

"Wixmor? You aren't by chance related to Bryce Wixmor are you?" Missy queried.

"Yes. He's my half- brother."

"The one that is the warden at Golga Correctional Facility?" Jeff asked in a surprised tone.

"Yes. Will you take these damned cuffs off me now?"

Missy unlocked the cuffs and immediately Royal rubbed his wrists, scowling at the two agents.

"Don't try anything funny, mister, or I'll have to take you down again." Missy warned.

"Two against one here, huh? I'll claim police brutality! You guys won't ever work in Law Enforcement again!" he sneered.

Jeff looked at Missy, then turning to Royal he informed him, "We can make sure you will never have a bruise to show anybody. Now, just sit down and answer our questions."

"Whaddaya want to know?" Royal said sullenly.

"First of all, why did you attack my partner? And who put you up to it?"

"Bryce's lackey did. Bryce wants you out of his hair and thinks if your girlfriend gets hurt, you will turn tail and run."

Missy asked the next question.

"Why Bryce? He's the head of the prison. He shouldn't be afraid of Jeff! He's been there for five years!"

Royal just stared at his two interrogators.

Rocking Royal's chair back against the motel room's wall, Jeff said in a determined voice, "Talk o me man, before I lose my temper!"

"Bryce has done more time on the inside of a prison than on the outside."

"What in God's name are you talking about?" Missy exclaimed, "How can he be a warden if he served time in prison?"

Royal, looking terrified responded, "He'd done his prison time in Canada. What he learned in prison was if you grease the right palms, you'll get places quickly. So he started with local politicians and graduated to Senators and Governors. They expunged his record. That is how he was able to get his present job."

Roy shook his head in bewilderment, "I went to college in the U.S. I worked hard and paid my way through it and got my degree in hotel management. He waved his hands, indicating the motel they were in and continued, "I'm the night manager here. I should be promoted to full time manager next month, but if you turn me in, it won't happen."

"Look Roy, tell me why this person would want you to get Tom out of the way?" Missy commanded.

"Bryce's second in command, Tim Effabee told me to do this. He said he is second in command at the prison. He saw you there today, getting cozy with Bryce and figured if you were attacked it might scare your man and keep his status safe."

Missy laughed in his face.

"Hah! You just tried to attack me. It looks like that promotion is trashed, now, unless you cooperate. I can't believe Effabee told you he's second in command! That guy is funny! He's a clerk in the Administration Offices. He's got a lot of nerve telling you that."

"I suppose the $2,000 he promised me is a lie too," he said glumly.

"Yes, that would be a fair assessment." Missy observed.

"He gave me the impression he that he and my step-brother were very close. I mean so close that Bryce would ask his opinion on matters and have him do highly confidential work." Roy sighed and leaned back in his chair.

"Did he elaborate on the highly confidential work he was doing?" Jeff asked his prisoner.

"I'm not sure. What I mean is, the guy said he was doing paperwork on the prisoners of special interest to the Warden. How confidential can that be? I'd imagine the Intake people would see it as well as the head guards and the Medical staff."

"Could he be talking about the high profile prisoners, or the more vicious prisoners?" Missy probed.

"I think both, from the way he talked. He was saying he just got the order to transfer some guy that killed his own brother."

Missy knew she'd hit gold. She looked at Jeff and saw his expression of satisfaction.

Casually, she replied to Roy, "That was a long time ago, wasn't it? It must have been at least two years ago. Besides, I think the guy got put way for 50 years or life. Does it matter where he spends his time?"

"I can't say I'm clear on the details, but I remember a guy getting convicted for killing a dispatcher in Anderson Falls. Do you think that's him?" Roy answered, "I guess it doesn't matter where you do your prison time, unless you plan on breaking out of the place."

"I don't know, maybe he is planning to help the convict escape" Jeff interjected, "Are you going to meet with this Effabee guy again? If you do, you can ask him."

"He's under the impression that if I meet with him, you're out of the picture, at least temporarily. He's hoping that I either scare you away or hurt you enough that you won't show up at the prison again" Roy explained.

"Let's have him think that."

"What else did he tell you?" was Missy's next question.

"From what Effabee told me, it is not you in particular that his sources care about; it's your boyfriend, Mickson. They saw the two of you go to Personnel together, and then they saw you go into his room here. They're hoping he'll be protective of you and take you away, leaving his job open for one of their cronies to fill."

Don't tell Effabee any of what has happened. Let him believe what he wants to believe." Missy instructed.

"Sure." Royal said, "How will I get in touch with you?"

"Contact Tom."

Jeff walked Royal Wixmor to the door and watched while his prisoner ran to the parking lot. He turned to Missy and observed, "I had a feeling Bryce Wixmor isn't really cut out for that job. He seems to be more of a paper pusher to me. So what's the plan now? Do we expose Wixmor and Effabee?" Jeff said.

"No, not yet. Roy is going to meet with Effabee. Effabee is under the assumption that if Roy meets with him that I'm out of commission. That fits perfectly with what I plan to do, which is watch and wait to see how these players react. Roy will meet with Effabee. You can observe how he is at work, while I keep an eye on him outside of the prison. You still need to get those documents, so stick to that part of the job. I'll try to determine who else would put Effabee up to all this."

"That sounds good. You better get back to your car before anyone notices that you are here." Jeff said.

I'll get in touch with you tomorrow night and we can compare notes again."

"Good night Missy."

"Good night Jeff."

Missy picked up her purse and walked out to her car. Jeff watched as she drove away.

Jeff had left the television on a sports channel to mask his conversation with Missy. The announcer was recapping the baseball game's exciting conclusion. "And in the bottom of the ninth inning, David Ortiz was clutch again. It was a rocket over the Green Monster in Fenway Park that led the Red Sox to victory over the New York Yankees by a score of 7 to 5."

"Way to go!" Jeff said as he turned the TV off, undressed and lay down on the Queen sized bed. He thought about all the events of the day and felt concern for Phil, hoping he wouldn't suffer another attack from the brutal guard.

Chapter 22

Jeff slipped his wedding ring on as he stepped off the elevator to the sixth floor near his office. As he walked down the hallway approaching his office, he slipped into the persona of Tom Mickson. Weaving his way toward his cubicle, with his morning coffee in hand, he passed Tim Effabee's desk & heard an audible gasp as Effabee jumped to his feet.

"Good Morning, Tom! You're here bright and early!

"Good Morning, Tim. It's a fine day out, isn't it?"

"Yes, yes it is. Say, how's your girlfriend doing? I heard she had a scare last night."

"Tim, I thought you knew I'm married. My wife is the only girlfriend I have. She's fine. I certainly hope she didn't have a scare last night!" Jeff said in a voice edging between surprise and annoyance.

"Uh, well, I forgot you're married. Who was that brunette you were here with yesterday?"

"Ann Cody? You should know her! She's the head of HR!" Jeff was having fun now, making Tim really work for any information.

"No, not her. Everyone knows her. I am talking about the woman that went up to the Personnel Office with you." Tim gave a superior look, as if he had caught Jeff red-handed.

"Her? She and her husband, Tony, have been friends of ours for years. She's friends with Ann Cody and heard there was a job opening here. I applied, Ann interviewed me, and Voila! Here I am! Missy drove up here with me so she could visit with Ann. She's as devoted to her husband as I am to my wife."

"Oh. Well, you two looked awful chummy." Tim retorted.

"We're good friends; that's all. What concern is it of yours about how she's doing, anyway? You don't even know her." Jeff turned away from Tim Effabee before he lost his temper. He went to his cubicle, sat down and started reading the morning emails. He could hear Effabee talking to Kimble about the episode in a voice loud enough for Jeff to hear every word.

"...and he looked like he was gonna hit me because I was talking about his girlfriend! He should be reprimanded, maybe even fired!"

Kimble looked Jeff's way, noticing him sitting calmly at his desk. Kimble turned to Effabee and in a stern voice said, "First, you knock him and Ann Cody down scrambling to the Warden's Office, acting as if you're someone of great importance and now you provoke this gentleman with your insidious remarks. I think you forget that my office is right here with the door open. I heard your entire exchange. Now go back to your desk and get those reports I assigned you completed! I had to answer to Ann Cody and the Warden for your rudeness yesterday. Trust me, they weren't happy."

Jeff stifled a laugh as he heard the conversation between the two men. He continued to read his email, sitting up straight when he received one from Missy. He read the message and read it again, absorbing every word. The email read:

"I observed Roy Wixmor meet with Effabee early this morning, about 3AM. Two hours later, I received word from Intel that Roy was found hanging from a tree, gutted like a deer. If that's the work of Effabee and his crew, I'm pulling you and Phil out right away."

Jeff typed a message back to her:

"Effabee confronted me this morning about you, calling you my girlfriend. I assured him we are just friends but he kept it up, provoking me until I had to just walk away or I would've punched him. I'm going to get those documents ASAP. Please contact Madeline and have her make the request for them to Kimble, asking that I specifically do the job."

He hit send and sat back for a moment, thinking about what he'd just read. He deleted the message, taking care to empty the email trash then the PC trash. After that, he began organizing his desk. He'd just finished when his phone rang. The sound of the phone snapped him back to attention.

"Good Morning, Administration Office, Tom Mickson speaking."

"Tom, you sound very professional. Good job. This is Kimble. Could you come to my office? I have an assignment for you."

"Right way, Sir," he said, hanging up the phone and making his way to Kimble's office. As he was passing Tim Effabee's desk, Effabee stood up to block Jeff's progress.

"Hey, Tommy Boy, are you trying to score points with Mr. Kimble just because he defended you and your girlfriend?"

Jeff sidestepped Effabee and slipped into Kimble's office. Tim Effabee followed him into the office, saying "I'm the Senior Clerk here, why does this 'nothing' get special treatment and special assignments? I deserve them!" stomping his foot for emphasis.

"Effabee, stop acting like a child. Tom's special

skills are in Document Research. That's why he was selected. Are those reports I asked you for this morning ready for my review yet? I can see by your body language they aren't. If you want to remain the Senior Clerk, then go get them done!"

Tim gave "Tom" one final glare and sidled past him whispering, "I'll get you for this, you slime. I'm gonna make you suffer. You'll regret the day you were born."

"My good man," Jeff replied in the perfect Tom Mickson persona, "I shall never regret that day! My life has been quite rewarding and I have enjoyed every minute of each day."

Tim Effabee's face grew a bright red with anger, which only intensified as Jeff calmly said, "I do say you should get your blood pressure checked. Your face is quite red."

Tim Effabee, furious, slammed the door as he left.

"I don't know what got into him," Mr. Kimble apologized, "I didn't expect my Senior Clerk to act in that manner."

"Apology accepted. That poor gent has some anger management issues. Now, you said you have a special project for me?"

"Yes," Kimble said, "You must have made quite an impression on Ann Cody. She's specifically asking you to do some document research for her. There's a special investigation going on concerning a guard and an inmate. Mrs. Cody wants you to pull the files listed and look for items that match the criteria she listed here." He handed Jeff an envelope.

"Follow the instructions in this packet. You can start on it after your lunch break. I'll make sure you have the necessary clearance to retrieve the files requested and I will make sure you aren't disturbed. I'm going to have Effabee in my office all afternoon counseling him on appropriate office behavior."

"Thank you for your confidence in me, Mr. Kimble. I won't let you down. I do have one question. When I've completed this, am I to report to you or Mrs. Cody, since this is her request?"

"This is a special request; Mrs. Cody may want to meet with you personally. Let me give her a call." He paused, listening. "Hello, Ann? Yes. It's me, Dean Kimble. Yes, I got the request. I just handed it to him. Our question is this: do you want him to deliver the results to me, or are you going to meet with him personally? Yes, I see. I'll relay the message. Thanks Ann."

"Well, Tom, Ann told me this is a highly confidential matter. That's why she chose you. She said your research skills are outstanding and because you're new here, you won't have any bias. So you will deliver all results from this assignment directly to her." Looking at his watch, he said. "It's 12:15. Why don't you go get some lunch? Plan on starting your research around 1:15 and you can work uninterrupted all afternoon. If you need to lock up any results you get, let me know and I will get you a locking file cabinet. If you don't complete everything today, you can start in again when you get in tomorrow."

Jeff replied, "Thank you, Mr. Kimble; I'll get right on it after lunch." With that, he left the office, avoiding Tim Effabee's desk on his way to the break room.

"Tom! Tom Mickson!" a woman's voice called. Jeff turned at the sound of someone calling his alter ego's name, and saw Ann Cody.

"How may I be of service to you, Mrs. Cody?" he said.

"Please, call me Ann. How would you like to go lunch at Frenchman's? I would like to make it a working lunch and discuss the special assignment I gave you."

"Yes, that would be nice, as long as I am back here within an hour. Mr. Kimble wants me to start the research around quarter after one."

"I'll stop by Mr. Kimble's office and let him know what we're doing. I'm sure you'll be back in plenty of time."

"Why don't you get the elevator and I'll check in quickly with Mr. Kimble."

"Okay."

Jeff headed for the elevators while Ann Cody went to see Mr. Kimble. A few minutes later they stepped out of the elevator in the front lobby of the building.

"Let's go this way, Tom", Ann said as she walked down a path between the two buildings. "The Plaza is over here." The path they were on opened into a large cobblestone area with a fountain in center. Water spewed from spigot creating a waterfall down marble steps. To the left of the fountain, there was an open air restaurant. Tables were gradually filling with patrons for lunch.

Once seated, Ann started with, "I highly recommend the blackened salmon salad, Jeff."

Stunned that she called him by his true name, Jeff nearly knocked over the water another server had placed in front of him.

"Detective Barone was in touch with me last night and brought me up to date on what has been happening. We had previously planned your special assignment so you could get into the files without suspicion. Now it's even more important to find out if Effabee is working alone or there are others behind this."

"Well, I should be able to look into his files this afternoon once I get back."

The waiter came and took their orders. "Try to get whatever you can about Effabee and the transfer orders. See if you can determine who approved the orders or if Effabee forged the signature."

"I'll start with the Personnel files and see what I can find." The two finished their lunches and started walking back to the office. They retraced the route they had taken earlier, entering the path between the two buildings. Four burly men dressed in black approached them.

"Hey there, Tommy Boy, that lady from Personnel can't save you now." They crouched ready to attack.

"Ann, duck!" Jeff shouted. Ann leaned down as Jeff did a roundhouse kick, connecting with the chin of one of the thugs. It knocked the attacker into the man next to him, sending both sprawling on the ground. The other two men ran off into the crowd in the plaza.

Jeff went to the two men still lying on the ground. Standing above one of the men, with his foot on the man's throat, "Who are you? Who put you up to this?"

The man made choking sounds from the pressure created by Jeff's foot. "I can't breathe", he choked out, "Let me breathe and I will tell you what you want to know."

Jeff eased his foot off the man's throat and grabbed him by the shirt, pulling the thug to his feet. Ann had her 9mm Glock trained on the other thug who was still unconscious.

"Let's start with your name, fella."

"My name is Joe Fish. Here's my ID." He reached in his pocket and retrieved his wallet, pulling out his Golga Correctional card. Jeff looked it over and handed it back to the man.

"Who ordered you to ambush us?" Jeff questioned.

"I don't know his name" insisted Fish. "I only know what he looks like. He was medium height, kind of pudgy with a bad haircut."

Jeff and Madeline looked at each other and said at the same time, "Effabee!"

The other man began to stir. He blinked a few times and said, "Effabee? What does that scum want now?"

Madeline leveled her gun at the man. "Let's start with your name, and then we'll talk about Tim Effabee."

"Lady, can you put that gun away first? It makes me nervous."

"No. I like making you feeling nervous. Now, what's your name?"

"Bill Messner.", the man said in a trembling voice.

"How did you become involved with Effabee?"

Madeline asked, stowing her gun back in her purse.

"Joe and I were working out at the fitness center a couple days ago. Effabee came up and asked if we wanted to make a couple of bucks on the side. We thought it was to help him move stuff or do some heavy lifting. He said no, it was to help him play a joke on some of his friends before they all met at a party. He showed us photos of you two and told us to bring you up to a camp on Lake Pleasant and drop you off. He said he would pick you up after a few hours and you'd all go to the party."

Joe continued the narrative.

"Yea, Tim said you'd get a big surprise when he picked you up. I thought you were all buddies and liked to play jokes on each other."

"Well", Jeff said, "He'll be getting the surprise today."

"Why don't you two get lost for the rest of the day", Madeline said, "Unless you want me to press charges for assaulting us."

"No way. You two don't scare us. We'll take you out, one way or another." The brawny thug said, leaning toward them, shaking his fist.

"We'll be back to finish this", his thin accomplice sneered. The two men sauntered out of the alley.

"I better get back to the office" Jeff said, "Tom

has a big project to work on this afternoon!"

"I'm curious how Effabee will react to seeing you return unscathed."

"It should be an interesting afternoon." Jeff waved goodbye and sprinted back to the office, getting there with minutes to spare. He stopped at his desk to pick up a notepad and pen, then made his way to Kimble's office. As Jeff neared the door of the office he could hear Tim Effabee making the announcement that Jeff wasn't back from lunch and wouldn't be in for the rest of the day.

Jeff knocked lightly on the office door. "Excuse me, Mr. Kimble, do you want me to start my project with the Inmate or Personnel files first?"

Kimble looked up from his work; first at Tim Effabee, then at Jeff. Effabee's mouth opened and closed a few times with no sound escaping.

"Mr. Effabee, I think you'd better verify your information. It appears Mr. Mickson is in our presence. Tom, why don't you start your assignment with the Personnel files? Here's the key to that cabinet. Warden Wixmor is expecting you to be doing your research in his office this afternoon."

Tim Effabee finally found his voice. "He's not allowed in Mr. Wixmor's office! I'm the only one that can work in there!"

"Have a seat, Effabee," Kimble said sternly, "We

have a lot to discuss."

Chapter 23

Kevin O'Hara sat at a metal table in a small room behind a Plexiglas window that separated him from the prisoners on the other side. A guard shoved a shackled prisoner into the chair directly across from him.

"My God," Kevin exclaimed in his southern drawl, "What have they done to you!? You've lost weight and look like you've been hurt really bad. Spike, what did you do this time?"

"Hey, Cuz", Phil said in his gravelly voice, "I corrected the guard on my name. He didn't take too kindly to the correction. My ribs paid the price, but it doesn't bother me. I'll get him back when I blow this joint."

"I've hired a lawyer for you, Spike. His name's Scott Egan. He'll be up to see you tomorrow."

"Look Kevin, it will just bring another beating down on me. Don't waste your time or money on a lawyer. The last one I had landed me here!"

"You need a new trial. The last one was a joke."

"I'm not worried about myself. How's my wife? Tell her I can do this time standing on my head, as long as I know she'll be waiting for me."

"No worries there, Spike. I'll see that she's taken care of."

"And my brother? How is he doing? Did he ever get that job he was looking for?"

"Yes, he started there this week. He's already made new friends and found the job quite enlightening."

"Tell him about the beating, he'll get my gang on the alert."

"Time's up, prisoner! Let's go! The guard pulled roughly on Phil's shackles, causing him to stumble.

"Get up, Maggot! I said time's up!" The guard yanked again on the shackles, dragging him to his feet.

"Take it easy, Screw!" Phil snarled, "I've got a witness here!"

"That means nothing", the guard retorted. He opened the door leading to the prison cells and pushed Phil through it.

"Open 518!" the guard shouted. The barred door to Phil's cell clanged open and the guard shoved him into the cell. The door slid closed with a bang.

Vito looked up from his bunk nervously. Phil waited until the guard walked away a distance before speaking.

"I saw my cousin from down South. He wants to get me a new trial."

He knelt by Vito's bunk and said in a whisper, "As long as I'm in here, I won't let the Screws hurt you. Or anyone else, for that matter."

"Thanks, man. I mean, Spike. There are some really bad dudes in here that want me dead."

Phil laid his hand on Vito's shoulder. "Look man, nobody gets by Spike. I've got your back."

Vito leaned up on one elbow and looked at Phil gratefully. "I'm glad somebody does. There are some wicked people in this cell block."

****

Lt. O'Hara dialed Detective Barone's cell phone number. She answered on the second ring.

"Detective Sergeant Missy Barone."

"Missy - This is Kevin. I went up to Golga to see Phil a/k/a Spike. It really does look like he took a beating. The guard that brought him into the

Visitation Room gave me the impression he beats the prisoners whenever he wants. He practically dragged Phil out of the room after our time was up."

"Do you think we should abort the mission? Is his life in danger?" Missy asked.

"No", Kevin said, "He seemed tough enough to handle whatever they dish out. My concern is that they can get to Vito under the guise of taking him to see a visitor." Kevin mused.

"The only family he has is Madge Flanders. I doubt she wants to see the man that killed her brother." Missy observed

Kevin reminded Missy, "Don't forget, even if Vito turned on his own twin, he is Madge's brother too. And he has become a Confidential Informant."

"I just can't fathom killing my own brother, for whatever reason. It's family! Drugs have an evil influence on people!" Missy exclaimed.

"They do. They make people who are otherwise good souls into evil incarnate. Drugs are not an excuse for killing, but people under their influence lose their minds." Kevin said somberly.

****

Jeff inserted the key into the lock on the cabinet labeled Personnel Files. Unlocking the cabinet and opening the drawer with the files A-K, Jeff thumbed through files until he located the one for Tim Effabee. Removing it, he placed it in a large envelope. Thumbing a little further, he located the file for Thomasina Karol. He removed that one and included it in the envelope. Closing the drawer, he locked the cabinet and said to Mr. Wixmor, "I need to review these files right now. I'll be back to return them and proceed with the Inmate files."

Wixmor glanced at Jeff in a distracted way. "Very well, Tom. Carry on. Just return the key to Mr. Kimble when you're finished."

Jeff left the office and stopped at a copier on the way to his desk. He made copies of the two files, putting them into a second envelope. When he reached his desk, he sat down to study the files. Effabee had been hired five years ago; before Wixmor became the Warden of Golga. He'd started in the Mail Room, then a year later transferred to the Administration Office as a clerk. Performance evaluations for that position were either satisfactory or unsatisfactory. Tim's were rated as satisfactory, even though the comments by his supervisors said he needed to improve in all areas, especially in the area of getting along with other employees. There had been several complaints from the females on staff, saying he made unwanted advances and threatened them with losing their jobs if they did not do as he wished. He had been counseled on that matter and went through the sexual harassment training as remedial measures for his behavior. Still, Tim was hard to get along with in the office.

"How did he ever get to do transfer orders for Bryce Wixmor?" Jeff thought to himself. "What is going on between them?"

He put the file back in the envelope and withdrew the one for Thomasina Karol (aka Mick Thomas). Thomasina had been hired fifteen years ago as a female corrections officer in Golga's women's facility. She had beaten a female inmate to death six years ago. At that time, she was suspended for a year without pay, and ordered to undergo Anger Management courses. When the year was almost complete, she returned as Mick Thomas, a male guard and assigned to cell block D. After several complaints from other guards and inmates in that cell block, he was transferred to cell block A. Jeff read and re-read the evaluations for Officer Thomas that praised him for keeping the inmates in line and reducing the amount of fights between prisoners for fear of Officer Thomas giving them a beating with his baton.

"Man, this is so wrong" Jeff thought to himself, "If we even think of laying a hand on one of our prisoners, we'd get fired. This guy gets praised? How screwed up is that?"

He closed the file, filled with disgust over the

corruption that was going on. "Wixmor must be at the bottom of this." He said to himself. Putting the file back in the envelope, he stood to return them to the cabinet. As he approached the warden's office, he saw Tim Effabee huddled with Bryce Wixmor. Jeff stopped, not wanting to be seen observing them.

"…Well, get rid of them for good! They're meddling with everything we've taken so long to do!" Bryce said in an irritated voice, slamming his fist on his desk.

"Yes, Sir," Tim said meekly, "This time they won't get away."

"Get out of my office and take care of them! I can't stand the sight of you!"

"Right away, Sir. I'll get right on it" Tim scurried past Jeff, not even noticing him enter the office.

"Good Afternoon, Mr. Wixmor. I'm going to return these files to the drawer and begin my research on the Inmate's files."

"Yea, whatever" Wixmor dismissed, not even noticing who he was talking with.

Jeff inserted the key in the cabinet, opened the drawer and returned the files to their proper places. He withdrew the key and went to the cabinet labeled Inmate Files and Correspondence. As he was opening the drawer, Bryce Wixmor suddenly came to life and asked, "Tom, what are you doing now!? I thought you were finished with your research."

"Oh, no Sir. As I explained when I came in, I returned the employee files to the cabinet and am beginning my research on the inmate files."

"Why do you even need to do this research, Tom? This facility is running just fine as it is. What possessed you to do this?"

"Warden, I was asked by special request of Ann Cody to do this project. If you have any concerns, I am sure Mr. Kimble or Ann Cody can address them," Jeff said calmly.

"We'll see about that, Mickson. My prison is one of the best in the nation. You can continue your research tomorrow – AFTER I talk to Kimble and that dame, Cody." Wixmor growled.

"Very well, Sir." Jeff gathered his files and left.

He dropped the keys off to Kimble, giving him a recap of the conversation he had with the Warden. Kimble assured him he would be able to continue the research without any further harassment. As Jeff neared his desk, his phone rang.

Jeff answered it with, "Tom Mickson here, how may I help you?"

"Tom, this is Ann Cody. Come to my office immediately and bring your research with you."

"Yes ma'am" Tom replied. He gathered his files and went up the elevators to the Ann's floor. As he neared her office, he sensed something was wrong. Normally, one could hear the cheerful chatter of the ladies that work in the Personnel Office. Not today. No light shed from the office into the dim hallway and the door to the office was shut. Jeff backed away and sprinted to the elevator. He went directly to Security and told them of his concerns. Two Security Guards rode the elevator to Ann Cody's floor with him. They approached the silent office and one of the guards drew his weapon, ready to fire it. Another guard walked ahead slowly, careful not to make any noise. When he got to the office door he stopped, in shock. Reaching for his radio, "Base station, this is Security One. Get the Police, and ambulance here right way! We have a mass murder on our hands." The second guard rushed to assist his coworker. Jeff followed at a distance. He reached the two guards and looked into the office. The young receptionist lay over her keyboard, riddled with bullets, obviously dead. The Secretary next to her was huddled down, crying and bleeding from the shoulder. Two employees that had been sitting in the waiting room were both dead from gunshot wounds. The guard who had his gun at the ready stepped into the office. He spoke to the secretary. "Ginger, honey. Look at me. Stay with me. The ambulance is on its way. Please, stay with me!" Ginger gave a frightened nod. "Is anyone in the back offices?" Again she gave a nod. The guard turned to his counterpart. "Draw your weapon. Have it ready in case the person that did this comes out here. I'm going to check the back rooms."

"Okay Chet, if you need help, holler."

The guard left the reception area and "Clear!" could be heard as he checked the rooms. After what seemed like an eternity, he returned. Ann Cody was with him, limping and holding on to him for support. She was bleeding from the lower leg. "Where is that ambulance and the Paramedics?" he shouted into the radio, "We have people that need medical attention, right now!"

Within minutes, the pounding footsteps of the ambulance crew could be heard running in the hallway. Two stretchers were wheeled into the office; the secretary was loaded on one and Ann Cody on the other.

The police detained Jeff for questioning. He answered their questions and was told he could resume work, but to be on hand if they needed him for further questioning.

Chapter 24

Jeff returned to his office, visibly shaken. He made his way to his desk and sat down, gripping the arms of his chair. His mind was whirling. If he had been in Ann's office right after she called, he could have been either wounded or dead by now. He had to alert Detective Barone and Lt. O'Hara. He pulled his laptop from its case and logged on to the secure email that had been set up. He sent Detective Barone a hurried message, detailing the events and asked her to get word to Phil so he could be extra vigilant. Jeff did not want to see his friend in danger or injured. After hitting send on the email, he returned the laptop to its case and went to get a cup of coffee. Several employees were gathered at the coffee bar, talking about the tragedy in the Personnel Office. One girl was crying.

"I just went to lunch with Diana yesterday. We were making plans to go to the Chicago concert this weekend," she sniffed, "now she's gone!" The young woman sobbed. A few of the employees around her hugged and led her to the employees lounge so she could sit with them and try to gather herself. Another man spotted Jeff and said, "I heard it was you who got the Security Officers to check the room. What made you do that, Tom?"

"Well, I was on my way up there because Mrs. Cody had called and asked me to report to her office. When I got off the elevator for her floor, it was strangely quiet. The other times that I've been up there, you could hear the radios and the chatter from her office. It struck me as odd. Then I noticed the door to the Personnel Office was closed. On my first day here, Mrs. Cody told me they never close that door; everyone is encouraged to drop by the office. That's when I felt something was wrong, so I alerted Security."

"Well aren't you just the big hero" sneered Effabee. "Too bad you couldn't save anyone. Okay, everyone gets back to work. There's nothing you can do here except waste my time."

A few employees wandered back to their desks, befuddled by Tim's callousness. Others stood their ground. Turning to Effabee, one man said, "Look Tim, we all know the people in Personnel. They're our friends. We're all in shock and are gathered together to support one another. How can you be so heartless?"

Tim retorted, "This is a place of business. Business continues whether there is tranquility outside our office or murder in Personnel. I'm in charge here, and you lowlifes will listen to me!"

Jeff tried to suppress a laugh because at that moment Mr. Kimble had come out of his office with his coffee cup in hand and was standing just inches behind Effabee, taking in the entire exchange. He coughed and tapped Tim's shoulder, saying "Excuse me Boss, but I'd like to get a cup of coffee and talk to my friends about what happened in Personnel."

Tim was so wrapped up in his own feeling of superiority that he did not recognize his supervisor's voice.

"Get back to work, or I'll have you fired!" he snarled.

Kimble had had enough of Tim's swelled head. He took Effabee by the shoulders and spun him around to face him.

"Mr. Effabee, need I remind you that I am your supervisor!?"

Tim sputtered, "But, but, uh, I was trying to get his unruly crowd back to work. They were just wasting time here talking about things they have no control over."

"Unless you were in another state, this is a big tragedy. The people gathered here are friends of the injured or dead. They need each other for support. And another thing, you should have been thanking Tom for alerting Security to the situation. They could have come in here and caused more bloodshed. The news just reported they've found one of the gunmen." Kimble turned to Jeff and said, "Good work, Mickson. I wish more of my staff were as alert as you are." Then he addressed the entire office. "There is a big screen TV in the employee lounge. You can go down to get news updates throughout the day. I just request that you go in groups of three and limit your time there to ten minutes every three hours. You can take your lunch in there as well. Thank you. Mr. Effabee you can return to work now."

Deflated, Tim Effabee slunk back to his desk and shuffled some papers around. Jeff returned to his desk to check his email on his laptop and saw a reply from Missy Barone. It read:

"Jeff, if you feel the situation is not safe, we will send in an extraction team immediately. If, however, you can continue with the assignment and are confident we can discover who is behind all of this, please follow the plan. I spoke with Madeline. Be assured, she will be fine and will return in a few days. She is determined to get to the bottom of this as well.

Kevin will be going to see Phil again today. He will brief him on the situation and warn him an attack on Vito may occur at any time and to be on high alert."

Good Luck,

Missy

Jeff hit reply and assured Missy he was still going through with the mission. He logged off, put his laptop back in its case and sat back with a sigh. The phone on his desk rang, startling him.

"Tom Mickson."

"Tom, this is Mr. Kimble. The Warden asked me to reassign the research that you're doing to Mr. Effabee until further notice."

"But I'm almost done with the research. In fact, I was bringing the results to Ann Cody when the shooting took place. I want this complete and my presentation to be polished upon her return."

"Mr. Effabee told me that the Warden instructed him to take over the project." Mr. Kimble stated.

"I don't mean any disrespect to you or Mr. Effabee, but wouldn't it be prudent to confirm this with Wixmor himself?"

"Effabee was quite adamant about the instructions." Mr. Kimble went on. "I'm going to be having lunch with the Warden in ten minutes; I'll discuss it with him then."

"Thank you, Mr. Kimble" Jeff said and hung up the phone.

"If he comes back from lunch and confirms that Wixmor wants Effabee to handle the research then I'll know that he and Effabee are in cahoots and I'll inform Lt. O'Hara and Detective Barone so they can handle it from that point on." Jeff thought to himself. He stood up and went to the employees lounge to eat his lunch.

As he sat at one of the round tables scattered throughout the lounge, his attention was drawn to the latest news report. "The tragedy in the Personnel office at Golga Correctional Facility has shaken the small community located near the prison. Many residents of the community are employees of the prison. Police are interrogating the gunman they have in custody. We will bring you updates as they happen. This is Lori Langorski reporting. Back to you in the studio, Fred."

Jeff finished his lunch and headed back to his desk. As he passed the elevators nearest his office, he saw Kimble returning as well.

"Hi, Tom! Did you have your lunch yet?"

"Yes, I ate in the lounge. I wanted to watch the news to see if there have been any new developments in catching the men that shot our friends in Personnel."

"And…?" Mr. Kimble asked.

"They're interrogating the one gunman they caught. There's no word on the outcome of the interrogation yet."

"Come into my office. I had an enlightening lunch with Wixmor."

Jeff followed him into his office and took a seat across from Mr. Kimble at his desk.

"At lunch, Wixmor seemed very somber. I think he has been deeply affected by the shooting in Personnel. He and Ann Cody have been friends for a couple of years. I did manage to ask him about the statement Tim Effabee made. He concurred that Tim does have a superiority complex and tries to be something he's not. He also said that since I had approved the reassignment, he wouldn't question it. You could have knocked him over with a feather when I told him I had never made such a reassignment! We both agreed Tim was trying to pull a fast one. Needless to say, you can continue your research this afternoon. That is, if you are not too shaken by today's events."

"To tell you the truth, I think research will calm my nerves. I'll get right on it."

Kimble handed Jeff the keys to the Inmate Files. Jeff left the office and stopped at his desk to retrieve his notepad, an empty envelope and a pen. As he started to make his way to the Warden's office to continue his research, he was practically bowled over by Tim Effabee for the second time that week.

"Get out of my way, Mickson. I have important work to do. What're you doing going into the Warden's office, anyway?"

"Perhaps it slipped your mind that I'm doing research for a special project assigned by Ann Cody. I'm continuing the research so when she returns to work, it will be completed."

"Ann Cody? I thought she was shot. She's not coming back to work, she's on her way to the morgue."

Remaining true to his undercover British persona, Jeff said, "My dear sir, she suffered a flesh wound. She will be back by the end of the week. Now, I must get going." Jeff turned and went into the Warden's office, leaving Effabee standing in the same spot, sputtering.

Jeff greeted the Warden and explained he was going to finish his research. He noticed that the Warden nodded in the same distracted way he had the day before. Jeff went to the cabinet that held the inmate files and retrieved the files for Vito Phenton and Donald Sarmanson. He put them in the empty envelope and left the office, again stopping at the copier to make copies of both files. Once he was at his desk, he slipped the copies into a separate envelope and put it in his briefcase. Opening Vito's file, he thumbed through the reports and trial documents that he was familiar with. He reviewed the confidential informant agreement regarding Vito. He saw the order to sentence Vito to the State prison and also the order to keep him separate from the drug lords he had turned over to the police. His eyes widened when he read the order to transfer Vito from the hospital directly to Golga Correctional Facility. It was signed by Tim Effabee, Warden of Golga Correctional Facility!

"No wonder he didn't want me to finish my research! He knew he would be discovered. But why would he take the risk in the first place? Does he have connections at the State Prison and the hospital too? I need to inform Missy right away." Jeff pulled out his cell phone and snapped a photo of the document, emailing it to Missy's phone. The last thing he remembered was pressing send. After that, everything went black.

****

"Sarmanson, you have a visitor" Officer Thomas said, as he rapped the bars of Phil's cell. "Open 518!"

"The name's Spike" Phil muttered in a low voice as the cell door slid back noisily. Fortunately, Officer Thomas didn't hear what Phil said. If he had, Phil would have suffered another beating after his visitor left. Officer Thomas was careful enough not to beat the prisoners when they were getting visitors. Phil shuffled to the opening of the cell and held his arms out so he could be cuffed for the short walk to the visitation room. Once cuffed, Officer Thomas led him to the drab cement room equipped with cubicles and phones for the visitor and prisoners to communicate with across a Plexiglas wall. Surveillance cameras were mounted in each corner of the room.

Phil saw Kevin waiting patiently at the furthest cubicle from the door. Picking up the phone, he heard, "Hello Spike, how're you being treated?" Kevin drawled.

"I'm holding my own. I'm keeping watch for the bums that want to hurt me, y'know." Phil hoped Kevin would pick up on the code he was speaking.

"Just remember, they could come after you at any time. Don't go outside without protection. If you get stuck, get help immediately." Kevin looked at Phil with a very serious expression.

"I gotcha, Cuz." Phil said, nodding. "I have it right here," he tapped his head then laid his finger next to the emergency button on his jumpsuit.

"Indeed you do." Kevin smiled knowingly.

Chapter 25

The back of Jeff's head hurt tremendously. He rubbed it and felt where blood had congealed. Opening his eyes, he took in his dim surroundings. He could see metal above his head and felt a trunk liner below him. Judging by the whine near his head, he assumed he was in the trunk of a car. "Thank God, whoever put me in here didn't bind my hands and feet." He tried to move slowly, so no one would sense him stirring. He felt around the trunk and located a tire iron. Hoping to disable a tail light, he started tapping at the back of the car. After a few minutes of drumming he had dented the area enough for the light to malfunction.

"Hopefully", he thought to himself, "they'll get pulled over and I'll be rescued." For good measure, he pressed the emergency button he had affixed to his lapel, doubting its usefulness in the trunk of a car.

Jeff felt the car slowing and making a turn. He recognized the sound of dried leaves and sticks snapping under the tires. The car soon came to a stop. Gripping the tire iron, ready to strike whomever opened the trunk, he could overhear two men.

"Look, the boss said to take him here and bury him. I didn't know he meant to bury him alive! I don't like it," the first man said.

"He also said he's going to give us fifty grand to do it! He said this is the guy that killed all those people up at Golga." The other man insisted, "Now open the damn trunk!"

Jeff steeled himself. As the trunk opened, he swung the iron with all his strength, connecting with the chest of the man opening the trunk. He felt a sickening thud and the man stumbled back into his cohort. Jeff jumped out of the trunk brandishing the tire iron. He swung again and this time hit the other man squarely in the jaw. The man crumpled to the ground, unconscious. Jeff grabbed a hat from the trunk, dug a small hole and set the hat on top of it. He leaned the shovel one of the men was carrying against a nearby tree, jumped in the car and drove until he reached the next town. Parking the car in the lot of a grocery store and sitting for a moment, he tried to think of his next move.

"Obviously, someone wants me dead. Why? Is there a leak in our operations and the same people that want to kill Vito discovered what I am really doing? Or is Effabee taking the attempted kidnapping of yesterday and ratcheting it up a notch? I have to get back to the motel and contact Missy." He thought to himself.

Jeff programmed the onboard GPS with the address of his motel. To his surprise, his captors had brought him closer to it, rather than further way. He drove the short distance to the motel. Once in his room, he sat down, overwhelmed with his discoveries and the recent events. His entire body started shaking, coming off an adrenaline high. Slowly, the tremors stopped as he realized he had been in shock since his episode in the trunk of the car. Reaching into his inner suit pocket, he was relieved to find his phone was still there. He dialed Missy's cell phone. She answered on the first ring.

"Jeff! Where have you been? We were supposed to meet for dinner at Mario's! You called and said to meet you there. You said you had reservations for us at five. I went and waited an hour. That had me worried!" she said.

"Missy, I didn't call you. The last thing I did was text you a photo of a falsified transfer order for Vito Phenton. Did you get it?"

"Yes, that's why we were going to meet. What happened?" her voice held concern this time.

"I was struck unconscious and stuffed into the trunk of a car. I used a tire iron to fend off my abductors and drove the car back here. Can you come over here right way? We really need to talk!" The words rushed out of Jeff's mouth.

"I'll be there in a flash", Missy assured him.

Less than ten minutes had gone by when Jeff heard Missy knocking on his door. He opened it as she rushed past him.

"Let me look at you! Is that a gash on the back of your head?" Missy cried, turning Jeff around, examining his wound.

"I'm okay, really. I'm just very concerned that my cover has been blown. Someone cracked me on the back of my head right after the text was sent."

"I forwarded it to Kevin and Senior Investigator Rennips as soon as I got it. They'll give us instructions on how to proceed. Kevin will be calling me shortly. Once I get the instructions, I'll notify you."

"What are we going to do with the car? Once those two thugs regain consciousness, they'll be looking for it."

"Either we can either drive it back to the spot where they were going to bury you and leave it there, or call the local police and let them deal with it."

"Let's let the police deal with it."

"Okay. I'll give them a call and let Lt. O'Hara know about what happened. Kevin will keep us apprised of the situation and what move we should make next."

"Thanks." Jeff rubbed the wound on the back of his head gingerly.

"That doesn't look good. I'm going to get a medic here to patch you up."

"Really, I'll be fine", Jeff protested, "I just need to shower and wash the dried blood from my hair."

"No, I think you need stitches, Jeff. It looks like a pretty good gash back there." Missy patted his shoulder and said, "Just let the medic take a look, for me, please?"

"Okay, I guess." Jeff conceded. "I don't like the looks of it." Missy stated again as she texted the home office for assistance.

A gentle knock sounded on the door. Missy jumped up and answered it. Bill Beetee, a well-muscled man, stood at the door with his EMT bag slung over his shoulder. "Jasmine said a team member needs medical attention?"

"Yes, Bill, come in, please."

The medic stitched Jeff's wound and told him to see his regular doctor when he went home.

****

"I am starved!" Jeff exclaimed.

"You know Jeff, I am too! Do you want Room Service or would you like to go to the diner down the road?"

"I could go for a pizza right now. Let's look at the room service menu."

They huddled over the menu and discovered a plethora of pizzas with several different toppings. They settled on a pizza half sausage and half cheese.

The meal was delivered and the two detectives ate.

Missy's purse vibrated.

She retrieved her phone from it, answering. "Oh, hello, let me put you on speakerphone."

She pressed a button.

"Are you still there?" Lt. O'Hara asked.

"Yes, Jeff is with me. Did you talk to Don Rennips?"

"Yes. I also spoke with Captain Egan. If Jeff feels up to it, let's move forward with the mission."

"Really, I feel fine", Jeff said with determination, "I want to get to the bottom of this. You can see the document Effabee used to transfer Vito

Phenton to Golga, but why did he do it? What was his motivation?"

"Jeff, see if there are any other suspicious transfers. Check on the health status of those inmates. If they're injured, find out which cell block they are in."

"I'll do that, Lieutenant. I'll check the files when I get to work in the morning."

"Jeff, get some rest. Missy, Ann Cody will be back at her job tomorrow. Why don't you meet with her at a spot outside of the prison and get her up to speed on all that's happening."

"That sounds like a good idea, Kevin. I'll call her."

"Yes. You can reach her at home or on her secure cell phone."

"Okay. Good night, Missy. Good night, Jeff", Kevin said as he clicked off.

Missy disconnected the call and put her phone back in her purse.

"I'll message you after I meet with Madeline tomorrow", Missy said as she went out the door.

Jeff lay on the bed, his head still tender. Feeling overwhelmed by everything that had happened in the last 24 hours, he felt concern for his friend, Phil. He hoped Phil was not in danger.

****

Phil and Vito shuffled along the food line with the other inmates. They slid their trays along the metal track, picking up their plates and utensils. As they neared the inmate who was doling out the food, there was a scuffle behind them. Phil leaned over to Vito and said in a low voice, "Stay low and near me. I was warned there may be an attack on you in the imminent future. When we get to the table, we'll sit next to each other at the end of the table. If another prisoner is out to kill you, I want you near me so I can protect you."

Vito looked at Phil, worried. "Spike, do you think Lester Gibson and the dealers have found out I'm here? Do you think they're here?"

"I know they are. That's why I'm telling you how to stay safe."

"They won't rest until I'm dead! I might as well die now," he moaned. "I can't get any peace."

Vito had just finished saying those words when a burly inmate stumbled near them, falling into Vito's arms. Phil saw the glint of metal in the inmate's hand and thrust his arm between the other inmate and Vito. The shiv intended for Vito became embedded in Phil's left arm. "Run, Vito! Run!" Phil screamed.

Vito broke loose and ran to the guard near the tables.

"Help us! My cell mate just got stabbed!" Vito yelled at the guard. The guard blew his whistle and spoke into the radio clipped to his uniform.

"Cell Block A, inmate lunch room, requesting assistance and medics, now!"

Within a matter of seconds, several guards descended upon the scene, along with medical personnel dressed in white scrubs. The guards cleared the area around Phil and Vito, pushing the unruly throng of inmates back so that Phil and Vito could be attended to by trained professionals.

"Sir", one of the medics said to Phil as he examined the wound, "Can you wiggle your fingers for me?"

Phil complied.

"Good, no nerve damage that I can see. Let's get this wound dressed and get you to sick bay so I can get an IV started."

"Please look after my friend, Vito. I think he's been hurt. Where is he?" Phil asked, looking around worriedly.

"The guards moved him back with the rest of the crowd when we arrived. Don't worry, you took the blow that was meant for him."

Phil jump to his feet shrugging off the medics. He scanned the crowd of inmates around him, looking for Vito. He saw Vito getting shoved toward a wall by a few angry inmates. Phil pushed his way past several of the other prisoners until he was close enough to Vito to protect him. One of Vito's attackers was saying to the cowering man, "We got your pal Spike outta the way, now it's your turn, traitor!" The man raised his fist to start pummeling Vito, as did the other two men with him. Phil gave a mule kick into the side of the first attacker's knee. A loud crack could be heard just before the man tumbled to the ground clutching his leg. The two men with him whirled around, in surprise.

"Anyone else want a piece of Spike!? Huh!? Because I'll give you what I gave this guy!" Phil yelled.

The crowd became silent. The only noise was the wailing of the first attacker on the floor with a broken leg. The guards moved in quickly, ordering the inmates back to their cells. The medics took Phil, Vito and the injured attacker with them to the prison's sick bay.

****

The head nurse tended to patients as they were brought in; the most urgent cases were seen by the attending physician first. When the medics brought the trio of inmates from the Cell Block A lunch room, Vito's attacker was given top priority because of his injury. His wailing did not affect his status; the inmates were notorious for claiming they needed medical attention, when it was just a ploy to stay out of the general population. They determined that Phil's wound gave him priority him over Vito since he had lost a significant amount of blood. Vito had a lesser stab wound and some bruises from the manhandling by his attackers. Phil and Vito were treated and released back to their cell block. Once they were in the cell, Vito spoke. "Spike, I owe you, man. Those guys would have sliced and diced me. You literally saved my life!"

Phil shrugged his shoulders. "I told you on my first day in here that I have your back. My word is good."

He sat down on his bunk and rested his arm on his lap. "I wanted to ask you – how did you end up in here? You don't seem very vicious."

"I deserve to be in here. I killed my brother in cold blood. The sad thing is, at the time I didn't think he would die, at least not the horrible death he endured. I was originally at the State Prison, but after I got sick and went to the hospital, they brought me here. I guess they re-thought things. I mean, I had a job and was good at it back at the State Prison. Here, the guards beat us and the other inmates try to kill us."

"We made it through today, buddy. I don't think they'll bother us again, unless they want to end up in the sick bay."

"I am glad you are my friend, Spike. I hope those guys really will leave me alone. I bet the drug lords and the others have found me again. The police told me they'd keep them away from me. They lied!"

Phil took Vito by the shoulders. "Look man, I told you I won't let anything happen to you. The cops didn't keep their promise. I will."

"I really hope you can, Spike." Vito said glumly.

Jeff woke up early, showered, shaved and ate a quick breakfast at the Dunkin Donuts around the corner and down the street from his motel. He purchased a coffee to go and drove to the office. He took his time getting there, curious about the reactions of his coworkers. He exited the elevator, straightened his tie, and smoothed his hair over his wound, observing the faces of the office workers as he passed. He strolled by the Warden's office, glancing in Wixmor's door as he passed, noticing Effabee sitting across from Wixmor, gesturing wildly. They both glanced up and saw Jeff. Effabee froze mid-gesture. Wixmor gasped. Jeff noticed their surprise and waved nonchalantly. He opened the door slightly and said, "Good morning gentlemen. I think I will be able to finish up my research this morning. I'll prepare my presentation and bring it to Ann Cody when she comes back to work tomorrow. Well, I'm off to the coffee bar, I need that morning coffee, you know!" He laughed. He closed the door and headed to the coffee bar with a backward glance, seeing the two men staring after him open-mouthed. Once he reached his desk, he sent a text to Missy. He told her about the reactions of Effabee and Wixmor. After he sent the text, he clipped his phone to his belt. He picked up the keys to the cabinets then started to walk to Wixmor's office to finish his research.

"Mickson, may I have a word with you, please? "Mr. Kimble asked.

Phil turned and walked toward Kimble. "Yes, Mr. Kimble, what can I do for you?"

"Step into my office."

Kimble closed the door behind him and offered Jeff a seat across from him at his desk.

"We received a very disturbing call this morning which explains the surprise you may have seen on our faces."

"Who received the disturbing call? What did they say?" Jeff was very curious.

"An unidentified caller made a call to my office phone at six a.m., stating you would not be returning to work – that you were indefinitely incapacitated. Obviously, those statements are untrue."

"Well, I'm here now. The call was probably a prank one."

"I am counting on you to make a professional presentation for Ann Cody. Will you be ready to meet with her tomorrow?", Mr. Kimble queried.

"Yes sir. I am finishing my research this morning on the guard's inappropriate actions. I will prepare the presentation this afternoon, and it will be ready to offer it to Mrs. Cody tomorrow."

"Very good. Why don't you get started now? If you need any other resources, please let me know."

"Thank you, Mr. Kimble" Jeff said as he left the office.

Jeff walked to the Warden's office thinking about the conversation he and Kimble had just had.

"Hmm", he thought, "Someone was sure I was injured enough that I would not be returning to work. Things are escalating. Once I'm finished with this research, I will contact Missy."

"Good Morning, Mr. Wixmor", he said in a cheerful voice, "How are you today?"

Jeff opened the cabinet for the Golga prison personnel and withdrew the files for Tim Effabee and Bryce Wixmor. He slipped them in the envelope he had for personnel files. As he turned to leave, he noticed Bryce Wixmor's right hand shaking uncontrollably as if to signal him. The left side of his face was drooping and Bryce's mouth was opening and shutting with incomprehensible sounds coming out.

"Mr. Wixmor! Are you okay?" he said urgently.

Bryce Wixmor's head bobbed sideways in a jerking motion.

Realizing the man was having a medical emergency, Jeff picked up the phone, dialing 911.

"Mr. Wixmor, help is on the way." Still keeping an eye on the Warden, Jeff backed toward the office doorway.

In an urgent shout, he called out the door, "Help! We have a medical emergency here!" Several employees came running. One identified himself as an EMT. Jeff told him he had called 911 and an ambulance was on the way. The EMT knelt next to Mr. Wixmor and said in a soothing voice, "Warden, I'm an EMT; I'm going to help you. If you can understand me, blink twice. Wixmor blinked twice and tried to say something, but all that came out was a gurgle.

"Don't try to speak. I am going to take your vital signs now." He took the Warden's wrist in his hand and noting the man's pulse rate, said "Does anyone have a flashlight?" Quickly, one of the clerks handed him a small key ring flashlight. "Bryce, I am going to look in your eyes now. Stay with me!"

Mr. Wixmor blinked twice again. The EMT flashed the light in his eyes, noting the reactions of his pupils.

"Warden, smile for me, please."

Bryce could not smile. "Raise your eyebrows for me. He could only raise the right eyebrow; the left one sagged.

A commotion could be heard at the elevators. It was apparent the paramedics from the ambulance had arrived. The EMT assured Mr. Wixmor he would be in good care now and would be on his way to the hospital. Wixmor blinked twice and closed his eyes. The paramedics came in and lifted him onto a stretcher, maneuvering it quickly to the elevator and down to the waiting ambulance. The siren could be heard as the ambulance sped off into the distance.

The clerk who had identified himself as an EMT, pulled Jeff aside. "Tom that was quick thinking. If Wixmor survives, he has you to thank. I'm pretty sure he had a stroke. If he did not get immediate attention, he would have died right at his desk."

"Thank you for stepping up and using your medical skills on him; it gives the paramedics a head start in helping him. Your manner with him was great. He didn't seem as anxious after you spoke with him. The hospital will be calling Mr. Kimble with an update on his condition."

Later that morning, Mr. Kimble assembled the employees in a large conference room.

"Good Morning, Ladies and Gentlemen. I have some very sad news. This morning, the Warden suffered a stroke. The ambulance was summoned to bring him to Mercy General Hospital. I just received a call from the hospital's emergency room. Mr. Wixmor died on the way to the hospital. All measures had been taken to revive him. He had suffered a major cerebral infarction and was declared brain dead after an EEG was performed. His family took him off life support. They will call us with the wake and funeral arrangements."

There was a solemn silence for a moment, then employees began murmuring to one another, feeling the shock of another tragedy that had happened in the same week as the shootings in Personnel. Still feeling numb, the group broke up slowly walking back to their desks.

Jeff copied the Effabee and Wixmor files, replaced the originals in Wixmor's office, and went to his desk to complete his research. He pulled out his laptop and sent an urgent email to Missy. He told her of the anonymous caller who said Tom Mickson was incapacitated and would not be returning to work. He also spoke of the stroke Wixmor suffered and his subsequent death. Putting the laptop back in its case, he turned to the files he had copied. He laid them side by side, so he could review them quickly. The first thing he noticed was Wixmor and Effabee had come from the same town. "Pure coincidence", he thought.

The town's name seemed familiar to him, but he could not recall why. He looked at the file a little further and noticed they had both started on the same day. "Another coincidence? Maybe." He turned to his computer and looked up recent work schedules for both men. The schedules revealed the two had schedules that were identical. It revealed they had both taken days off at odd times during the past three weeks. Quickly, Jeff printed out the schedules and slipped them into the envelope with the copies of their files. He tapped out an email to Captain Egan's private account asking him about the town the two had come from. He sipped his now cold coffee and began preparing his presentation for Ann Cody.

****

"Open 518!" Officer Thomas commanded.

"Sarmanson! You have a visitor!" Officer Thomas rapped his baton on the cells bars. "Come on, make it snappy! I'm done with my shift in ten minutes!"

Phil walked to the cell opening, held his arms out patiently, the left arm still bandaged. Officer Thomas snapped the cuffs on him and led him to the visitation room. He shackled him to the ring on the metal table and turned to leave the room.

"Officer Pole will bring you back to your cell."

Phil sat in the metal folding chair waiting for his visitor. Kevin O'Hara was escorted into the visitation room and sat opposite Phil, behind the Plexiglas. They both picked up their phones at the same time.

"My lands, Spike! What happened to you!?" Kevin said in his southern drawl.

"Aw, someone tried to hurt my pal Vito and I protected him. It is nuthin' to worry about. The other guy is in worse shape than me. I broke his knee" Phil growled.

Kevin spoke in a voice just above a whisper, "He's okay? They didn't get to him did they?"

"No, they didn't get close enough", Phil replied in a quiet voice, "Did he make a report this week?"

"Yes", Kevin answered, "He checked in. Part of his report was about your injury."

"Don't worry about me. I can take care of myself. I'll just be glad when I can blow this joint as a free man."

"I'm working on that, Cousin. Your lawyer is doing some useful research; he should have it done tomorrow."

"Good. He probably wants to move on to the next case too."

"Sarmanson! Time's up! Let's move it!" a burly guard announced. Phil waved his shackled hand in a goodbye to Kevin and walked back to his cell next to the big guard. As they neared the cell the guard leaned down face to face with Phil. "The brass sent me in. Just listen to me and you'll be fine."

"Stick it, Screw!" Phil muttered.

The guard, still close to Phil's ear, whispered, "Does Paul Z. Meyers mean anything to you?"

Phil stopped in his tracks, stunned, but happy. "You – you – Paul!" he stammered in utter amazement.

"Yes, Sarmanson, now get in the cell. I'll be back for you later!"

"Open 518!" he shouted.

"Okay, Officer Pole," came the response.

The cell door clanged open and Phil shuffled inside. Officer Pole removed the cuffs and called for the cell door to be shut.

After a moment, Vito asked Phil, "Who was that guard? What happened to Officer Thomas?"

Phil answered Vito with, "Officer Thomas' shift ended. That was Officer Pole."

"Geez, he looks big", Vito observed.

"You ain't kidding, man. I heard one guy crossed

him and he dragged him away in cuffs. The guy wasn't heard from again. We just have to do what he says or else," Phil made a slicing motion to his neck.

"I believe you. He looks like a giant!" Vito said in awe.

Chapter 26

Jeff hit the save button on the desktop computer. He had reviewed his report and felt confident he could make the case for guards to have better training in anger management, rather than taking their frustrations out on the inmates. He pressed the print button, retrieved a folder from the drawer and rose to pick up his printout. As he reached the printer, the familiar beep of an incoming email sounded on his phone. Opening the message, saw a reply from Captain Egan. Eagerly, he opened the email. It read:

"Jeff,

The name of the town you describe is Bellmants. The latest survey of urban crime listed Bellmants as a community that has seen a rise in drug trafficking over the past eight years. We considered that along with the regular activities of Effabee and Wixmor. In addition, the reports sent to us by Detective Barone regarding Royal Wixmor's confession led us to take a close look at their respective bank accounts. We noticed that on the days you reported the two men took leave from work, the bank accounts showed very large deposits and withdrawals. We also noticed that today, Bryce Wixmor's account was closed and a deposit matching the amount that was in Wixmor's account was deposited to Effabee's account. An agent from the Financial Crimes Unit is on their way to speak with him as I write this. Please keep him occupied until the agent arrives; we think he and Wixmor are involved in drug trafficking.

Keep safe.

Scott"

Jeff closed his email program. He picked up the completed presentation, heading towards Kimble's office to let him review the information. He stopped at Tim Effabee's desk first. Effabee was on his smart phone, using a banking application, muttering, "Hurry up and transfer! What is taking so long!?" he banged his fist on the desk.

"Tim, I just wanted to stop by and extend my condolences about Mr. Wixmor. I know how much you admired him." Jeff shook his head sadly, "He will be sorely missed."

Still focusing on his smart phone, Tim didn't answer, muttering, "Hurry up, hurry up, hurry up!"

Jeff coughed and repeated his condolences.
Tim finally looked up at Jeff and said, "Yea, yea, he'll be missed, he'll be missed." His attention returned to his phone. "Yes! Now we're talking!"

"Did you just win the lottery?" Jeff queried.

"You might say so, Tom. Yes, you can say I did."

"Congratulations. Is it enough for you to retire?"

"Probably, but I won't retire. The benefits here are too good for me to quit. I have to admit that I'll have the upper hand, knowing I can up and quit whenever I choose. I'll apply for the Warden's job."

"Good luck to you, Tim."

A man in a dark suit with a briefcase approached them. "Mr. Effabee?" he said, looking at the two men.

Jeff nodded to Tim and said, "Well, "I'll leave you two." He moved off toward Kimble's office. As he was leaving he heard the agent introduce himself. The man spread several sheets out on Effabee's desk. Jeff could not stop and look back at them; it would certainly blow his cover. He knocked lightly on Kimble's door.

"Come in."

Jeff entered the office, handing Mr. Kimble the report. "Here is what I have prepared to give Mrs. Cody tomorrow. If you'd like to review and critique it that's fine with me." Mr. Kimble took the presentation, sitting at his desk as he looked it over.

"Very well put, Tom. I think Ann will be impressed. You make a strong case for future training." He handed the file back to Jeff.

Headed back to his desk, Jeff noticed Tim Effabee's face was flushed red with anger and the veins in his neck were bulging. The agent sitting with him was speaking softly, pointing to different parts of the sheets spread out in front of them. Jeff could hear Tim becoming more and more agitated.

"No! You can't say or do that! It was the Warden, not me! He directed me to create that account," he pointed to another item on the sheet in front of him, "and make that deposit!" Slamming his fist down on the desk, he demanded, "How did you get these reports, anyway! - Is nothing private anymore?"

The agent remained calm and said in a near monotone voice, "The Judge granted us a subpoena for these records. Nothing is private when drug money is involved. We traced this back to when you both lived in Bellmants. The spike in drug trafficking happened after the two of you became friends."

"How would you know when we became friends? Huh?"

"May I remind you that our investigators are very thorough and that Bellmants is not a big town? People love to talk. They were only too happy to let us know you and Wixmor were an item."

At this, Tim sprung from his chair.

"How dare you malign the dead!? Bryce Wixmor was a good, kind man. He treated other people with respect. We all loved him!" Tim, consumed with anger, reached in a drawer and pulled out a snub nosed gun. He swung around to face the agent. He was just about to fire the gun, when the deafening sound of a .357 Magnum went off. Tim screamed in pain and clutched his arm where blood was spurting out. The agent now had his gun out and pointed at Tim Effabee's head. Lt. Kevin Leestaude O'Hara strode forward, his service revolver in his hand.

"What in Heaven's name is going on out here?" Kimble yelled, bursting out of his office. The employees in the office crowded around Effabee's desk, craning their necks to see what had happened. "Did you see it happening?" one employee asked the other.

"Please, everyone, back up. I need to secure this crime scene. An ambulance has been called." Lt. O'Hara strode purposefully toward the desk. "Please, move back!"

The crowd moved back and within minutes the ambulance crew was in the office for the second time that day. They wheeled Tim Effabee out and loaded him into an ambulance, ready to speed off to Mercy General.

Lt. O'Hara turned to the agent who had been meeting with Effabee.

"What brought on your investigation of his financial records?"

"We have been monitoring Effabee closely. He has been having large deposits and withdrawals recently. We suspected illegal activity. The fact is, Mr. Effabee cleaned out Mr. Wixmor's account without proper authorization."

****

"Open 518!" shouted Officer Pole.

Vito's eyes shot open when he heard the cell door opening. He sat bolt upright, frightened that this was the end for him. Officer Pole's large figure filled the opening of the cell.

"Phenton, Sarmanson, get up! Let's go!"

Phil looked up at the guard.

" Just a second, Screw." he growled.

"I said, get up!" The guard repeated. Phil jumped up and approached Officer Pole and Vito. Officer Pole connected the two men via a chain attached to their shackles. He led them to an empty, darkened hallway.

"What's going on?" Vito asked.

"Shh!!" Officer Pole turned and whispered, "Just keep quiet and watch!"

Vito shrank back, afraid of getting beaten by the burly guard.

"Okay", he whispered, just don't hit me! Please!"

Phil leaned over to Vito reassuringly whispering, "There's nothing to worry about. This screw is not Thomas. This one has a brain."

Officer Pole signaled them to follow. Silently, they moved forward edging around a corner. Officer Pole held his hand up, stopping them. He pointed to an open area a few yards ahead. There were four or five prisoners there, looking around, confused.

One prisoner, obviously the group's leader pulled out a cell phone and punched in a number. Putting the phone to his ear, he listened for some time, and then said, "Tim, this is Gus. Where the hell are you? I have four buyers here, like I told you I would yesterday. They want their product now! We're at the spot you told me to be. Get down here!". He pressed another button and slid the phone back into his jumpsuit.

"Guys, I left a message on his phone. He should be here any minute. Do you have the money?"

The other four prisoners reached into their prison garb and produced wads of money that they gave to the leader. He counted each prisoner's bills and nodded, satisfied.

"Okay, boys, it's all there. Now we just have to wait for the delivery."

He walked into the dark hallway, looking down it anxiously. "Where are you!?" He said angrily. No answer came.

"Hank, get back in here, I want my money back! I'm gonna find a different dealer; this guy isn't dependable and I need my fix."

The others agreed with the man who spoke, all demanding their money be returned. Phil, who had been observing the entire scene, staggered back, shocked to see Captain Scott Egan enter the open area. Officer Pole stepped back to support him.

"Do you see who that is!?", Phil exclaimed in shock.

Chapter 27

The three men retraced their steps hurriedly. When they reached the cell, Officer Pole spoke in a low voice, "I was really shocked when I found out; I didn't want to believe it myself. This proves my worst fears about him."

Phil, still visibly shaken said, "I trusted my life with that man. How could he have betrayed us? I trusted him for years and so did Jeff! Does he have any idea about this?"

"Shh, don't blow your cover! Jeff doesn't know yet that Egan is involved in these illegal activities. He thinks your Captain is on the right side of the law; he's been doing his part in the Administration offices. I haven't been briefed on his activities for a few days, but if things are as intense there as they are here, he could be in danger."

Phil stiffened at the thought of his best friend being in harm's way. "Shouldn't you get him out of there, if he's in that much danger?"

"Well, Phil, he hasn't hit the panic button and we haven't had any reports from that sector yet. I do think he should be informed about the perpetuation of the drug ring, so he can be prepared for anything that comes down the pike!"

"Seriously, somebody better get word to him quick! Remember, Captain Egan assigned us to this mission! So, has he been in this drug ring from the start? I mean, from before we arrested Vito?"

"Apparently not. If he was, don't you think he would have either shot Vito or tried to stop his arrest?"

Phil thought for a moment then said, "Yeah, you're right; I'd better stay in character or my cover will be blown."

"Open 518!" Officer Pole demanded. The cell door made a loud noise opening. Officer Pole unchained the two men once they were in the cell. They moved toward their bunks and sat down.

"Close 518!", Officer Pole shouted. The door closed with a grating noise.

After the guard left their area, Vito whispered, "What was that all about? Why did he take us to that hallway where that prisoner was doing a drug deal? And that man that walked in to talk to the prisoner? He looked awfully familiar…almost like that Captain that arrested me a couple of years ago!"

Phil put a finger up to his lips, signaling Vito to remain silent. He knelt next to him and said, in barely a whisper, "It was Captain Egan."

Vito stared at him in disbelief. "How would you know anything like that, Spike? You don't even know the guy!"

Phil coughed, then spoke in his true voice, "He's my Captain in Anderson Falls."

"Holy smokes! You're one of the detectives that investigated Gary's death! You, you ...Did you come here to kill me?" Vito started to back away, nervously.

Phil said calmly, "You have nothing to worry about. I was sent here to protect you. You have to keep my identity a secret. I'm Phil Glass. But while we're here, I'm Spike Sarmanson, got it? I cannot let the guards or the other inmates know my true identity; it will blow the entire mission!"

"Okay, okay, Spike! I'll do whatever you say! You can trust me. All this stuff just blows my mind."

****

As the brochures advertise, Mercy General Hospital's Intensive Care Unit is an efficient, unit staffed with caring nurses. The nurses were gathered at the Nurses' Station, giving reports at the change of shifts for the night. They had discussed the condition and prognosis of all the patients, except one.

Nurse Bondi was giving her report on her patients. "And in room104, we have Tim Effabee. He is a former clerk from Golga Correctional Facility. His right hand suffered severe trauma from a gunshot wound. He was brought in at noon and went directly to surgery. The hand had suffered so much trauma that it had to be amputated. He was brought into our unit at 2:30 pm and started to wake up from the anesthesia around 4:30 pm. I don't think he realizes his hand was amputated because he keeps pressing the call light and asking why we bandaged over his fingers. I thought the ER Doctor told him his hand would be amputated. Somebody slipped up."

"Well", the Nursing Supervisor said, "I will call one of the social workers for this unit and ask them to sit with him so they can explain the surgery to him and help him adjust to the loss of his appendage."

"Thank you", Nurse Bondi said. "He is one of the most obnoxious patients I have ever encountered! He presses the call light to find out where his fingers are, he presses it again almost immediately to ask for his boss, then again to tell me to fill out new transfer orders for prisoners."

The nursing supervisor replied, "Diane, he may be

in shock, or denial over losing his hand. Try
to bear with him. I spoke with the doctor that is
treating him and he told me Mr. Effabee should be
stable enough to go to the general recovery floor
tomorrow." She glanced at the patient's chart,
"Unless of course, his temperature spikes over
103 again tonight."

"Thank you. I will do his vitals again before I
leave tonight." She excused herself to go and take
his vitals right then. As she headed toward room
104, another nurse ran past her, Shouting "Code
White! Code White, room 104!" Nurse Bondi
sprinted to the room as did several orderlies and a
few other nurses. The scene in the room was
chaotic. Tim Effabee was standing in the middle
of the room making unholy noises. They were the
mixture of a screech, a wail and some kind of
guttural noise. He had pulled the IV lines from
his arm, causing it to bleed, the bandage was torn
from the stump on his right arm and was flung on
his hospital bed. The patients in the nearby rooms
had all pressed their call buttons and were
shouting for their nurses. Finally, a male orderly
was able to wrestle Tim Effabee to his hospital
bed and hold him down while nurse Bondi
injected him with a strong sedative. He thrashed
for a few seconds more, then the sedative took
effect. He laid still. Nurse Bondi cleaned and
dressed his wounds. The Intensive Care Director
consulted with the attending physician to make
sure they had orders for a mild sedative until the
patient was able to meet with his social worker.

The doctor instructed the night nurse to put the sedative in his IV Drip, and left to write up the incident and his recommendations. Nurse Bondi looked at her truculent patient, now sleeping soundly. She returned to the nurses' station to write up her notes on the incident and finally go home. The nursing supervisor took her report when she completed it and commented, "That was an exciting end to your day. I bet you don't get many nights like that!"

"No", Nurse Bondi said, "Nor do I want many like that. That man, no matter how obstinate, must have some really serious issues for him to act out like that!"

"I heard he had an attacked a federal agent and his hand was shot during the scuffle."

"I guess he's lucky to be alive", Nurse Bondi observed, "Better to be without a hand than dead. I assume once he is well enough to leave the hospital, he'll see Golga prison from the inmate's perspective."

"Maybe. Have a quiet night. See you tomorrow!" The nursing supervisor waved good night and went her way. As Nurse Bondi walked to her car, she thought how lucky she was that the male orderly was there to overpower the unruly patient. "Maybe I should take those vacation days I have to use", she thought to herself.

****

Jeff put his presentation in an envelope and tucked it into his briefcase. It had been a very hectic day. He needed to meet with Missy and determine what their next move would be. If Phil could keep Vito safe and find out who was trying to kill him, they could be with their wives right on schedule with what the detectives had originally predicted. It would be just under a week they had been away, if everything went smoothly. Jeff stopped by Mr. Kimble's office to say good night where he found him straightening up some papers on his desk.

"Oh, Tom, please come in. I'd like to talk to you for a moment before you leave."

"Sure, Mr. Kimble. What can I do for you?"

"As you and everyone else here knows, Mr. Effabee will no longer be working here. He had several projects that were in the works. I am trying to divide them up between our remaining clerks. I just got the resignation of two of the female clerks here. They said they wish to work in a safer environment; I can't say I blame them. Anyway, Tim had a stack of transfer orders that needed to be completed and signed by the Warden. If you could get them completed as much as you can, then we can have them ready for the Warden to sign once he's appointed. They are in a stack in the corner of Tim's desk; you can pick them up tomorrow morning if you want to take on this assignment."

"Sure, I'll help out whatever way I can." Jeff thought to himself, "What luck! I can see if Tim was forging other transfer orders, and what type of prisoners he was bringing in."

"I'll check with you tomorrow after you get started on the project to see if there are any additional resources you need. Get a good night's rest!" Mr. Kimble said, taking the elevator that deposited him in the parking garage. Jeff got on the elevator that brought him to the main lobby. He dialed Missy's number on his way to his car. She answered on the second ring.

"Hello, Jeff! I've been waiting for your call! Kevin gave me his version of all that happened today – I'd like to hear yours."

"This afternoon, Mr. Kimble gave me one of Tim Effabee's projects he had on his desk. It is a stack of Transfer Orders for prisoners. I accepted the assignment. Now, I can see if he was forging more than just Vito's transfer and I can see what type of prisoners Tim Effabee was having transferred here. If he was doing anything illegal with the transfers, we can use that against him after he gets out of the hospital."

"We will need to have evidence showing he has been transferring potential drug ring leaders and actual drug leaders to sell to the prisoners who are also users." Missy informed Jeff.

"I can be on the lookout for drug dealers and users included in the transfers." Jeff offered.

"Do you want to meet for dinner and go over what you have up until now and make plans for the next step?" Missy asked.

"That sounds good. I have some thoughts I'd like to bounce off you. Where would you like to meet?"

"I heard there's a place called Gene's Variety; it has a grill and serves dinner until eight. It's in the Plaza just a few miles east of your motel. If you want, we can meet there in a half an hour."

"Great! I can run my presentation past you too. I think you will find it enlightening."

"See you there!" Missy hung up, put on a light sweater and headed to the diner. She arrived there just as Jeff was pulling into the parking lot. They walked into the diner together.

After they were seated, Jeff turned to Missy and said, "This has got to be the busiest three days of my life! Getting married wasn't as hectic as these past few days. I did my research on Bryce Wixmor and Tim Effabee. I found Effabee forged Vito's transfer orders. I have a stack to go through tomorrow that he was working on. I'll see if any of those are forged. I also found out he had set up some bank accounts and not only was laundering drug money, but he transferred every penny in Wixmor's account to his personal account minutes after Wixmor left in the ambulance."

"If we can get the bank records from the financial crimes unit, we can put Tim Effabee away for a long time."

The waiter came back and took their orders for dinner. Jeff showed Missy the papers he had prepared for Ann Cody. Within the packet were documents proving that Tim Effabee and Bryce Wixmor were involved in the laundering of drug money.

Missy flipped through the pages of the presentation stopping to read the inserted pages before she closed the file and handed it back to Jeff, "This is indeed very enlightening. I am sure Ann Cody will get it to the right people for their perusal. If you find any other supporting documents, call me and I will have her get them to the right people immediately."

The two detectives ordered coffee after they finished their meal and were sipping it in companionable silence. Missy's phone rang, startling both of them.

"Hello...yes he's here. They what? Who? You have got to be kidding!! That isn't funny at all! Really? I have got to get Jeff up to speed in this. Things are happening too quickly." She went on to tell the caller about everything that had happened in Jeff's office that day, pausing to listen before ending the call.

"Jeff, we need to go for a ride. C'mon let's go." She paid the tab and hurried to her car with Jeff right beside her. Starting the engine, Missy roared out of the parking lot.

"Where are we going?" Jeff asked, confused.

"I just had to get out of that place where we could be overheard. I can't take any chances with what I have to tell you."

Chapter 28

"Now I'm really curious. What do you have to tell me?" Jeff said in an anxious tone, "I hope Phil's okay."

"Phil is fine", Missy reassured Jeff. "I have other mind blowing news for you".

"Go ahead, hit me with it."

"Phil has been busy these past three days." Missy recapped the close call Phil had while protecting Vito, then finished with the revelation about Captain Egan.

"I can't believe that! Are you sure? That man saved my life two years ago! Are you sure he was not doing undercover work?" Jeff was astonished at the allegations he just heard.

"My boss, Don Rennips checked out the tip. It is reliable. I found it hard to believe, myself. When Paul, Phil and Vito witnessed him making the deal, we had to believe it."

"What will the people at the station think now!? A man we all respected and trusted is no better than the thugs we bring in off the street." Jeff shook his head. "You cannot trust anyone anymore!"

"Jeff, Kevin and I have your back. I swear on my mother's eyes; you can trust us!"

"Thanks, Missy. Believe me, I will be glad when all of this is over!"

"So will I Jeff, this has been a very busy week!"

They pulled into the plaza where Jeff's car was parked.

They said good night and each drove off to their motel rooms.

"This was really a lot to take in", Jeff thought to himself, "I don't know if Erma will believe me when I tell her all that has happened. It is so unbelievable!"

Jeff made the final turn off the highway to go to his motel. Just ahead, he saw three fire trucks, sirens wailing, heading toward his motel, which was now engulfed in flames. A traffic cop waved him to detour around the activity. Jeff lowered his window to speak to him.

"What's happening here? I have a room booked in this motel!"

"Sorry sir. The whole motel is a loss. You'll

have to move along so the fire company can put out the flames."

Reluctantly, Jeff decided to reveal his true identity to the cop. He reached over the seat to make sure his jacket and briefcase were in the back, reached into his briefcase and pulled out his badge, showing it to the cop. Examining it closely the traffic cop realized who he was talking with. "Detective Weston, why didn't you show me this right way?" He handed the badge back to Jeff.

"I am working a special assignment and did not want to broadcast that I am in law enforcement."

"Okay, I'll let you through, just be careful, it is crazy by the motel."

"Thanks, please don't say anything about my status."

"I never saw you." Was the response.

Jeff drove as close as he could to the motel. Fire trucks were spraying the blaze, trying to douse the flames. The motel was a total loss. Jeff made his way back to the plaza he had just come from.

Pulling out his phone, he dialed Detective Barone.

"Missy, the motel I was staying in burned to the ground. A cop directing traffic told me the motel was a loss. I am going to book a room at the Best Western. My clothes were in the motel room - I know; I sound like I am whining about petty things; this is just so unexpected! Sorry."

Missy was saying something to her husband that Jeff couldn't quite make out. Finally, she said, "Jeff, where are you right now? Tony and I want you to stay with us. I'm going to call Don Rennips and have him FEDEX a credit card to us so we can get you some clothes. "

"I'm at the plaza where we met for dinner. I can't impose on you two, I'll get a room at Red Roof in Pleasant Village."

"No!" Missy said adamantly, "We're going shopping. Tony just called a friend who owns the local Men's WearHouse and he's going to meet us there. Just sit tight. We'll be right over to get you."

Ten minutes later, Jeff saw Missy's car pull into the parking lot. She hopped out of the passenger's side and jogged over to his car. Jeff lowered his window so she could speak with him.

"Here's the plan Jeff. Follow us back to our house, then we'll go in my car to Men's WearHouse. Tony will drive."

Jeff nodded, put his window up and followed the Barones to their home nearby. It was a large ranch style brick home on about an acre of land. A long, wide driveway led to a three car garage. Flowering bushes lined either side of the driveway. A flagstone sidewalk branching off the right side of the driveway led to the entrance of their home.

Tony stopped his car and signaled for Jeff to park near the third bay of the garage. Jeff pulled up and parked his car. He got out and walked over to Missy and Tony.

"I sincerely appreciate all you are doing for me", Jeff said as he shook hands with Tony.

"Missy has been telling me what a rough mission you are on. That was such a bad stroke of luck, having your motel burn down and lose all your clothes. My friend owns the local store here. He'll fix you up with some suits to wear to work. Hop in and we'll go over there now."

Jeff got in the car and sat back, relaxing a moment. The day had been a hard one and he was glad that Missy was in control right now. He felt grateful that she and her husband were so kind to him.

"We're here!" Tony announced as he pulled up to the shop. "Larkson is right over there."

They got out of the car and walked over to the store. Larkson was unlocking the door. He turned as they approached him and greeted the trio. Putting his hands on his hips, he looked Jeff up and down.

"Hmm, you look like a 33 waist 29 length. Let's get you some clothes. "

Jeff was surprised that the man could get his waist and length measurements without even using a tape measure.

"You are amazing! Those are my exact measurements!" Jeff said in awe.

"Oh, you'll make me blush! I've been measuring men for many years, you see."

Larkson walked over to a rack of suits and selected a dark blue one, then selected a pale blue tie and a pink shirt.

"Try this on, please. I think you'll look simply fabulous!"

Jeff took the clothes to the fitting room and reluctantly put them on. He looked at himself in the mirror and was surprised, he actually looked good. Missy and Tony nodded their heads in approval. Tony commented to Larkson, "Man, he looks good!"

Missy asked, "How about fixing him up with a few more suits? All his clothes burned in the fire that consumed his motel today."

"You poor thing", Larkson said to Jeff. "Leave it to me, we'll get you a few more suits, some undies and a couple pair of jammie's so you don't have to sleep naked!" He bustled off, selecting, suits, shirts and ties, brought them back for Jeff's approval, and then disappeared again for a few moments. When he returned his arms were full of satin pajamas, designer underwear and several pairs of socks. He even had a toothbrush, toothpaste, electric razor, shampoo, conditioner and a man's hairbrush.

"Wow, you thought of everything!", Jeff exclaimed, "You are good!"

"Thanks", Larkson replied, "Any friend of Tony's is a friend of mine. And I take good care of my friends."

Missy took out a credit card to pay for everything but Larkson refused to take any money. "This will be my donation to the homeless. I can write it off."

"Thanks Larkson", Jeff said, "Once I get home I will send you the money for all of this."

"No, just donate it to a homeless shelter or to your favorite charity, that's all I ask."

"I will. You really are life saver!"

Larkson smiled and did a slight bow. "It was my pleasure."

"Jeff, bad luck is following you", Missy quipped, "First you are kidnapped, then you and Madeline are attacked, and your motel is burned to the ground.

"It has been a bad week so far." Jeff admitted. "I'm so close to finding the truth behind all this, I can't stop. I can't let Captain Egan win this time. I hope Phil and Vito are safe."

Chapter 29

Nurse Bondi pulled into the parking garage at Mercy General Hospital. She waved to the guard in the booth by the Visitor's Parking Area and drove forward to the Employee parking. Stepping into the hallway connecting the garage and the hospital, she took the elevator to the first floor. She wanted to stop in and see her friend, Greg Joshua. He had always been a good friend, always willing to listen. Greg had given her sound advice in the past and was always there for her. Today, she needed his counsel. She also wanted to make sure he would be on duty because she may need his presence on the floor to prevent chaos from erupting. She knocked on the door to the Security office and walked in.

"Greg! Good; you're here!" Diana greeted Greg.

"Diana, it's good to see you! What brings you here tonight?"

"I wanted to stop in before my shift so I could talk to you." She explained, "One of the patients I am assigned to have been so unruly, it verges on violent. He just had some surgery and when he woke up from the anesthesia, he started acting crazy. He jumped out of bed, pulled out his IV lines and ripped his dressing off. It took two orderlies to hold him down so I could inject him with a strong sedative. I'm nervous that if one of the orderlies isn't on duty tonight that this patient may overpower us, possibly harming someone. Do you think you could include my area on your rounds tonight, please? I might need your physical presence to keep this fellow in line."

Greg looked kindly at his friend and said, "Diana, that's what they pay me to do. I will make some extra trips to your floor to make sure everything is under control."

"Great. I have to go start my shift but I'll see you later then. Thanks for your help." Diana said. She went to her floor, not worrying about what her unruly patient might do. Greg would protect her.

Nurse Bondi went to the Nurse's station to get her reports and check on the patients she would have that night. The assignment included Tim Effabee. Nurse Regina Yak updated her. "The social worker had gone in to see him. He was startled to see Mr. Effabee had gotten out of bed and really caused damage. This time, he had slammed the IV Pole through a widow, shattering it and sending shards of glass everywhere. He tried to walk through the window! By this time, his arm was bleeding pretty badly and he shredded the skin on his legs and feet trying to get through the window and thrashing around in his room. He struck the social worker when he tried to subdue him. This time it took three nurses and two orderlies to restrain him. His attending physician is not on duty tonight, so we have a call in to the on-call doctor but haven't heard anything yet. Getting orders for a strong sedative could take a few hours. If he puts his call light on, please make sure you're accompanied by another nurse or orderly. This patient is definitely a threat. We are also trying to get the doctor that is on call to order restraints. I suspect the arm that had the IV line in it now has a serious infection."

****

Phil lay on his bunk. There had been no attempts on Vito's life for the past day. He hoped the attacks were over. Closing his eyes, he tried to sleep. Finally, sleep overtook him; it was a restless sleep. Jolted awake by Vito's loud cry of help, he jumped off his bunk. Vito was being pulled out of bed by Officer Thomas. Phil launched into Officer Thomas, tackling him hard.

"Get off me, you scum! I'll beat you to a pulp!" Mick Thomas snarled.

Phil, atop the rogue officer, swung his fist and

knocked the man out.

Panting, he asked Vito what had happened.

"He came up to the cell, used a key to open it instead of calling for the powered opening of the cell door. He slid the cell door open just a little and squeezed through the opening. He was talking to me in a very low voice, "The Boss wants you dead. He's paid me well to make sure you die. It will be my pleasure!" That's when he started dragging me off the bed trying to break my legs. Of course, I called for help." Vito finished.

"And I thought you were finished with the death threats and attacks! I need to be more vigilant. Are your legs okay?"

"Yes, they're just gonna be a little sore. If you hadn't taken him down, he would have beaten me to death!"

Officer Thomas stirred, rubbing his jaw where Phil had punched him. Phil kneeled on Officer Thomas' chest.

"Unless you want me to break your jaw, you'll stay down. I'll break it if you move an inch."

Officer Thomas glared up at him. "I'll put you in Solitary for this!" Turning to Vito, he added, "Consider yourself dead. Without this brute near you, it will be easy to beat you to death. Heh, I think I will make it a slow, painful death for you." He smiled an evil smile. Phil put his foot against Officer Thomas' throat and called out, "Officer,

Pole, hey Officer Pole!"

Footsteps could be heard running down the hall. Officer Pole appeared at the cell door, slid it back, stepped inside and asked, "What's going on in here? Officer Thomas, what are you doing in this cell? You should be on rounds now."

Vito spoke. "Officer Pole, this guy" he pointed at Officer Thomas, "tried to kill me. First he was going to break my legs then beat me with his baton until I was dead."

Officer Pole asked Phil to step aside. He leaned over Officer Thomas and relieved him of his sidearm. "I think the Captain of the Guard should be aware of your negligence in doing the rounds. Let's go have a chat with him."

Officer Thomas got up slowly, glaring at Phil and Vito.

"Once an order is put out on you guys, there's no hope for you." He was led out of the cell by Officer Pole down the hallway to the Captain of the Guard's office. Once inside, Officer Pole and Officer Thomas met with their supervisor. Officer Pole recounted the events as he knew them.

"Thomas, what have you done now!? Do you realize this is the third infraction in the past two months? What drives you to beat the inmates?"

"That scumbag was giving me a hard time. He needed to be shown who the boss is and who he needs to respect."

"Not by breaking his legs, Mick. That is way too extreme. We are going to have to involve Human Resources this time. You're dismissed; now get back to work."

Officers Thomas and Pole left the office and went back to work.

"Look, Pole, when a kill order goes out on an inmate, they won't quit until it is carried out. Vito's life is over. He might as well save himself the pain and just commit suicide!" Mick Thomas sneered.

Officer Pole turned to him and said in a calm voice, "Nobody is going to touch Vito. Got it? I can bet you heard what happened to the inmate that tried to stab him and then beat him to death? Trust me; he's out of circulation for a very long time. I doubt he will ever be able to walk right again."

"If you are trying to warn me and the others to stay away from Vito, it's not happening." Mick said with contempt, "The Boss put the hit out on Vito the day he was transferred here."

Now he had Officer Pole's full attention.

"Who's the 'Boss' you are talking about? What's his name?" Officer Pole asked with urgency. To prove his point, he took Mick Thomas by the shoulders and shook him.

"Who is he!? Tell me now!"

Mick Thomas' response was an evil smile. He removed Officer Pole's hands from his shoulders. "It really doesn't matter what I tell you. The order is out there." His words came out in a hiss.

"I hope you enjoy being a desk jockey, Officer Thomas. If you don't give me the name of this boss, you will be behind a desk until you retire. I can pull some strings and make that happen. Unless, of course, you cooperate."

Mick Thomas bowed his head and kicked the floor with the tip of his shoe as he thought.

"It's the father of the clerk that does all the transfer paperwork. That's all I am going to tell you." He turned and walked away.

Officer Pole walked quickly to a deserted hallway and pulled out his secure cell phone. He punched in Missy Barone's phone number.

"Hello… Missy? Yes, this is Paul Z. Meyers. Yes, posing as Officer Pole. I just got some critical information for you. The person that put out the hit on Vito Phenton is the father of the clerk that does the transfer paperwork in the Warden's office. You are in contact with our operative in that office, right? Have him find out who that clerk is and who the clerk's father is!"

He disconnected the call, satisfied that Detective Barone would get the information he wanted.

Chapter 30

Jeff was up and dressed before Missy came out to the kitchen.

"I hope you don't mind me helping myself, but I brewed a pot of coffee. I saw it on the counter here and couldn't resist!"

"No, I don't mind; make yourself at home. You'll be staying here until the mission is completed. Speaking of which – I got a call last night from Paul Z. Meyers. He's posing as a guard at Golga Correctional. He was given some vital information that he asked for you to act on. The information he needs from you concerns Tim Effabee or perhaps the clerk before him. He needs the name of the clerk who had processed the transfer orders for the Warden. If you can get that information, we can wrap this case up."

"I'll talk with Kimble today. We'll see what he says." Jeff snapped his fingers. "Hey, Missy! If Kimble is reluctant to share that information, maybe you can ask Madeline, in her capacity as Ann Cody, to look it up!"

"You know, I probably could. Let's see how far you get with Kimble. I don't know how much Madeline knows about the databases the Human Resources people use there. But that is a good thought."

During his drive to work, Jeff thought about how he would approach the subject with Kimble. He decided he would gather up the transfer orders at Tim Effabee's desk first, using that as a segue way to asking him about former clerks.

When he walked in the office, the atmosphere seemed much more somber than it had been two days ago. The normal chatter about which group of friends would be going out for lunch and what shopping spree was planned was replaced by talk of who was going to attend the services of friends that had been killed. Jeff went over to Tim Effabee's desk and saw the stack of transfer orders. He picked them up and a small box fell to the floor. Setting the documents back on the desk, Jeff leaned over to pick up the box and examine it. The box was partially open. There was some sort of signature stamp in it along with a slip of paper. Examining the paper, it was clearly a note on letterhead. Jeff read the note:

'Son, here is the signature stamp you need to make the transfers I want you to facilitate. This will make them look authentic.

Dad' (with the initials SDE next to it)

Jeff glanced at the letterhead and nearly choked. He leaned on the desk to steady himself. The letterhead was that of Captain Scott Egan. "I have to call Missy right away! Wait until she hears this!" He examined the signature stamp. It was the signature of Bryce Wixmor, Warden of Golga Correctional Facility. "This is mind blowing. I really need to talk to Missy." He pulled out his phone and dialed her secure number. She answered on the second ring. "Detective Barone."

"Missy! This is Jeff. Tim Effabee has been forging stacks of transfer orders. And I think I know who his father is – Captain Egan! Can your investigators from Bellmants verify this for us?"

"Whoa! Slow down there Jeff! What made you come to this conclusion? Did somebody tell you this?" Missy countered.

"Kimble had asked me to finish up the transfer orders Effabee was working on. I noticed a signature stamp, partially hidden next to the orders. The signature stamp was that of Bryce Wixmor, which, in itself is innocent enough. But, and this is serious. A note to Tim was on Captain Egan's letterhead telling him to complete the orders using the stamp, signed 'Dad' and had the initials SDE next to it."

"Holy smokes!" Missy exclaimed, "Sit tight! I am going to conference call my boss, Don Rennips, and we can hear what his thoughts are."

Jeff heard a series of clicks and short tones, then Missy's voice again. "Don? Jeff? Can you both hear me?"

"Yes," came their answers.

"Okay. Jeff will you please tell Don what you just told me?"

Jeff recounted all that he told Missy to Don Rennips. Once he finished, Don let out a low whistle. "I am not usually a man to swear, but Holy Shit! Jeff, take a picture of the contents of that box and text it to me. Once I determine this is truly the working of Captain Egan I will text you with instructions. Okay?"

"Yes, Sir. I can take the picture right now." He clicked a picture of the note and signature stamp.

"Done", he said.

"Text it to 555-1212 and I will look at the photo. I will get in touch with our field office near Bellmants. They will have the resources to find out if there is a familial relationship between Egan and Effabee." He clicked off.

"Missy, I'll talk with you later; I'm going to send that text right now."

"Be careful out there, Jeff. I will talk to you shortly." Missy disconnected their call.

Jeff sent the text to Don Rennips right away, and then took the stack of orders and the box with the stamp and note back to his desk. He put the box containing the incriminating items in his briefcase, took his coffee cup and went to the coffee bar, trying to act normally.

"Good Morning, Tom." Kimble called from his office.

"Good Morning, Mr. Kimble."

"If you need any help with those transfers, please let me know."

"I will. I'm just getting my coffee before I start working on them." Jeff called back to Mr. Kimble.

Jeff poured himself a strong cup of coffee and made his way back to his desk. He began looking at the transfer orders, reviewing them briefly as he put them in date order. There was only a scant amount of inmates that were not convicted of drug dealing or money laundering and other crimes that were quite violent. Jeff made a note of this. He found it hard to concentrate on his work when he was still trying to come to terms with the fact that Captain Egan may be Tim Effabee's father. Finally, he was able to pay attention long enough to get the forms in chronological order, checking each form for completeness and sorting the ones that had been signed. He noticed that the ones that were signed all looked like a stamp had been used, rather than the actual signature. "Hmm", he thought to himself, "I'll have to see if Missy has the jurisdiction to take these forms to a handwriting expert. Then we can determine if they are legitimate or not."

Jeff's cell phone buzzed. Looking at the caller ID, he saw it was Missy Barone.

"Hello, Missy. What did you find out?"

"Hi Jeff. I just got a call from Senior Investigator Rennips. His field agents have worked quickly and found that Effabee was adopted shortly after he was born. St. Agatha's Orphanage handled the whole thing. It seems a sixteen-year-old girl from a prominent family was found to be with child and the father was listed as Scott D. Egan. He met the young lady and one thing led to another. The girls' family hid her away, giving the story of the young lady going abroad for studies. She had private tutoring for the nine months of her pregnancy and once the baby was born, he was sent to St. Agatha's Orphanage. Mr. and Mrs. Broderick Effabee adopted him right way. The Effabees lived in Bellmants until Mr. Effabee died about15 years ago. Tim and his mother moved to Keese Trailer Park just a few miles from Golga. Tim got a job there but kept returning to Bellmants and met frequently with Bryce Wixmor. Now that you have come across this information, we can confirm that Effabee and Egan are related."

"Okay, so they are related. I feel bad for Captain Egan. Here's what I am having a hard time understanding: How did Scott Egan pass any background check if he had any connection with a drug ring?" Jeff asked.

Missy answered, "Simple. If you are already headed to the Police Academy and pay off enough people and you can pass the most comprehensive background check. That's what it looks like happened."

There was a pause as Jeff grappled with the realization that the man he trusted, the man who had saved his life just two years ago could be part of a drug ring.

"Jeff...are you there?", Missy asked.

"Yes I am here. I refuse to believe what I saw. Well, let me rephrase that. The signature stamp, sure, anybody can get them. But somebody had to have a gun to the captain's head or be threatening one of his family to have him write that message on his letterhead. Can you ask the handwriting expert if it was written under duress?"

"Sure, but we know he's Effabee's father and Paul Z. Meyers has confirmed that the Boss, as they call him, ordered Vito transferred to Golga and has a hit out on him now."

"I guess you're right; I have to believe what you say", Jeff said dejectedly, "What could be so powerful that he went to the dark side?"

"I don't know why he would do that, Jeff."

"Excuse me, Tom, how are those forms coming

along?"

Kimble had walked up to Jeff's desk and was standing next to him.

"Oh! Mr. Kimble! I'm sorry. My sister was just talking to me about some problems with her boy." Jeff quickly closed the phone, put it in his pocket, but did not hang up. "Oh, these forms? I was just about to bring them to your office. I have them in chronological order. "This pile", he indicated the one in front of him, "has all been signed and looks like it's ready to be filed. This other pile," he pointed to one on the corner of his desk, "needs the Warden's signature."

"Very good, Tom. I thought it would take a couple days to get this organized. Thank you for being so efficient. I'll take them from here." Kimble put one pile cross-ways on the other and took them back to his office. Jeff quickly took the phone out of his pocket and checked to see if Missy was still on the line. "Missy?" Jeff said, hoping she was still there.

"So I'm your sister with a troublesome boy now, eh? I must say, you are creative! Hehe" she laughed.

"I wasn't sure how Kimble would react to me saying I was talking to you about a drug ring that involved his boss, the Warden and one of the employees he supervised."

"I suppose a sister with a troubled boy is easier to

explain than why we suspect illegal drug activity going on right in the office he supervises. Now, regarding Captain Egan, I think we are going to have to turn that part of the investigation over to Senior Investigator Rennips because he has more extensive resources, both in the field and in the research center. Does that work for you?" Missy asked.

"I guess it's going to have to be okay. I would just like to stay abreast of all the developments, only because I have had such faith in the man and I feel completely betrayed by him." Jeff replied sadly.

"Jeff, cheer up. We will be bringing down a huge drug ring by the roots. You must feel good about that at least."

"I don't. I've known and respected Scott Egan since I was in the Academy. Now, everything I respected about him is turning out to have been a lie. It doesn't feel good bringing him down." Jeff said bitterly.

"I wish I could say something that would ease your pain," Missy said softly, "but this time the truth really does hurt. I don't know when Captain Egan got started in this mess, or why, but he has been on our radar for the past six months. It really hit home when we heard chatter that he engineered the transfer of Vito Phenton. The problem was, and is, that we need hard proof that he actually did it. We've been monitoring

Effabee's hospital room to see if Egan goes to see him. So far he has not. He has to make a move soon because there's supposed to be another drug deal tonight. Paul will be on the lookout for him there. I'm sure they know Vito is an informant because the people Vito has given us information on have been taken out of circulation. Egan sees that encrypted information and then passes it along. Now the dealers are so few, they are all under his protection. Thus, the reason for a mafia style hit on Vito. They don't want to take a chance on him informing anyone besides Captain Egan about the drug ring he and his cronies are in, especially since Vito saw him last night. Vito's life is in serious jeopardy and we have to take measures to keep him safe. We've sent Pail Z. Meyers in undercover as one of the guards.   Phil has saved him twice in the past three days!"

"I guess this is really serious, isn't it? What's the next step?"

"I spoke to Don Rennips. He wants to attack the situation from three sides. He will equip Paul Z. Meyer's undercover uniform with a body camera. If they are following a schedule, the next drug deal should go down tonight. The second approach is for you to get the orders back from Kimble. Do it under the guise of filing them or preparing them further for the final signature. Once you have possession of them, examine them for any possible trail back to Egan. Photocopy those orders and we will have Madeline pick them up. She'll make sure Don Rennips gets them. He will be able to use his resources to ferret out any connection to Scott Egan."

"I'll do my best to get the orders back from Kimble. I still don't want to believe the Captain is behind this!"

"It's a hard pill to swallow. Call me if you find any link in the paperwork to Captain Egan. I will talk to you tonight when you come home, anyway." She hung up.

Jeff sat at his desk a moment digesting all he and Missy had just talked about. It was difficult to accept, after thinking his superior was an honest man for so many years. But Jeff had a job to do, so he could get home to his pregnant wife. He straightened his tie, stood and went to Mr. Kimble's office. The forms were sitting by his overstuffed Inbox.

"Excuse me Mr. Kimble, I would like to review those transfer orders one more time for accuracy. May I take them back to my desk?"

Kimble looked up from his work. "Hello, Tom. Sure, you can take the orders for as long as you need to. I have a stack of work to get through that is more pressing than the transfers right now."

"Thank you." Jeff said. He picked up the stack of orders and headed back to his desk.

Once situated at his desk, he texted Missy and told her he had the orders. Then Jeff began examining the stack closely. They all were completed properly, except for the fact that the box reserved for the reason for transfer was suspiciously empty on almost every form received in the last six weeks.

"Why are all of those boxes empty? That should've raised a red flag, even with Effabee when he was reviewing them for accuracy. I'll have to talk Missy and then to Kimble about that." He thought to himself. He texted his query about the orders to Missy and told her Kimble should be aware of the missing information. He snapped his phone shut and went to lunch. Checking his phone, he was pleased to see Missy had replied to his text.

"Jeff, that is definitely an error even Effabee should not have missed, unless he was instructed to leave that box blank. Please compare the forms that do have the box completed. Who are they signed by? Are the new prisoners coming from local PD's or from other facilities? Let me know and I'll report this to Don Rennips. He can have an agent make some calls to the facilities that supposedly were transferring inmates to Golga. Let's see what turns up there."

Jeff dialed Missy's number. "I think I should point out that error to Kimble, don't you?" Jeff asked.

"Yes, Jeff, that's an error he needs to see, regardless." Missy said

"I still want to find out how Captain Egan became involved in all of this. That's the one thing that really bothers me!" Jeff grimly said.

"We'll get to the bottom of this!" Missy declared, "Then you will feel better about the whole thing. Show Kimble your latest findings and see what he has to say. Who knows? We may be surprised if we find out they are supposed to be blank!"

"Okay, I'll tell you how it went when I get to your house tonight."

"Bye!" Missy said as she hung up.

Jeff put his phone in his pocket, gathered up the forms then went in to see Kimble.

"Good Afternoon, Mr. Kimble. As I was reviewing these forms, I noticed that almost every form was missing information under the Reason for Transfer heading. Does that box get completed upon intake of the inmate?"

Kimble looked up sharply. "Let me see what you're talking about!"

Jeff handed Mr. Kimble a sampling of the orders with the missing information.

"I compared these with forms from three years ago. The older forms were complete. These," he indicated the stack Kimble was reviewing, "Have nothing entered under that heading."

Kimble looked at the form closely. "Please bring

me a form from 3 years ago," he asked. Jeff left to retrieve the document. He returned a few minutes later placing the contrasting forms side by side for Kimble's review. Kimble shook his head slowly and let out a long sigh.

"What was Effabee thinking? He knew that the box needed to be filled out by the facility sending us the prisoner. I knew he was lazy, but this takes the cake!"

"Could there be another reason for leaving it blank? Have you ever had this happen before?" Jeff asked.

No" Kimble said slowly, "Because if someone did arrive at Intake without that section completed, the person handling it would contact the facility sending the prisoner here to get the reason for the transfer."

"That makes sense. Let me ask you something; is it always the same person that handles the intake process for new prisoners, or is it on a rotation?" Jeff asked.

"Normally it's the same person. Of course, if that person is sick or on vacation, someone will fill in for them."

"Thanks. I will put the older forms away now, if you want."

Kimble handed Jeff the documents.

Jeff refiled the older transfer orders, went back to

his desk and pulled out his presentation that he was to give to Ann Cody. He called Mr. Kimble and told him he was going to see Ann Cody and give her the report.

Dean Kimble wished him luck and said goodbye.

This time when Jeff exited the elevator, light poured out the open door to the Human Resources office, along with friendly chatter.

Jeff greeted the receptionist and asked for Ann Cody.

"I'll let her know you're here; please have a seat" The young lady said. Jeff sat on a chair to wait for Ann. A few moments later, the receptionist called for him and led him to Ann's office.

"Gloria, please make sure we are not disturbed. This is an important presentation Mr. Mickson will be giving."

"Yes, Mrs. Cody," came the reply as the receptionist left the office, silently closing the door.

"Tom, let's see this presentation."

Jeff spread the papers on her desk for her to review. As he did so, in barely a whisper she asked if he had anything new to report.

Jeff nodded yes, then said, "And on these orders you can see there is important information missing," he tapped the papers for emphasis, "on the transfers of the inmates and is not acceptable. I call your attention to this empty box here." He tapped the page again.

"I think I follow you. Thank you for the research; you did a good job." She pressed a piece of paper into his hand.

Jeff walked quickly to the bank of elevators. He made sure the elevator was empty before he stepped into it. He stood with his back to the surveillance camera that hung in the corner. He unfolded the paper, reading it slowly.

"I spoke to Don Rennips about your latest discoveries. When you go to Detective Barone's tonight please call me at the secure number I have.

M"

Arriving at his floor, Jeff exited the elevator and put the note through the shredder on his way back to his desk. The message light on his phone indicated a new voice mail. Listening to the message, he heard, "Tom, this is Mr. Kimble. I just spoke with Ann Cody. She wanted to commend you on your research and will be bringing it to the attention of the Board and Training Program Director. Well done! Keep it up and you'll be considered for a promotion quickly." Jeff smiled to himself, pleased that he was able to use the skills he learned in college to create an acceptable presentation. He looked at his watch. I was time to put his papers away, straighten up his desk and head to the Barone's. Once there, he would ask Missy to give Madeline a call.

Chapter 31

Nursing Supervisor Regina Yak reviewed the blood test results that came back from the lab on Tim Effabee. His white blood cell count was very high, indicating an infection. The other report showed blood poisoning. Effabee's prognosis was grim.

"If we can get him calm enough to have Dr. Mottle put a PIC line in, Dr. Xander wants him on a new drug that will combat his infection. He said the arm may have to be amputated if this does not work; let's just hope we can ward off the blood poisoning." The lab report stated

"That's a tall order," Regina thought to herself, "We'll do our best to fulfill it."

She put the report down and headed to the patient's room.

Nurse Bondi had just finished cleaning Tim's

wounds and changing the dressings as Regina walked into the room.

"Good Afternoon, Mr. Effabee, may I take a moment of your time? We need to discuss a treatment program for you."

Tim Effabee looked at her sullenly and said, "Do I have a choice? What are you going to do, put me in a coma?"

Remaining calm, Nurse Yak said in an even voice, "Mr. Effabee, I just received the report from your blood test. It shows you have a serious infection, bordering on blood poisoning, due to the fact that you ripped out your IV lines twice. Dr. Xander wants to try a new drug that will aggressively battle your infection. Dr. Mottle will install a PIC line, making it much easier for us to do blood draws and ensure the new drug is working. If you rip this line out, you will be putting your life in danger."

"I need to get back to my job! I need to get the transfer orders done!" he said in an agitated voice.

"Mr. Effabee, please don't get upset! We're doing our best to help you. If you allow us to follow the program I just told you about, it will speed up your recovery and your return home. Then you can resume your work schedule. If you continue to be uncooperative, we may have to amputate your left arm, simply to stave off this infection. What's it going to be?" Regina Yak gave him the ultimatum.

"So, will this new drug make me feel better than I do now? I feel horrible. I have to get back to work! So I guess the answer is that I'll try this crazy line or whatever you called this new treatment."

"I'll call Dr. Mottle and have him get his team ready to put the line in. Nurse Bondi will prepare you for the procedure. Do you want something to calm your nerves?" Regina asked.

"I don't know. Is it really necessary? It's not something that will make me freak out while I'm getting it done, will it?" Tim started sounding nervous.

"Normally, I would call it a routine procedure, but in your case, I think a Valium will keep you calm since you do need to be awake."

"Okay, when will they do it?"

"If Dr. Mottle can assemble his team right away; you can have the procedure done before you eat supper."

Regina left the room to make the necessary arrangements. She whispered a prayer that Tim Effabee would be more compliant once the doctor put the line in.

****

Paul Z. Meyers donned the prison guard uniform, carefully placing the body camera that was part of his ID badge. He clipped the badge carefully to his shirt pocket, placing the earpiece Don Rennips provided to him earlier that day.

"Testing, one, two, three. Can you hear me?"

"Copy you fine, Paul. Let's get this show on the road." Don Rennips answered.

"I'm going to shut it off until I get to the prison. I don't want it losing power in the middle of the deal."

"Good idea, Paul. We'll be here when you go live again."

Paul left his apartment, got in his Monte Carlo and drove to the prison. He slowed at the guard shack, as the guard checked his ID, waving him through. Parking his car, he went into the guard's office, clocked in and turned his camera on.

"We're live." Paul said softly.

"Copy that", he heard in his earpiece.

"Officer Pole, you're on rounds in Cellblock A. Officer Thomas will be backing you up tonight."

"Hey, Pole. It's going to be a bumpy ride tonight. The natives are restless!" Officer Thomas hissed.

"I can handle it, Mick. No worries." Paul said in his sweetest voice, just to irritate him.

"Yea, you say that now. Let's see what you say by the end of this shift! I'm sure you'll be seeing things differently." Officer Thomas threatened.

"I don't get riled by your empty threats, Thomas. I'll be seeing a few things differently by the end of the shift, that's very true. You don't know how true!" Paul turned and left the office. He walked the long corridor to Cell Block A. He noticed that what Officer Thomas said was true. The inmates did appear more restless than usual. He made his way to Cell 518. Once there, he motioned to Phil to come to the door. Phil came forward, quickly and silently. Vito was sleeping as Phil asked Paul what was going on.

"There's supposed to be another drug deal tonight. I came prepared to get the evidence we need to bring down as much of the ring as possible."

"How do you propose to do that? Who do you hope to bring down?" Phil asked, not convinced Paul could pull this off.

Paul patted his pocket lightly. "Have you seen the latest in body cameras? Take a peek at the ID badge. "

"What the hell? Oh, I see it. Will it be able to catch all that we saw a couple of days ago?"

"Yes, this is a high end camera. It'll pick up Egan walking in the room, just as he did the last time."

Paul explained.

"I wish Captain Egan wouldn't show up. It's disheartening to find out he's just as bad as the drug dealers we bring in." Phil said with a touch of sadness in his voice.

"Yes, it is. You need to be very, very careful; especially tonight. I'm sure there will be another attempt on Vito."

"I'll stay close to him." Phil walked over to Vito's bunk and shook his cellmate by the shoulder. "Wake up, Vito, we need to talk."

Vito stirred but did not awaken. Phil shook him harder. "C'mon man, wake up!" He said loudly.

Paul Z. Meyers heard the urgency in Phil's voice and turned to go to back the cell.

"Open 518!" He shouted. The cell door banged open, Paul striding in quickly in response to Phil's shouts.

"He's not waking up!", Phil cried.

Paul pulled his flashlight from his utility belt, turned it on and opened one of Vito's eyes, shining the light in it.

"Good, his pupils respond to the light." He felt Vito's neck for a pulse and found a weak one. He stood and said into his radio, "We have a medical emergency in 518! Get the medics here right away!"

"Copy that", came the crackled response.

"Hehehe", Mick Thomas said to no one in particular, "When the boss wants a hit done, it gets done," He picked up the desk phone and punched in a number.

"Boss, consider the hit successful. Whatever the cook put in Vito's food did the trick. Medical attention won't get to him in time." He heard a slight beep as he hung up.

Paul and Phil were keeping a close eye on Vito Phenton. His breathing was very shallow. "Pick him up! We need to get him to sick bay right now!" They picked him up and ran down the corridor to the elevator that brought them to sick bay. The elevator doors opened to reveal a wide room with gurneys separated by curtains. Nurses were hustling to and fro attending to their patients.

"We need help here, right away!", Paul shouted.

A nurse and an orderly appeared within seconds.

"What's going on?", The orderly asked.

"I'm just guessing, but I think he's been poisoned. His pulse is weak and breathing very shallow."

The nurse and orderly took Vito from the two men, put him on a gurney and started him on oxygen and an IV. Paul and Phil stepped back into the elevator, satisfied that Vito was in good hands. Once the door slid shut, Paul turned to Phil and told him what Officer Thomas had said.

"I think we have to let the guards, as well as the prisoners, believe Vito is dead. They all know about the hit that that was put out on him. If they believe he's dead, they may relax enough for us to catch them tonight. I just got word in my earpiece that Officer Thomas was recorded via phone tap confirming with the boss that Vito is dead. He'll be taken to the FBI field office Interrogation Center."

Phil walked slowly to his cell, head down with shoulders slumped. The prisoners nearby called out, asking what happened to Vito. Dead," was all Phil said in a distraught voice, "Now leave me alone."

Phil slumped down on his bunk. Paul walked out of the cell, called for the door to be closed then went to the guard's office.

He walked up to Mick Thomas and said angrily, "Why didn't you send the medics? What is wrong with you?"

Mick Thomas replied, "Oh, I thought you were kidding" in his most innocent voice, "I thought you were just seeing how quickly they would respond."

"Either way, you failed miserably. Now a man is dead and that's on your shoulders!"

At that moment, four FBI Agents entered the office. They approached Officer Thomas, "Are you Mick Thomas?"

"Yea, what's it to you?", he sneered.

"You have the right to remain silent. Anything you say, can, and will be held against you...." The lead agent read him his rights as he pulled Officer Thomas' hands behind his back and placed him under arrest.

"You are under arrest for aiding and abetting the murder of Vito Phenton and for illegal drug dealing."

"Wait! I was doing what the big Boss told me to do! Arrest him!" he yelled as he was led away.

****

Jeff parked his car next Missy and Tony's Buick. He picked up his briefcase and suit jacket from the passenger's seat before heading into the Barone's home.

"Jeff, how was the rest of your day? Did you come across anything else we should talk about?"

"Madeline wants us to give her a call so she can go over the discoveries that were made today.

"Let's have dinner first. Then we can call her and really concentrate on what we have to discuss."

"Good idea." Jeff agreed. "I'd like to relax a little before we give her a call. It's been a stressful day."

"Come and get it!" Tony called from the kitchen, "I made my special tortellini soup!"

Missy and Jeff took their seats at the kitchen table. Tony dished out the soup and the three new-found friends devoured the delicious meal.

After cleaning up the dishes, it was time to get back to business. Missy's secure cell phone rang, interrupting the brief silence.

Answering her phone, Missy listened closely, nodding her head and saying, "Yes," "Okay", and, "I'll do that" throughout the short call. Once she disconnected the call, she turned to Jeff and relayed the events at the prison. She finished with," So Don said Vito will be fine and the guard was arrested who coordinated the attempt on his life was arrested."

Jeff blew out a long breath. "Is Vito going to be okay? What about Phil? Is he okay? Is his life in danger too? Remember, he has a pregnant wife waiting at home for him!"

Chapter 32

Two orderlies put a safety belt on Tim Effabee after they helped him on to the stretcher that would carry him to the Radiology Department. "Take this belt off me, you lousy bums! I don't need that on me!" Tim Effabee shouted.

"Sir, it's hospital policy that we put the safety belt on you. We don't want you to fall off and injure yourself. The older orderly said in a soothing voice, "We're almost there now."

The orderlies made two more turns then went down a short hallway to the Radiology Department. They stopped at the check-in desk and informed the receptionist that Mr. Effabee had arrived for his procedure. She picked up the desk phone, called Dr. Mottle to tell him his patient had arrived, then asked the orderlies to bring the patient into the first room on the left. The X-Ray table in the room had a white sheet draped over part of it, with a medium sized pillow at the head of the table. Two technicians and Dr. Mottle greeted them. "Mr. Effabee, I am Dr.

Mottle. We are going to be installing a PIC line in your arm today. My assistant will administer a dye in your vein, so I can see where the line is going. Are you ready?"

"As ready as I'll ever be.

This better not hurt!" Tim shouted.

The Doctor's assistants made a sterile field around Tim Effabee. The Doctor was gowned and had sterile gloves on as did his assistants. "Okay Mr. Effabee, we be as gentle as possible. First, could you please stretch your left arm as far as you can? We will be using a strap to hold it still, any movement of it could be dangerous." The doctor injected a numbing agent into Tim's arm so he would not feel the PIC line going in. Tim Effabee complied with the doctor's instructions. One assistant strapped his arm down snugly while the other assistant prepared the injection of dye.

"You are doing very well, Mr. Effabee. Now my assistant will give you an injection of dye. His other assistant stepped forward.

"Mr. Effabee you are going to feel a pinch." She said as she began the injection, "You may feel a little pressure as the dye is injected, then you may get a warm feeling all over your body. Here we go." She said as she depressed the syringe's plunger.

"You are doing fine. Keep taking slow breaths. Dr. Mottle, we are ready to implement the PIC line." Dr. Mottle stepped forward. Another sterile blanket was laid out with a needle and a very thin catheter on it. The doctor took a handheld fluoroscope and moved it over his patient's arm.

"Mr. Effabee, it looks like you have an excellent vein to put this in. The catheter will travel up it to the vena cava. Then you will be all set to get your needed treatments done each day."

Dr. Mottle inserted the needle that had the tip of the PIC line on it into a vein in Tim Effabee's left arm. He began threading the catheter through the vein to the vena cava, just above the heart, watching the fluoroscope as he carefully guided the line to its destination. The tip of the catheter reached it final destination. Dr. Mottle put sterile caps on the two short tails on the end of the line that was hanging from Tim's upper arm. "Mr. Effabee, you are all set. Now your nurse can administer your medications and do blood draws without having to poke your arms anymore." He patted Tim's shoulder kindly, then called the orderlies to bring him back to his room. The orderlies loaded Tim on the stretcher and began the trip back to his room. Tim looked curiously at the two short ends flopped over the bandage taped over the spot where the PIC line was inserted. To him, the ends looked similar to Christmas lights. One was colored red, the other blue. "I hope they don't poison me with the new drug or let all my blood drain out", he thought to himself. The orderlies reached his room and transferred him into his assigned bed, and then stopped at the nurse's station to let the supervisor know he was back in his room. Nurse Yak thanked them as they left. She checked Tim's chart, retrieved the new antibiotic treatment for him, and then walked to his room to start the treatment. "Hello, Mr. Effabee. You may remember me from earlier today. I am Regina Yak, the Nursing Supervisor on this floor. I have your first treatment of the new antibiotic Dr. Xander ordered for you."

She carefully hung the plastic bag that contained the antibiotic fluid on the IV pole and connected a sterile IV line to the bottom of the bag, weaved it through the fluid regulator and was about to connect it to Tim Effabee's PIC line when he became very agitated, flailing his arms and screaming, "What are you doing to me? You are trying to kill me! I know it!"

With that, he knocked Nurse Yak down and savagely ripped the PIC line out. He began bleeding profusely. Nurse Yak was screaming for help. Tim Effabee picked up the IV pole and used it like a battering ram, trying to break the window near his bed. Two orderlies came running in to see what all the commotion was about. Tim swung the pole like a bat, striking the first orderly and knocking him off balance. The second orderly tackled Tim to the floor. Nurse Yak, who had crawled out of the room, returned with a syringe in her hand.

"Hold him down! I have a sedative injection." She

tried to maneuver close enough to him so she could administer the shot, but he was screaming and wriggling around. Pulling out her cell phone, she called Security. "I need you in room 104 STAT!! We have a violent patient that has gone berserk!"

Two more nurses came running into the room.

"Try to hold him down", Nurse Yak commanded. The nurses tried to help the orderlies, but it seemed like Tim Effabee had superhuman strength. Finally, two burly Security guards appeared in the room. One took Tim's stump and held it behind his back, while putting his knee in the center of the wild man's back. He straddled the violent patient while his equally burly partner held Tim's bleeding arm straight so nurse Yak could administer the sedative. She moved in quickly and gave him the injection.

"Get away from me, you fiends! I know you are…. trying……….to……k…." Tim's body slumped down, the sedative having taken effect.

"Nurse Bondi! Please get some towels and a tourniquet to stop the bleeding!" Nurse Bondi did as she was instructed. "Nurse Jones! Call Dr. Mottle and Dr. Xander! Tell them both that Mr. Effabee has ripped out his PIC line and is losing blood rapidly. Tell them we are attending to him as best we can. Mr. Joshua and Mr. Gregory, could you help me get him back in his bed, please?"

The two security guards carefully lifted Tim
Effabee into his bed. Nurse Bondi returned with
the tourniquet and several towels, fresh dressings
and the IV nurse. Nurse Yak took the tourniquet
and put it on Tim Effabee's arm. The bleeding
slowed drastically. She then used the towels to
sop up the blood that had pooled under his body.
Nurse Bondi wheeled a dirty linen cart next to
Regina Yak to collect the bloody linens. The
orderlies stayed nearby in case Tim Effabee had
another violent episode.

"Thank you all for your assistance in restraining
this violent patient. He has lost a tremendous
amount of blood. We will need to give him a
transfusion."

Nurse Bondi opened a file folder and reported to
Regina Yak that the patient had A negative blood
type. "I called the Phlebotomy department and
asked them to bring up two bags of it for the
transfusion." They will be here shortly."

She set the IV pole upright. "Thank you, Nurse
Bondi." Nurse Jones came into the room, a little
out of breath. "Dr. Mottle is on his way right now.
Dr. Xander is on the second floor. I texted him
with what you told me to tell the doctors. I
imagine he will be here shortly." "Good. Let's get
the monitors hooked up to Mr. Effabee again. We
are going to have to watch him closely. Nurse
Bondi, would you and Mr. O'Day please stay with
Mr. Effabee? We need to monitor his vital signs
closely. He has lost a lot of blood and the lab

reports show he has a serious infection. We cannot administer the new stronger antibiotic Dr. Xander ordered to combat the infection Mr. Effabee has in his system. If Dr. Mottle can get another line into Mr. Effabee, then we will attempt to administer the antibiotic again. "

"We will keep a close eye on him." Nurse Bondi replied, "Did Dr. Xander order an anxiety reducer medicine for him? We could try to have Mr. Effabee take it by mouth or by injection, whichever you deem best."

Regina Yak thought for a moment as she studied the now sleeping Tim Effabee. "As long as he is sleeping let's just let him sleep. I will get in touch with Dr. Mottle and Dr. Xander and see what they think is best to do. Once we have the orders from them we can proceed."

"We will wait for his word.", Nurse Bondi and Mr. O'Day, the Orderly agreed. The two caregivers sat on the plastic molded chairs next to Tim Effabee's bed. The rhythmic beeping of the heart monitor was the only sound in the room besides Tim Effabee's heavy snoring. Dinner was served to the pair in the room, since Dr. Xander wanted at least two people in the room with Tim at all times. He gave orders to sedate his patient immediately if he showed signs of becoming aggressive again. Nurse Bondi and Mr. O'Day had just finished their meal when the heart monitor started beeping. It indicated that Tim's heart was beating much too fast. The monitor

showed the heart rate climbing very quickly.
"Code Blue! Code Blue!", Nurse Bondi yelled.
Mr. O'Day removed the blankets and the hospital
gown covering Tim Effabee's chest, a crash cart
was wheeled up to the bed. Nurse Bondi took the
paddles of the defibrillator, called out, "Clear!",
and then applied the charge. Tim's back arched as
he received the shock. Nurse Bondi looked at the
heart monitor as the beeping slowed to a normal
pace. "Sean, what is his BP?" Sean O'Day
reported, "160 over 100 and dropping. It looks
like it is returning to normal." After a few tense
moments, carefully watching the heart monitor
and the blood pressure monitor, the machine
returned to its normal rhythmic beeping. Tim
seemed to be resting peacefully, his arms at his
side, head turned toward the monitors. The
Phlebotomist entered the room along with an IV
nurse who quickly inserted an IV in Tim's good
arm then hung two bags of blood. The nurse and
Phlebotomist left as quickly as they had come.

"That was frightening, wasn't it, Sean?" Diana
Bondi observed. "It certainly was! You did a good
job saving Tim's life! "Sean O'Day returned.
They sat near Tim Effabee's bedside and kept an
eye on the monitors, prepared to revive their
patient if he had another cardiac episode. Tim
became restless, tossing and turning. Suddenly his
eyes shot open. He leaned up on his elbows.

"I saw it! I saw it!" he cried out. Nurse Bondi
jumped to her feet as did Sean O'Day. "Mr.

Effabee, please, try to stay calm", Nurse Bondi said in a soothing voice, "What did you see?" she smoothed the blankets covering Tim Effabee's legs and waist. "I saw the most wonderful light! It was as bright as the sun, but it didn't hurt my eyes. Then I was surrounded by it, and felt such an indescribable love. It was amazing! I was forgiven for all the terrible things I have done. Nobody said any words, but I knew it. Now I am going try to make the rest of my days on earth count. I only hope I can make amends for all the evil I have done. I am truly sorry for having behaved so badly here. I am so sorry." Tim laid down again. He looked truly peaceful this time as he slept. Diana looked at Sean and said in hushed voice, "He had a near death experience! I wonder if it truly changed him." "We'll see soon enough. It looks like he's waking up again." Tim's eyes fluttered open. He laid quietly before speaking.

"Nurse, may I sit up? I can think clearer when I am sitting." Nurse Bondi went over to his bedside to make sure there were no wires that would restrict him from sitting. Once she was satisfied, she raised the head of his bed slowly, until he was in a sitting position. "How is that? Do you feel dizzy or nauseated? If you get the sweats or chills let us know right away, please."

"Thank you. This is good. I don't feel any dizziness and the temperature of my body is comfortable. He relaxed a little, rubbing his head with his hand. "Mr. Effabee, may we put an IV line in your arm, so we can resume the antibiotic for your infection?" Sean asked. "Sure, but I feel okay. I bet the infection has left me." Tim answered.

Nurse Bondi queried Tim, "In that case, will you let the Lab take another blood draw to check for the level of infection?" "No problem." Tim answered. He reached his arm out and said, "Draw all the blood you need."

****

Vito Phenton woke up slowly in the prison sick bay. He felt like he was in a bad dream, unable to really focus on anything. The voice of a doctor broke through the fog that clouded his mind.

"Mr. Phenton, wake up! Look at me!" The doctor clapped his hands in front of Vito's face.

"Vito! Look at me! Come on, wake up!"

Vito blinked his eyes, trying to focus on the man leaning over him, speaking loudly.

"Good Vito, blink your eyes again."

Vito blinked once more.

"Where am I? What happened to me?"

"Vito, do you remember anything before waking

up here in the sick bay?" the doctor asked in a gentle voice.

Vito thought for a moment then said, "I remember having my dinner and laying on my bunk in the cell. Then I woke up here."

"We pumped your stomach and have been monitoring your vital signs. You were lucky the guard and your cellmate brought you here right away."

"Yeah, I think there are some bad dudes out there that want me dead."

"That almost happened. Be careful when you return to your cell. I'm going to keep you here today to ensure that all the poison is out of your system." The doctor told Vito.

"Okay, I guess. Would you let Spike know I'm okay? He's the only friend I have here." Vito laid back on his bed.

"Sure, we'll get the message to him. You should rest now."

****

Scott Egan's desk phone rang, startling the Anderson Fall's Police Captain.

"Egan here", he said as he answered the phone.

A squeaky female voice sounded on the other end, "When are we going to make the exchange - my cameraman has the goods hidden in the false battery pack on his camera!"

"Lori, calm down. I got the money three nights ago. When and where do you want to meet?"

Meet me at four o'clock at the studio. It will appear that I am doing a follow up interview on the Gary Phenton homicide. You know, one of the stories about how the investigation ended and where everyone is now. After the interview we'll walk to your car. That's where we can make the exchange. Don't be late!"

"Take it easy, Lori. How much of a cut is this cameraman getting? I have to give my contact at the prison a cut too, you know."

Lori Langorski's squeaky voice got even squeakier as she said emphatically, "My cameraman gets a straight cut of $500. Then you and I split the rest. You can figure out what you'll give your prison contact!" she hung up the phone abruptly.

Egan replaced the receiver on his phone and leaned back, satisfied that within a year he would be able to retire and live comfortably with all the money he was making. He picked up the phone again and called the hospital where his son had been taken.

"Good morning, you've reached Mercy General

Hospital. How may I direct your call?"

Disguising his voice, Egan asked for patient information. An older lady, obviously a volunteer, cheerily answered, "Patient Information. How may I help you?"

"I would like to know the condition of Tim Effabee please."

"One moment", the volunteer said as she typed the name into her computer. There was a short pause then the lady spoke in a somber voice.

"I'm sorry, Sir. You'll have to speak with his family about his condition. I cannot tell you."

"I am his father! Tell me what is going on with my son!?" Egan practically shouted.

"Sir, please remain calm. I am going to connect you with the nursing supervisor on your son's floor." The line went quiet for a few seconds and then the familiar dull trill of a phone ringing through sounded. It was answered after two rings.

"Regina Yak, Intensive Care Unit."

"Hello, my name is Scott Effabee," he fibbed. "My son, Tim is a patient at your hospital. I want to know how he is doing!" he exclaimed.

In a soothing voice, Regina Yak said calmly, "I think it would be best if you came down to the hospital."

"Why? What is going on there that I have to

travel thirty minutes in order to get some answers?" Egan was becoming agitated.

Still in a calm voice, Regina Yak said, "You really need to meet with me here. I cannot give you the information over the phone. Can you come here now?" she asked.

"I live thirty minutes away from you and I have to be at a very important meeting at four o'clock! Why do I have to drive all the way out there?" he said just a bit too loudly.

"Well if you are his father, I can see the family resemblance, Mr. Effabee. I still cannot give you any information over the phone. You must come here." Regina Yak insisted.

"Oh, alright!" Egan slammed the phone down, grabbed his keys and sprinted to his car. He started it up and squealed out of the parking lot in the direction of Mercy General Hospital.

****

Don Rennips looked at Kevin Leestaud O'Hara and Missy Barone as they all removed the headphones they had used to listen to the phone tap on Scott Egan's office phone. He let out a long whistle. "Wow, this just keeps getting better and better! Lori Langorski is that TV reporter! Tim Effabee was the clerk at Golga Correctional.

From what Jeff Weston reported, Tim Effabee was creating false transfer orders for incarcerated drug dealers so they would be sent to Golga and then they would be introduced to the drug ring there. Scott Egan somehow got a copy of Bryce Wixmor's signature and had a stamp made from it. That is what Effabee used to sign the orders. Once he is out of the hospital, we'll bring him in for questioning. I'm going to call Mercy General shortly to see how Tim Effabee is doing."

Missy nodded her head and said, "I guess he was ready to shoot the FBI agent when Kevin got to the scene. I don't know how much more bloodshed there would have been if Kevin hadn't showed up!"

Don Rennips continued, "I'm going to call Paul Z. Meyers and have him pose as a guard one more time. This time he will be a guard at WANN TV. He will be wearing a body camera, so we'll have video evidence of Scott engaging in illegal activities."

"Do you think we'll have enough dirt on Egan to bring him in? Can we use the footage from Paul's body camera too?" Kevin asked.

"I'm sure we can use it against him. Let's get our equipment ready for this afternoon – I definitely think we should wear the bulletproof vests. If we are dealing with a drug cartel, it could get nasty. Let's bring some extra cuffs too."

The trio went their ways to collect the gear they

needed.   They gathered the vests, extra handcuffs and some extra ammunition for the firearms they had on their persons.   Once it was loaded into an undercover vehicle, they met again.

"I am going to call Mercy General now and get a status on Effabee.   Hopefully, he will provide us with information on the drug ring within the prison, such as which guards are involved and who in the Administration is corrupt." He picked up the receiver and called his contact at Mercy General.

"Good Afternoon", he said in response to the greeting he heard on the phone. "May I have the Security Office, please?"   He rubbed his chin as the call was transferred.

"Hello, Joshua? This is Don Rennips. I would like to get the status on Tim Effabee's condition and when he's expected to be released."   There was another pause.

"What? That's terrible. You were able to subdue him?" He listened intently to his contact at the hospital. His face took on a quizzical look and his hands shook. "Well, this changes a lot of things. Thanks for the information." Don's hands still trembled as he hung up the phone.

Kevin asked, "What did he say that has you so worried?"

Don cleared his throat, giving the two detectives a recap of what the hospital had reported to him.

"Effabee says he is a changed man and will cooperate with us. I think he will be a great asset in uprooting the bad seeds at the correctional facility."

"If he is truly willing to help us, we can get his testimony about how deeply involved Egan is in the drug dealing." Missy offered.

"That's right!" Kevin agreed, "That will take a big bite out of the drug trade we've seen in that area. Let's hope he has changed his ways."

"We can bring him in once he is well enough to talk with us here," was Don's response.

Chapter 33

Scott Egan's car squealed around the corner in the parking lot of Mercy General Hospital. Hastily parking, he ran in the direction of the main entrance to the hospital.

The receptionist at the front desk looked up at him. "Good Afternoon. May I help you?"

"I'm here to see Regina Yak. Get her for me quickly!" Scott demanded.

The receptionist remained professional even though she was taken aback by his rudeness.

"Do you have an appointment with her?"

"I want to see her now! I talked to her on the phone this morning. I have things to do! Just get her down here now!" He slammed his hand on the counter separating them, in an effort to intimidate the young lady.

"Excuse me sir, but you will have to take a seat while I contact Nurse Yak."

The receptionist's calmness infuriated Scott Egan.

"I will not sit down! Get on the phone and get her down here right now!" This time the volume of his voice caught the attention of Joshua Gregory as he was walking by. He turned and looked at the red-faced man who appeared ready to explode. Josh walked over to him, put his hand on Scott's arm and said in an even voice, "Sir, why don't you come with me? We can straighten this out in my office."

"Don't touch me!" Scott exclaimed, angrily brushing Joshua's hand off his arm, "Just get Regina Yak down here, NOW!"

Josh knew how to handle volatile people. His voice remained even, but he gripped Scott Egan's arm in a vise-hold.

"Sir, let's just go to my office and we will get this matter cleared up. We can use my office for you and Nurse Yak to meet to discuss whatever it is you have to talk about." This time he herded Scott Egan out of the reception area and into the Security office, using his grip to steer the unruly character away.

Sir, please have a seat here", Josh said as they entered his office. "I'll give Nurse Yak a call and let her know you are here."

"I don't have time for sitting down! Just get Regina Yak!" Scott still sounded agitated.

"You can have a seat, or I can escort you off the hospital grounds. It's your choice." Josh's authoritative voice had the proper effect. Scott Egan sat uneasily in the chair Josh had indicated.

"Good. I'll call Regina now." Josh picked up the phone and dialed a number. "Hello, Regina. I have a man in my office that says he spoke to you this morning and was told he had to come meet with you." Josh put his hand over the mouthpiece and addressed Scott Egan.

"What is your name?"

"Scott Effabee." Egan lied.

"He says it's Scott Effabee. Um-hmm, okay, well he's in my office." Josh answered Regina. "Five minutes? I'll tell him. Thanks, Regina."

"Mr. Effabee, she's in the middle of something. She'll be down in five minutes to see you." Josh sat in the chair across from Scott.

"I don't have five minutes! I have to be at an important meeting! Take me to her!" he yelled.

Josh stood up and leaned his muscular frame over Egan. "You still have the option of being escorted off the grounds, Mr. Effabee. Now keep your voice down."

Josh sat down again, crossing his legs as they waited for Regina to arrive. Scott kept looking at his watch and tapping is foot. Finally, Regina appeared in the doorway, her uniform splattered with dried blood.

"Regina Yak, this is Scott Effabee." Josh introduced.

"Mr. Effabee." Regina said in greeting.

"Okay, now that I am here," Scott demanded, "just tell me what you could not say on the phone! I have an important meeting at 4:00!"

"Certainly, we can talk now. Could I please see your identification? It is for security purposes." Regina Yak gave Scott a sweet smile.

Scott looked trapped. He fumbled with his wallet, not sure how to wriggle out of his lie. Then he brightened.

"Uh, well, I forgot it. I was so worried about my son! You can understand that can't you?"

"Actually, no." was Josh's reply, "How do you forget your license when you know you are driving anywhere? I don't buy it. Who are you and what makes you so interested in a patient at this hospital?"

"Look, I just found out he is my son! He was put up for adoption 30 years ago and I just found out he was alive. They told me he had died at birth! Imagine my surprise to find out one day that I have a son, and then the next day to hear he is in the hospital!"

Regina Yak stood her ground, saying, "Still, we

need to verify that you are who you say you are. Mr. Effabee, do you have any ID showing who you are?"

Scott Egan pulled his wallet out again, removing his Driver's license.

"I am Scott Egan. I got a girl pregnant 30 years ago. The baby was adopted by a family with the last name of Effabee. I was supposed to meet him today, then I found out he was admitted to this hospital."

"Do you have the proof that you are his father with you?" Josh questioned.

"It is in my briefcase on the back seat of my car. I have to get back home for an interview on WANN TV for 4:00, why can't you just trust me!"

"Mr. Egan, or Effabee, whatever your name really is - if you cannot produce proof that you are indeed related to the patient in question, we cannot give you any information. We are bound by HIPA laws."

Scott Egan looked from Regina to Josh and held his hands up in surrender.

"If I can use your computer for a few moments, I will show you the documents proving our relationship."

Josh and Regina studied him silently, looked at

one another and gave a nod.

He sat at the computer and entered a website, gave a satisfied nod, showing the nurse and security guard the information on the screen.

"Mr. Egan, this looks valid. I will gladly answer any questions you have" Regina said.

"Is Tim still here? Can I see him? What's going on with him?" The words rushed out of Egan's mouth.

"He is here and being cared for by an excellent staff. We can go back to the unit together. If he is awake, you may visit with him. I ask that you don't upset him and please keep the visit brief. Tim is still in critical condition."

They left Josh's office together. As they approached Tim's room Regina asked Egan, "Are you nervous about meeting your son for the first time?"

Scott answered distractedly, "Yes, I guess so."

"Well, here we are. Remember, don't upset him and please keep the visit short. Nurse Bondi is attending to his IV right now, but you can enter the room." Regina stepped back, allowing Scott to gain entry to the room.

Tim looked up as Scott approached. He made an audible gasp. "What are you doing here? I gave you your money! I don't want to be involved in your dealings anymore. I'm a changed man!"

Tim's voice trembled with fear. The heart monitor started beating rapidly.

Nurse Bondi addressed Scott, "Sir, please leave the room. You are upsetting my patient."

Regina Yak had observed the interaction between Scott and Tim. She stepped into the room.

"Excuse me, Mr. Egan?? I thought you had never met this man before. It seems as though you two know each other quite well!"

Tim spoke up, "This is an evil man! He has been dealing drugs at Golga Correctional Facility. He and the Warden had me forge papers so people were brought into the prison that could be coerced into dealing drugs there. The latest transfer they made me do was so they can kill an informant. You have to stop them!"

"Tim, I am your father. You were given up for adoption thirty years ago. I have come to tell you I am here for you."

"No, you're not! You're here to see if the drug deal is going down tonight. Nurse, this man is a criminal!" The monitor beeped at an even faster rate.

Nurse Bondi stepped between Scott and the hospital bed. "Please leave the room immediately. You are upsetting my patient!"

"Don't you know who I am? I am the police chief of Anderson Falls! I am here to see my son!"

Regina Yak had seen enough. She quietly dialed Josh's emergency number for the second time that day. He responded immediately and he walked with Regina as they entered Tim Effabee's room where another confrontation was taking place.

"I will not leave!" Egan said adamantly. "This is my son and I want to talk to him!"

Tim leaned up on his elbows, "My father was John Effabee. This guy may have created me, but he is not my father! He controlled Bryce Wixmor. He made Wixmor get entangled in the drug trade at the prison. I was nothing more than a pawn, doing their dirty work. I've changed. I won't do it anymore!"

Scott started to step toward Tim, enraged. Josh's strong hands gripped Scott's arms and steered him away from the hospital bed and into the hallway.

"Mr. Egan, you were asked nicely to leave the patient's room twice. I am going to escort you to your car and see you off the hospital grounds. Let's go." Josh pulled Scott's arm behind his back and led him away. Tim's heart monitor resumed its steady beeping, indicating his heartbeat was back to normal.

Josh escorted Scott Egan to his vehicle. He informed Egan that his inappropriate behavior had brought about serious consequences, meaning he was barred from entering the hospital while Tim Effabee was a patient there. Although Scott protested, Josh remained firm. He saw Egan off the property and alerted the guards. Scott drove angrily off the property heading to his meeting at WANN TV.

****

Paul Z. Meyers donned his WANN TV security guard's uniform and prepared for his assignment. He had the body camera ready to record whatever happened that afternoon. A voice crackled in his earpiece, alerting him that he should get in position. He went to the guard's meeting room to get his *"assignment"*.

"Paul, you'll be working the Langorski interview. Make sure the interviewee doesn't get unruly. Lori can really push people's buttons during her interviews. Also, if it is done outside the building, make sure there aren't any whackos trying to get on camera. We want this interview to look as good as her last one."

"No problem, Sir. I'll keep a close eye on Ms. Langorski." Paul said as he left the meeting room. He wound his way through the station to the studio where Lori Langorski was set up to do her interview. As he neared the studio, he saw Lori talking intently with her cameraman. He made sure his camera was on as he got closer to the pair and he heard Lori whisper angrily to the cameraman, "I told you that five hundred is all you are going to get! You are lucky I am giving you that much. Do you have the product?"

The cameraman snickered and hissed, "As soon as I get the money, you get the product." He patted the false battery pack. Lori handed him a thick envelope. He examined the contents. Satisfied, he unhooked the battery pack and she took a plastic bag filled with a white powdery substance.

Tell Egan the street value on this is $100,000. I expect a much bigger cut next time we meet."

"Oh, I'll tell him, but don't expect anything more than you've been getting." She slipped the plastic bag into her large handbag then walked to the studio.

Paul pressed a button on his earpiece. "Did you get all that?"

"Yes," the voice crackled back. "Now catch Egan buying it from her and we can bring him in!"

Chapter 34

Jeff and Tony sat in the Barone's spacious living room discussing the scores from the previous night's baseball games. Missy came in and sat next to her husband. The three friends chatted a little more, then Missy turned to Jeff and reminded him of the call they were to make to Madeline.

"That's right. We better call before it gets too late." Jeff said as he glanced at his watch.

"You two make your call. I know your group is onto something big. I have some things to do in the garage anyway." Tony said. He stood and left the room.

Missy took the phone from an end table and set it on the coffee table between her and Jeff.

"I'll put her on speakerphone so we can have a normal conversation." She pressed the speakerphone button and heard a dial tone. Missy punched in Madeline's secure number and waited while it rang.

"Madeline Gilmore here."

"Hello, Madeline. This is Missy Barone with Jeff Weston. You asked Jeff to have us call you this evening."

"Yes, I did. It seems as though so much has happened just in the last day or two!" Madeline said with wonder in her voice.

"You aren't kidding!" Both Missy and Jeff exclaimed at once. "First, finding evidence that Captain Egan could be Tim Effabee's father; then Tim pulls a gun on an agent and ends up in the same hospital where Bryce Wixmor died." They went over everything else they had learned that day.

"That's not all. We have Tim Effabee's cooperation in bringing down the drug ring at Golga.", Madeline said excitedly.

"Well, with that deposition and the evidence Paul brings to the table, we will have a slam dunk prosecuting Scott Egan." Missy said, delighted.

****

The makeup technician finished applying the lipstick and blush on Lori Langorski's face. He removed the cape that covered her blue and gray pantsuit, patting her shoulder, pleased with his work.

"There you go Miss Langorski, you're all set to do your interview. I must say, you look great."

"Thank you, Raul. I don't know how I'd do it without you. Did anyone prep Captain Egan?" Lori asked.

"My assistant tried to put a little lip color on him and a bit of blush, but he shooed her way. He will not look very good once he is on camera. He has his uniform on too; that's going to make him sweat under those hot lights!" Raul predicted.

"I plan on asking him some hard questions; that alone will make him sweat!" she laughed, walking away.

The director noticed Lori and a cameraman in close conversation with their backs to him. He observed the cameraman hand Lori a bag containing something the size of a sandwich.

"I hate to break this up, but we have a show to do, Miss Langorski. Please take your place. We are ready to do your intro," the director instructed.

The two looked up, startled, a guilty glance passed between them.

"I'm on my mark." Lori said, scurrying to the spot designated for her.

"Thank you." The director said sarcastically,

"Now, in three, two, one…"

"This is Lori Langorski, WANN TV. My guest today is Captain Scott Egan, head of the Anderson Falls Police Department. We are doing a follow up report on the murder of Gary Phenton, by his twin brother, Vito that occurred two years ago. Welcome, Captain Egan."

The camera swung to the chair where Captain Egan was sitting. He looked into the camera and said, "Thank you Lori, it's a pleasure to be here."

Lori wasted no time making her guest feel uncomfortable.

"Captain Egan, as I understand it, Vito Phenton was convicted of murdering his brother and several drug related crimes. Is that true?"

Captain Egan coughed, taken aback by her departure from the script he had rehearsed, and said, a little hesitantly, "Yes, you know that. It was in all the papers two years ago."

Lori continued, "And he was sentenced to do 50 years to life in the State Prison, correct?"

Captain Egan looked uneasy, "Again, yes. That is also public knowledge." He ran his finger under his collar, nervously.

Lori went on doggedly, "If that is so, why is he doing time in Cell Block A at Golga Correctional Facility? Cell Block A is for vicious criminals. He was a model prisoner at the State Prison. How did that happen?"

Beads of sweat could be seen on the captain's forehead. He took out a handkerchief and wiped the sweat from his temples.

"Lori, I am a Captain at a police department. I am not a prison administrator. Perhaps you should be speaking to them." He wriggled in the chair.

"Captain Egan, it was you who took a personal interest in Vito going to the State Prison, not Golga. I am sure they notified you when he was transferred. Also, there have been rumors of a drug ring at Golga Correctional that has roots all the way from the guards to the Warden. If you were so concerned about Vito, how could you let him get transferred and involved in this drug ring?"

Captain Egan's face was red with anger and his nervousness was evidenced by the sweat pouring down his face. He reached for his handkerchief and dabbed his face again. He raised his hands in surrender.

"You've got me stumped Lori. These are questions for the prison administration and the Warden of the correctional facility. I don't know anything about a drug ring. I haven't talked to Vito since I sent him away two years ago!"

"That's odd." Lori hammered away at the captain, "The prison's visitor log shows you up there two weeks ago and the prison surveillance cameras show you in conversation with Vito. What do you have to say about that!?"

"That's it! This interview is over!" he jumped up and stormed off the set.

"Wait!" Lori called as she followed him with her cameraman in tow, "I have more questions!" She kept following him even after the director yelled, "Cut! Go to a commercial break!"

Paul Z. Meyers followed the trio as they made their way out of the studio, dodging cameras and studio personnel, hopping over cables that ran along the floor until they reached the parking lot.

Lori, Captain Egan and the cameraman slowed to a stop near the captain's gold Buick. Paul stayed in range of the trio so he could capture everything with his body camera.

Panting, Scott Egan said to Lori, "Have you got the goods?"

"Yes," she snarled, "Where's my money?"

"You'll get your money once I have my cocaine."

Lori reached in her bag and withdrew the bag her cameraman had given her. She handed it to the Captain. He opened it and tasted a fingertip of the powdery substance. Satisfied, he reached in his back pocket, pulling out a thick envelope. He handed it to Lori. She opened the envelope and counted the contents.

"It's been a pleasure doing business with you. Same time next week?" she said smugly.

"Absolutely. Now I have to get this to my contact at Golga. He tossed the package on the front seat of his car and got in. Just as he was closing the door to his car, an FBI van screeched to a stop ahead of him. An FBI car followed. The lights were flashing, but the siren was silent. Don Rennips got out of the car, gun drawn.

"Scott Egan, you are under arrest for drug trafficking. You have the right to remain silent…." Don finished reading him his rights as he handcuffed the former Captain and herded him into the waiting car. Paul's earpiece crackled, "Good work, Paul. Now we can bring the team at Golga Correctional home."

Paul watched the Captain get taken away with a bit of sadness. He couldn't fathom what would cause someone who was so steadfastly a man of honor to turn to such a despicable way of life. He shook his head and went to his car. As he drove to the FBI substation he continued to think about the events that led to this point. "It all started with a pillbox." He said to himself, "And now it ends in Cellblock A."